A WAR
of
HER OWN

A WAR
of
HER OWN

by

Sylvia Dickey Smith

CRICKHOLLOW BOOKS

Crickhollow Books is an imprint of Great Lakes Literary, LLC, of Milwaukee, Wisconsin, an independent press publishing quality fiction and nonfiction.

Our titles are available from your favorite bookstore or your favorite library jobber or wholesale vendor.

For a complete catalog of all our titles or to place special orders, visit our website:

www.CrickhollowBooks.com

A War of Her Own
© 2010, Sylvia Dickey Smith

Cover design by Amanda Cobb (www.amandajcobb.com).

Publisher's Cataloging-in-Publication Data
(Prepared by the Donohue Group, Inc.)

Smith, Sylvia Dickey.
    A war of her own / by Sylvia Dickey Smith. – 1st ed.

      p. ; cm.

    "A World War II novel" – Cover.
    Includes bibliographical references.
    ISBN: 978-1-933987-11-8

    1. Women – Social networks – Texas – Orange – 20th century – Fiction.
2. World War, 1939–1945 – Social aspects – Texas – Orange – Fiction.
3. Shipbuilding industry – Texas – Orange – 20th century – Fiction.
4. Consolidated Steel Corporation (Orange, Tex – Fiction. 5. Twins
– Psychology – Fiction. 6. Historical fiction. 7. American literature –
Women authors. I. Title.

PS3619.M5379 W27 2010
813/.6

First Edition • Original Trade Paperback

To Glenda Dee Dickey,
("Chocolate Ann")
one of the bravest women I know.

Thanks, Sis, for always loving me
and being there for me.

Chapter 1

Orange, Texas.
1924.

It was early Sunday morning and the sparrows were beginning to flitter across the backyard, stopping to peck and scratch for the slightest morsel of food. Marie stuck her head out the screen door and looked cautiously around. Overnight, a light snow had fallen. It wouldn't last long, though. No one who lived in Orange, Texas expected snow to stay on the ground for more than a few hours. By noon, it would all be gone. A brown rabbit hopped across the backyard, stopped to wriggle its nose, then continued its journey, leaving a trail of tiny footprints in the snow.

Mama was over near the barn tossing dried corn to a flock of clucking hens, while Ivan and Robert, Marie's good-for-nothing older brothers, hunkered around the pot-bellied stove inside, laughing and talking ugly. Papa'd chopped the wood and built the fire before leaving for the creosote plant. He'd come home that evening smelling like old coffee brewed in oil. No telling where her younger sister Edith had gone.

But the morning's peaceful calm belied the panic Marie felt as trickles of warm blood ran down the inside of her thighs. Clutching a gray wool sweater tighter against the cold air, she fled down the back steps of the old homestead toward the outhouse, ducking behind a large bush when Mama grabbed a chicken, skillfully wrung its neck, and headed back to the house. Hopefully, she wouldn't notice the once virgin snow now stained with Marie's tainted blood. If Mama saw it, maybe she'd think the red drops came from the sacrificial chicken. For Mama, a devout Pentecostal, it wasn't Sunday without church and a fried chicken dinner.

Soon as Marie heard the backdoor slam, she ran farther down the path, breathing hard, each quick breath visible in the cold air.

She reached the toilet in the nick of time, for the blood flowed heavier now, down her legs, into her shoes, and onto the ground. She grabbed the rough-hewn door handle and pulled, but it was latched from the inside. Probably Edith had gone in and locked it so Mama wouldn't make her come kill chickens.

Edith couldn't kill a chicken. Edith couldn't kill anything. She even rescued crickets when they got inside the house. She'd cup them in the palm of her hands, carry them outdoors and let them go. "Play your fiddle," she'd say as they hopped off and struck a chord for freedom.

Marie tapped on the weather-beaten door. "Okay, Edith," she whispered. "I know it's you in there. Open the door. Hurry, I need to get in before Mama sees me."

Edith raised the latch, stuck her head out and grinned, dimples shining. "What's your hurry, Toots? You don't want to kill chickens, either?" Then she looked down at Marie's feet. "Good lord, Marie, is that chicken blood? Or is all that coming out of you? You're not dying are you?"

"Shh, no, I'm not dying, honey, but don't be so loud. I don't want anyone to hear us. Can you run fetch me a pile of rags while I get out of these bloody clothes?"

"Sure, come on in." Edith sniffed away her tears as she swung the door wide, grabbed Marie's arm and helped her up. "I'll go get the rags and be back in a hurry, just hang on."

"Also, wet a couple of the rags, okay? But be sure Mama doesn't see you. Oh, and on the way to the barn, can you cover up those drops of blood?"

"Sure. And don't worry, I'm good at hiding," Edith giggled and darted off toward the barn.

SYLVIA DICKEY SMITH

Marie couldn't keep from smiling at the biggest understatement she'd ever heard. Edith vacated the area when it came time to do chores. That's when she got the urge to visit *Miss Jones*—the outhouse—and stayed until the dishes were washed, wiped, and put away. Uncanny timing that girl had.

While Marie waited for the rags, she pulled down her blood-soaked underwear for inspection. She felt guilty when she saw the tiny mass Madam Tousant said to look for, but she also felt relieved. Then again, it just didn't seem right to put it in the toilet like it was shit. But since she knew of no other place to dispose of it that the dogs wouldn't dig up or the chickens peck, she dumped it into the rank pit below—along with a piece of her heart.

Backed to the rough bench, she hiked her nightgown and sat on the hole. She smelled and felt the blood as it dripped into the foul-smelling cesspit below. Her stomach cramped something awful. She wrapped her arms around her middle glad for the pain, because it told her she'd been successful. Her life hadn't come to an end like she thought it would when her monthly curse didn't come. She hoped it also meant Sol would appreciate her sacrifice and wouldn't leave her now that she'd rid herself of the problem.

The door opened and Edith stepped up into the outhouse, her arms full of rags, and one by one handed them to Marie, who commenced cleaning herself. Once finished, she tossed the bloody rags, along with her step-ins, into the pit.

As if Edith read her mind, the younger girl said, "We both need to take a big shit to cover up the bloody rags, or when Papa or Mama see them, they'll ask questions." She pulled down her own drawers and plopped on the other hole. "Now, tell me what you did to yourself, Marie. I hadn't seen that much blood since Ivan stabbed Mama's hand with a kitchen knife."

"Keep your voice down, Edith," she said, putting a finger to her lips. "I'll explain it all to you one of these days."

Innocent so far, Edith left no doubt in anyone's mind that she wouldn't stay that way for long. The baby of the family, two years younger than Marie, she tested every rule given by Mama and Papa. Not a bad kid, Edith simply loved life—a life without rules. Rules seemed of no consequence to her. Nor did any standards set for young ladies.

Marie loved her little sister, but alongside the love, she harbored resentment that Edith got away with things she never dared test. To add insult to injury, Edith's hair, the color of the darkest of midnights, hung down her back in long radiant curls, while Marie's dull dishwater blonde hair refused to even grow, let alone curl.

That day, Marie hadn't a clue what Edith knew about how babies were made—or not, as the case may be—but Marie certainly didn't plan to be the one to hand her that information on a silver platter. Besides, she doubted she'd ever need to teach her rebellious little sister anything about the birds and the bees. She'd learn soon enough without Marie's help.

Weak with blood loss, Marie grabbed Edith's elbow and they marched together up the path to the house. "And if you tell anyone about this, I'll wring your neck." Marie warned.

"Cross my heart and hope to die. Besides, I'll even keep Mama busy till you get to the bedroom."

* * *

Life went a little smoother for several weeks, although Marie wondered why the smell of coffee still made her sick in the mornings.

When her monthly bleeding didn't return and people started talking about her getting fat, Marie gathered her courage and prepared to tell Sol. Sol had demanded that she end the pregnancy, and she'd learned from Madam Tousant which herbs would do what was needed. She'd thought she'd taken care of the situation without anyone finding out she'd lost her cherry to Sol, and Marie had hoped to resume her *good girl* status in the community. She kept Sol at arm's length, still hurt he'd wanted to end it all. But something was still growing inside her.

SYLVIA DICKEY SMITH

The next evening, she ran into him downtown in Orange, in the middle of a group of girls and a blond-headed boy in a sailor suit. When Sol saw her coming, he turned around and walked briskly the opposite way. Marie hurried to catch up. When she did, she grabbed his arm, bringing him to a stop. The rest of his companions had turned the corner and were out of sight.

Trying not to let the tears come, she begged, "I know I lost the baby. I saw it. I held it in my hands. But I swear I still have another one growing inside me. Feel my belly." She pulled his hand to her stomach.

He looked startled.

She held his hand there. "I must've been carrying twins and lost only one. But it's too late to take the herbs again. You have to marry me, Sol. People are already starting to talk."

Sol, several years older than Marie, jerked his arm away and spat out, "I don't give a good goddamn, Marie, whether they talk about you or not, or how many babies you have. I'm not marrying you. I told you I still love Irene Meade. If I can't marry her, I won't marry anyone."

He spoke so loudly, passersby paused to look at the tall, thin young man with dark eyes and dimpled chin. Not handsome by any means, but with an ego that attracted attention—and had convinced Marie he was as great as he thought he was.

"But Sol, Irene broke your heart, and now she's engaged to someone else."

"It's her or no one." He leaned down to Marie and at first she expected a kiss, but instead, he whispered in her ear. "Besides, how do I know you haven't slept with some other guy since I got in your pants?"

Without stopping to think, Marie popped him in the mouth, as hard as she could. Then she turned, fearful he'd return the blow, and walked away briskly.

She held the panic inside all the way home, and then threw herself across the bed and cried. Edith, awakened by the sobs, put her arm around Marie and rubbed her back, but never asked why she cried. Although Edith had a devil-may-care attitude about society's expectations of her, at the same time she held maturity beyond her years. And her love and loyalty to family and especially to her older sister Marie knew no bounds.

By the time the early-morning sun slanted through their window the next morning, Marie had a plan.

If people at Mama's church found out about the baby, Mama would never be able to hold her head up there again, and that would kill her. But Marie knew that Papa had been worried about his old aunt Gertie, who lived alone in Hartburg, a rural community outside town. Marie would tell them she'd go take care of the old lady for a few months. That's what she'd do.

When she told Mama and Papa, they couldn't have been more pleased. Mama even helped Marie pack.

"This is the nicest thing you've ever done, Marie. You've made your papa very happy." Mama carefully folded the last dress and tucked it in the suitcase. "Who's going to take you?"

"Sol will. I know he won't mind." Truth was, she hadn't asked him yet, but didn't dare admit it.

"That's nice of him. Here, here's a nickel to help pay for the trip." Mama pulled the coin from her apron pocket.

Marie knew just how few nickels Mama possessed and hated to take it, but did anyway, not knowing what she faced.

"How long you plan on staying?" Toothless gums showed through Mama's smile.

Marie counted six months forward in her head. "I'll see how it goes. Don't worry. I'll be fine. If I need anything, I'll write." She walked out the door, holding her head up with a confidence that was the opposite of how she felt inside.

Sol must have seen her coming down the road, for no sooner was she inside the picket fence of his mama's big white, two-story house on Border Street than he stepped onto the wide front porch. The screen door slammed behind him. If she hadn't known better, she'd

SYLVIA DICKEY SMITH

have sworn steam rose from the top of his head.

"What the hell do you think you're doing?" He pointed at the tan suitcase in her hand. "You sure as hell aren't moving in here with me and Mama."

"I didn't come to move in with you. I came to ask if you'd take me out to Hartburg so I can stay with my aunt until after the baby comes. That way, folks won't know my shame, and afterwards, I can still hold my head up in this town. At least you can do that much."

Sol had enough chivalry left in him to hitch Old Molly to the wagon and do what she asked.

They rode the twelve miles in silence except for the clip clop of horse hooves on the roadbed, and the occasional plop, plop of horse dung as it fell under the wagon wheels. The foul stench lingered in her nostrils and churned her stomach, but pride forced her to swallow whatever came up in her throat.

When they finally arrived in Hartburg, Sol followed directions as told, but stopped the wagon a good quarter mile from the house. He sat on the driver's bench like a puffed-up toad frog, waiting for her to get down.

"You're not taking me all the way?"

"This is as far as I go. You're lucky I brought you this far. I almost stopped a few miles back."

"I can't believe you'd make me walk that far carrying a suitcase, not to mention your baby."

"Believe it or not, this is as far as I go." He clicked his tongue at the horse and pulled the reins as if to turn around.

"Okay. Wait. I'll go." She threw him a disgusted look, but with little choice, eased herself down to the ground. "I made a mistake. You're no gentleman. You're nothing but a bastard." She grabbed her suitcase, spun around and headed up the long path to the house. The sound of the horse-drawn wagon echoed in her ears, grew faint, and then, nothing.

Hartburg was *country*. And Blind Aunt Gertie's house was *country country*, and even older than Aunt Gertie. Marie had visited a number of times over the years with her family. The well-worn floors creaked every time anyone took a step, and sometimes at night, when no one did. The place had been modernized with electricity and running water, but other than that, the house looked its age—old. Since she had been a little girl, Marie's favorite spot had always been the swing on the front porch.

Everyone had started calling the old woman *Blind* Aunt Gertie since cataracts had stolen her eyesight years ago. Now she was ninety years old. And although age had also taken its toll on her hearing, Marie had noticed that Aunt Gertie heard what she wanted to. She existed day-to-day, barely aware the world turned around her, stubbornly insisting no one would ever force her out of her own home. She'd been born there, she'd die there, and she dang well better be buried in the yard behind the house.

Marie looked back at the road. No sign of Sol or the wagon. She looked around, happy to see the porch swing still there, swaying slightly in the breeze like ghosts were relaxing on it. She went inside. But the minute the screen door slammed behind Marie, the musty smell of an old person too feeble to bathe, and certainly unconcerned with dust and mold, made her dart back outside and lose what food she'd kept down so far that day.

It had been a while since she'd visited, and now that she saw the condition of the house, she felt ashamed she hadn't come sooner. The place looked like one abandoned for decades—dust, clutter, threadbare curtains covered in cobwebs, rat droppings everywhere.

She found Aunt Gertie sitting in her rocking chair near the big picture window in the living room. Cloudy eyes stared out as if she could see the trees bursting open with new growth, excited that winter had eased into spring. Her thin, unwashed white hair straggled down her back, and she wore a dingy nightgown she must have had on for days, weeks perhaps.

"Aunt Gertie," Marie called out, unsure whether or not her aunt could hear her, but not wanting to frighten her either. She stepped closer, tapped her aunt on the shoulder and helped the gnarled fingers find Marie's eyes, nose, mouth, and chin, until, at last, recognition set in. The toothless old woman smiled and clapped her hands with delight.

Sitting beside Gertie's rocker was the cherry lamp table with its large brass claw-and-ball feet Marie had always loved. Every time she visited she'd ask where it came from. Gertie would only smile and say a secret lover no one ever knew about gave it to her years ago. Marie reached over and flipped on the Tiffany lamp, wishing she knew the story behind the table. She nudged the wiry hair off her aunt's face and pinned it back up into the topknot from which it strayed. "I'll make us a cup of hot tea, okay?" she asked quietly, happy to see Gertie nod. The old lady's hearing was still good.

The small unkempt kitchen held a dilapidated table and two chairs, kerosene stove, and a cabinet with two gray enamel dishpans full of dirty dishes on top. Marie found enough water to prime the pump, then pushed and pulled the rust-colored handle until she'd collected a bucketful of fresh water. After ladling enough water into a blue-and-white granite teakettle, she struck a match and lit the stove. Waiting for it to boil, she scrounged around inside the cabinet until she found a tin of stale tea leaves. Soon, she carried two cups of the steaming hot, dark liquid into the sitting room.

When Gertie raised the cup to her lips and sipped, sheer delight flashed behind her sightless eyes. A spot of color flushed her ghost-white cheeks. "Ohh, that's good," she said, with a sigh. "It's been a long time since anyone made me hot tea. Thanky, sweetheart. You're a good girl."

They sipped slowly, reveling in the drink and the company of the other. When their cups were both empty, Marie set them aside, took her aunt's hand and rested it on Marie's growing belly. "I'm having a baby," she said, trying to sound firm, but her voice broke a little. "I need somewhere to stay until it's born."

Aunt Gertie folded her arms and rocked an imaginary child left and right, back and forth, humming a lullaby as she did so. "Baby?" She uttered the word as if describing a first-time miracle, but Marie knew this pregnancy was no immaculate conception.

Delight in the sightless eyes of her aunt made Marie want to cry.

"You stay here as long as you like, sweetheart." Aunt Gertie glowed with the idea of a baby in the house, and looked as if she grew younger by the minute.

Bless her heart. She had always been a strong woman, never married, never wanted to marry, an independent cuss who swore she didn't need a man. Marie never had understood that, but a new regard for the old aunt formed in Marie's heart.

The two settled into a routine. Over the next few months, Marie cleaned both the house and Aunt Gertie, and did the cooking. At night, they'd sit side by side in the porch swing, Gertie's crooked fingers resting on the growing belly of her great niece, alert for any movement inside the womb. Each time the baby kicked, Gertie laughed, clapped her hands and hummed a tune.

In time, Marie met a few neighbors on her way down to the corner store where she picked up a few groceries with her aunt's meager pension check. Likely the folks guessed Marie's predicament, but were too polite to ask. She wondered what they said behind her back.

One day, the preacher from a nearby Baptist church came to call at the house. After brief formalities, he grabbed Marie's hands and looked her in the eye, but his gaze kept straying to her belly. "Jesus gave his life on the cross for your sins, you know," he said, as if telling her something she hadn't heard every day of her life. "Here, let me read you what the Bible says about it here in John Chapter Three." He read a passage familiar to Marie, and then looked to see if she'd been swayed.

She hadn't.

"If you confess your sins before God and ask Jesus to forgive you and come into your heart as your personal lord and savior, He will."

Marie just looked at him.

"If you do, you will spend eternity in a heaven where the streets are paved with gold," he explained, his eyes sparkling with the gold of which he spoke.

Before he left, he shared plans for a new church building in case she wanted to make a donation.

She didn't.

The days grew longer and her days of confinement grew shorter.

On one particularly hot summer day, wilted and weary, she sat on the front porch in the dilapidated swing and nursed an ache in her lower back. The pain had started the night before and still hadn't eased. Mindlessly, her bare, puffy feet nudged against the porch each time the swing went back, and then she lifted her legs and let the momentum carry her forward. The unwelcome visitor inside her womb seemed to find comfort in the peaceful, hypnotic movement. Either that or the baby slept, for the kicking had slowed and finally stopped a couple of days ago. She rubbed her belly with one hand and with the other, fanned herself with an old newspaper. Her half-empty glass of lemonade rested on the porch railing, within easy reach. Condensation pooled around the bottom of the glass and dripped off the railing to the porch, below. Listless, she stuck her finger under the flow, caught a drip and put it in her mouth.

Her mind wandered to Sol. She hadn't heard a word since he'd dropped her off months ago. She wondered if he and Irene had gotten together, and if not, would she still stand a chance with him after this?

Heavy and lethargic, she'd sat and swung and stared off into space for most of the afternoon when, down the road, a movement—something red—caught her eye. Someone headed their way. Marie stopped the swing with her foot, and sat motionless, holding her breath, hearing only the sound of her pulse in her ears. Maybe Sol came with a marriage proposal.

As the figure drew closer, she realized instead of a man, it was a girl dressed in a red blouse and brown trousers. She carried a small suitcase in one hand and seemed to hold a cigarette in the other.

Marie shielded her eyes with her hands and squinted harder.

Oh lord, she'd recognize that blouse anywhere, the same one she had outgrown several years ago and passed down to Edith.

A speck on the shoulder of the blouse sealed the deal. The visitor coming down the road was indeed her little sister, Edith. The object on the girl's shoulder could be nothing other than the heart-shaped mother-of-pearl brooch she'd handed down to Edith last year on her birthday. The girl never went anywhere without that infernal cheap pin. She'd told Edith the tiny red stone set in the middle was mere colored glass, but the way Edith acted, an expensive, perfectly cut ruby adorned the center. The closer Edith got to the house, the easier Marie could see what else the girl wore—a big impish smile.

Marie eased her awkward, lumbering body up out of the swing, one hand on the chain, the other supporting her back. A twinge grabbed her around the middle as she straightened to a standing position. She stopped to catch her breath, then moved to the edge of the porch and waited, watching.

Marie knew the exact second Edith saw her belly and the real-ization hit. Edith's jaw lost its hinge and fell open. By the time she stepped up on the porch, her eyes looked as big as her mouth.

"How come you didn't tell me you were having a baby? If I'd a known, I would've come out here with you."

"Mama doesn't suspect, does she?"

"She doesn't know what to think since you didn't write. She's worried sick, told me to come find out what's going on."

"You better keep your mouth shut about this," she said, rubbing her belly. Her own sarcastic, hateful voice startled her. Up until now, she'd spent the last few months convincing herself this was all an unfortunate accident. Once she had the baby and gave it away, she'd resume her rightful domain as *the good sister*. At night, when she tossed and turned to find relief from the weight of the baby stretched from bladder to rib cage, she reminded herself of her good-girl status, that she didn't deserve this. People like Edith, who never played by the rules, and their no-good brothers, Ivan and Robert, who were just plain lazy and mean were the ones who deserved to pay for their sins. Not someone like her who never even talked back to Mama or went to bed without her face washed or her teeth brushed. She had complied with every rule ever given her, so she must be more worthy than the rest.

But all that had changed that afternoon upstairs at Sol's mama's house when he sweet-talked her into sleeping with him. He said if she would, he'd be able to get over Irene, and she'd been dumb enough to believe him. Afterwards, the whole thing left her repulsed, so full of shame she'd run all the way home and locked herself in her room. Now, she was paying the price for her one and only sin.

She looked at Edith and put her hands on her hips. "And tell me, just who do you think you are, smoking cigarettes? You're too young to smoke."

Edith ignored the question and blew the smoke in the direction of Marie's face. "For your information, smarty pants, I'm just two years younger than you. I can smoke if I want to. Anyway, that's beside the point. What I want to know is why you didn't tell me you were having a baby? I'd have come with you."

"And gotten you in trouble with Mama? No, thank you. You do well enough all on your own, sweetie. Besides, I didn't want you here." Marie looked down at the suitcase still in Edith's hand. "Well, now that you're here you might as well come inside and put away your things." She opened the screen for Edith. "How long did Mama say you could stay?"

Edith ignored the question and headed inside, but before Marie could follow, another cramp caught her in the back, took her breath away. A tiny trickle of water rolled down the insides of her thighs.

She stopped outside the doorway, afraid to move.

There went another trickle.

Edith came out, pitched her half-smoked cigarette off the porch and grabbed Marie's arm as a gush of fluid washed down her legs, dripped through the cracks and onto the ground below.

"Uh oh, your water broke. That means the baby's on the way.

Here, let me help you inside."

Annoyance rumbled inside Marie. "Listen to *Miss Know It All,*" she said. Then the realization hit. Rather than annoyance, it was pure terror she felt. She also realized how grateful she was Edith had come.

Meanwhile, Edith grabbed her by the arm, helped her inside and over to a daybed by the window. She yanked off the covers as Marie crawled in, then Edith reached over and pulled the threadbare curtains closed.

"Thanks," Marie muttered. "No sense in the whole world witnessing the price I have to pay for my sin."

"Oh, Marie, don't be so dramatic," Edith laughed. "Shoot, you just got caught, that's the only difference between you and most other girls."

Blind Aunt Gertie sat across the room looking out a window, seeing nothing. Her hands lay in her lap squeezed into tight balls. "Take care of my girl, take care of my girl," she whispered over and over, as if God needed reminding. The creaking chair rocked back and forth, back and forth, back and forth.

"Don't you have a midwife or someone who can come help?" Panic coated Edith's voice. "We need someone who knows what they're doing. I sure don't know how to deliver a baby."

"An old man, a Doctor Mosquito, lives next door. He said he'd come deliver the baby. Run over and tell him to hurry." Marie clenched the sheets and squeezed tight. "Hurry, I said. Another pain's coming. Tell him to come quick."

"I'm going, I'm going. Don't do anything until I get back with the doctor." Edith darted out, letting the screen door slam behind her.

Not doing anything until the doctor arrived sounded like a good idea to Marie, but she doubted her ability to comply, as another contraction tore through her gut. She grabbed the sheet and clenched it tighter.

God, no one told her it hurt like this. Poor Mama came to mind,

SYLVIA DICKEY SMITH

she'd been through the same thing seven times. Marie wished now she'd have listened to Mama and kept her legs together.

The next contraction came at the same moment Edith darted back in. Out of breath, she squeaked, "The doctor's on his way. He just had to put on his shoes."

"I don't care if the doctor has his damn shoes on or not. Tell him to just get here."

"He's coming, Toots. Hang on." Edith wiped the sweat off of Marie's forehead.

The contraction soon passed, but another sensation took its place. "Look, Edith, down between my legs. It's like . . . like I feel something sticking out of me. Now it's moving, Edith, it's moving. What is it? Look?"

"Moving? It can't be the baby. They don't come that fast."

Surprised that Edith sounded as if she knew so much, Marie felt even more surprised when her younger sister reached over and yanked the sheet up, spread Marie's legs wide and looked. If Marie hadn't been in such pain, she'd have been embarrassed to death.

For the second time that day Edith's mouth dropped open. "There's a tiny blue leg sticking out," she yelled. "Babies aren't supposed to come that way. Now what do I do?"

She dropped the sheet and sprinted to almost collide with the doctor who was just entering the room, bag in hand. "Get over here, Doctor, quick. Something's wrong, bad wrong. I thought the head came out first."

The bald, potbellied man rushed to the bedside, his loose shirt-tail flapping. "It should. What's the problem?"

"The problem is the baby's leg is sticking out of my sister," Edith bellowed, her face redder than her blouse.

"It's a footling breach," he said after he checked under the sheet, "and the baby's other leg is caught up inside her. We could've turned the baby earlier, but it's too late now. All I can do is try and work the other leg free. Hold on, this will be a tough ride, honey. I'll do the best I can." Marie opened her eyes long enough to see the doctor shake his head with concern, then he set his bag on a nearby table, rolled up his sleeves, and bent to his task.

Lost in a fabric of pain that went on forever, time became one long thread for Marie that led nowhere except deeper into a bearing down, unfruitful force that ripped her apart. In between contractions, the doctor reached up inside her and pushed, turned, pushed again, further each time until from somewhere far away, he said, "There, I've got the other leg out. Good work, Marie, just a little bit longer. Now push, hard."

How the hell did he expect her to push harder when she lacked the strength to even breathe? Drenched in sweat, she heard herself scream, and wondered where the energy came from to do even that. She writhed, yelled how she'd kill Sol, adding a string of profanity ugly enough to bring pink to a sailor's cheeks.

She tried to push, but her body refused to follow what her brain and the doctor told her to do. Exhaustion took control. Unable to follow his order, she tried to hold back the pain. Going into it felt like more than she could bear. Still she tensed, pulled back, tried, hoped, and prayed the pain to go away.

It only grew stronger.

In an instant, her body made a decision all its own. It took control over her as if to say, w*hat the hell, go into it. What you've done hasn't worked, so now I'm in charge. Hold on. Here we go.*

She—it—they—whatever the gender—plunged her headlong into a bottomless pit of red pain. It grew darker, more intense than before, more than she ever thought possible. Nothing existed but pain—not even sound. From a place so deep inside her she didn't know it existed, the urge to push grew, took control and defiantly ordered the pain to hurt more and her to push harder. Somewhere in the back of her brain, she knew she squeezed Edith's hand and somewhere even further back, feared she crushed the bones in those slender fingers. But try as she wished, her vise-like fist refused to release the hand of her little sister.

In the pain-induced fog, she saw Edith who stared, hollow-eyed,

SYLVIA DICKEY SMITH

from Marie's vagina to her face and back again. The doctor stopped to blink away salty tears, and then resumed his work.

After an eternity—no, more than an eternity—even in the midst of the pain, Marie felt a shift inside her and knew the child came out. But she heard no cry. Newborn babies always cried, at least those born alive did. Shameful hope took shape and grew by the second. Maybe the baby hadn't survived the birth, which resolved the whole issue. She could go on with her life like all this never happened. Unable to resist, she rose up on her elbow to look.

"The little tyke's too exhausted to cry," the doctor said as he wiped out the bloody infant's eyes and mouth. "The heartbeat and breathing are strong though. The good Lord helped us. We got us a healthy baby."

Marie couldn't imagine the good Lord had anything to do with the baby's health. If He had, the infant would've come out head first, like they were supposed to. Retribution's what it was, plain and simple—God's way of getting back at her.

"Look, Marie, it's a girl," Edith said as she clapped her hands and jumped with joy.

"I don't *want* to see her," Marie cried and turned her face to the wall. "I can't keep her."

Chapter 2

Orange, Texas.
Summer, 1943.

It seemed like some towns came with their own gravity—towns like Orange, located in the deepest southeast corner of the state of Texas. Cross the Sabine River, heading east, and a person would step into Louisiana, smack dab in Cajun country. Go just a few miles south, and that person would step into Texas' northernmost waters of the Gulf of Mexico.

The Sabine River ran right down through the middle of town, wide and deep enough for a an ocean-going vessel, making Orange a prime spot for the shipping trade. Built with money from that commerce, Grand Victorian-style homes lined the streets of town. In and around town, towering virgin pines, ancient gnarled oaks draped with Spanish moss, and bayous full of cypress and water tupelo trees made the town a living, breathing Shangri-la.

The richest men who lived in Orange, some of them arriving as post–Civil War carpetbaggers from Pennsylvania, bought up all the nearby timberland for a pittance, and then made millions from prime long-leaf yellow pine. Working for them became the most coveted jobs in town, but most people were as poor as a mouse kicked out of church. The times demanded a stern code of conduct, and, at least in public, the manners of polite society were strict and exacting. All a man had to do was say the word "damn," and folks fell out in horror.

Set back by the Great Depression, Orange saw hard times. Even the aristocratic, proud people nearly starved to death. About the only thing the small town did during those years was make babies and scrounge for food. Those lucky enough to own land survived by growing their own crops, and the really lucky were able to keep a milk cow for the wee ones. A couple of Northern companies moved to town to establish shipyards along the rivers, supplying a small number of naval destroyers to England, but not enough to keep the town alive.

Then, in December 1941, the Japanese attacked Pearl Harbor, and all hell broke loose.

Shipbuilders were awarded major contracts to build vast shipyards in Orange. Overnight, the yards hired anyone who walked through their gates—black and white, men and women, skilled and unskilled. News of the plentiful jobs spread fast. Barefoot, hungry, desperate people from the backwoods of Texas, Louisiana, Tennessee, and Arkansas flooded a town soon stretched beyond its limits. Almost overnight, the population exploded from 7,500 to well over 65,000.

The question arose where to put them all. The answer was in thousands of hastily erected and cheaply built houses, ramshackle shelters erected atop river sand pumped in to fill up mosquito-infested marshland. Undaunted by the poor accommodations, work shifts buzzed and bustled around the clock, and at the launching of each new ship, the yard and the town went wild in celebration.

Life was good again—but not for everyone.

Not for Bea Meade.

She'd grown up in the grip of the Pentecostal church, where she learned when a person fell from grace it likely came as the result of one stupid error in judgment. She didn't know it could happen so slowly she might not even know she was falling until she hit the ground.

Her life changed directions so slowly the summer of '43. Only later did she see that day as the start of her fall. Later, if she looked back, if she licked her finger and ran it down a mental list of unfortunate events, it stopped at that point to say, that's the day the slide began. The day she learned to hate.

It was the day her husband Hal staggered in after midnight, smelling of stale beer and piss, puked all over the bathroom, then yelled at her to get up and clean the puke instead of laying there crying like she always did.

She got up out of bed, dragged herself to the bathroom, and cleaned up the mess, then dumped the foul-smelling rags into a kitchen sink full of hot soapy water and started scrubbing.

Hal came in behind her, stuck his head in the icebox and pulled out another beer.

"I don't care what you say, I don't cry *every* night," Bea argued back.

"Nah, but most nights you do." He popped off the bottle top and swigged.

"Don't you think you've had enough of that stuff?"

"Listen to Miss Know It All," he mocked, prancing around the kitchen like a show dog expecting to win first prize. "Lemme ask you this. How come you just lay there like a bump on a log when I touch you at night? There's this woman at work, and she knows what a—"

"She knows what? What a man wants?"

"Forget it." He finished off the beer, tossed it in the garbage, and shook his auburn-colored hair. "How come you're not thankful for where we live? Thousands of people in this town still live in cardboard shacks, but you think you're Miss Bitsy Rich, and ought to be livin' in one of them fancy houses down on Green Avenue. Well, I got news for you, honey, we ain't never . . ." His slurred words trailed off, and he turned and stumbled out of the room.

She slammed a rag against the rub board and scrubbed. The house was a dump. She'd heard how they'd chopped down thousands of cypress trees from the marsh and then filled it with wet sand pumped in from the river bottom. Before the sand could even dry out, they'd poured unreinforced concrete, expecting it to serve double duty as streets and drainage. These rows and rows of crappy houses, ugly as an Army barracks, went up overnight.

She tossed the rag into the sink she'd filled with rinse water and proceeded to scrub another. "Don't tell me I'm not thankful," she'd yelled at him, sprawled on the couch in the other room. "I'm thankful

I have a dry place to lay my head at night. That's why we need to pay the rent on time. If you don't bring your paycheck home, I can't."

She finished the laundry, dumped it in the clothes basket, and went back to bed. Hal came in a few minutes later, still reeking of beer. When she turned her back, he slapped her ass and said, "Roll over."

She did, and hated every jab he shoved into her.

Afterwards, he fell back onto his side and within minutes, snored.

She turned out the light and cried.

Most nights she cried, and always had. No one ever understood why.

The next morning she awakened with two consuming thoughts: the pail of dirty diapers in the bathroom and relief that another night had passed. She slipped the heart-shaped brooch—the only thing that ever brought her a semblance of comfort—from underneath her pillow, tucked it in the cigar box on her bureau, and stumbled to the bathroom, fearful she might awaken Hal.

A couple of minutes later she watched the water swirl out of the toilet, marveling again at the miracle of indoor plumbing. At least they had this luxury, which made her feel a little bit rich for the first time in her life, and helped take her mind off the enemy, who everyone else believed to be Germany. For her, a deeper, more seditious adversary chewed at her insides.

She shoved the mass of thick, blonde hair off her face and stared at her reflection in the medicine cabinet mirror. *Get a grip on yourself, toots. Just because you can't sleep at night, don't forget the blessings you do have—like sweet Percy, sleeping in the next room.*

After she washed and dried her face, she took her housecoat from the nail behind the door, slipped it on, and then tied the sash as she walked across the hall into the baby's room. Percy lay sprawled on his back, arms out to his sides. A tiny bubble rested on pink lips that curved into a smile. She eased the door shut and headed through the small living room, sparsely furnished with discards from neighbors and friends.

A rocking chair sat at a right angle to the pale-blue, coffee-stained couch she'd shoved against double windows. Irritating spring-roll shades on the windows forever sagged low, thwarting her attempt to keep them raised. Mismatched end tables on each side of the couch held not-to-be-outdone mismatched lamps. The bare floors were spotlessly clean but refused to shine, regardless of how much she scrubbed the unfinished wood.

She gave the room a quick once-over and spied a rubber ducky on the floor. With a quick, but precise movement, she bent to pick it up and tucked it into the pocket of her housecoat.

After checking the mousetraps and tossing out two of the little destructive devils, she went to the kitchen sink and scrubbed her hands until they ached.

Eager to get Hal's breakfast ready before Percy woke up and screamed for his, her first task, the one she dreaded even more than emptying mouse traps, was lighting the infernal oven on the small four-burner stove. She struck a match, turned on the gas, and waited for the small explosion. Even though she expected it, the blast made her jump back just like it did every time she lit the dang thing. She glanced behind her, hoping Hal hadn't come in and laughed at her foolishness. She hated the way he made her feel like such a child.

She lit the burner under a teakettle full of fresh water and, while that heated, spooned coffee into the drip pot. The strong smell of the local brand gagged her, but Hal wouldn't drink any other kind, and complained if she made it too weak. "Baby, it don't take near as much water to make a pot of coffee," he'd say, teasing. But she knew he meant business.

By the time Hal walked into the kitchen, eggs were scrambled and hot buttermilk biscuits had been flipped over on a plate so they wouldn't sweat. Mama hated thick, soggy-bottom biscuits. In her mind's eye, Bea could recall how Mama would pinch off a small piece of the dough, pat it flat, place it in a pan of hot grease, and turn it over to coat both sides. The results were thin biscuits with crispy tops and bottoms and soft tender insides. Bea swore that's why Hal asked her to marry him—for her mama's biscuits—hoping one day Bea's would be as good. Of course, Mama had cooked many years by the time Bea came along, for she'd been what Mama had called her change-of-life baby. Good Lord, she hoped she didn't have a baby at that age.

She rested Hal's food on the table in front of him.

He poured the hot coffee in his saucer to cool, and then slurped it down while he scanned the *Orange Leader's* daily war coverage.

Bea fixed herself a cup of the strong liquid, wishing she could sweeten it with a big spoonful of sugar. Rationing didn't allow for such luxuries. Instead, she topped it off with a dollop of cream and eased into the chair beside Hal.

He didn't blink.

Lost in loneliness, Bea sipped her coffee and allowed her mind to wander to the day's chores.

"Better catch the news," Hal said, more to the room than to her. He switched on the old Emerson radio, and the announcer's voice filled the room with the urgency of a world and a war far away from Bea.

"Do we have to listen to news about this infernal war so early in the morning?" she asked, and put her hands over her ears.

"Hush. Listen," he said, scolding her like a child. He turned the volume louder as the announcer recounted how yesterday the local Coast Guard had sunk an U-166 submarine off the banks of the Mississippi River. Hal bit off a mouthful of biscuit and chewed while he talked. "Them Krauts are getting mighty close, baby. At least our guys got this one. No telling how many others of 'em are out there."

"Today's payday, Hal, so if you could—"

"Mm hmm."

"—if you come straight home after work, I'll have time to walk down to the rental office and pay this month's rent before they close. We're late, you know. And the man said if we don't keep up, he knows lots more people with money in their pockets that want a place to live."

"Yeah, yeah, I'll try." Hal sopped his plate with a piece of biscuit to catch the last puddle of Steen's syrup. "But as soon as I get off, I gotta go see a dog about a man."

Hal always had someone he needed to talk to about something. "Don't wait supper for me," he added.

"Hal, Mama's gone now. We don't have her to fall back on." Bea brushed a sprig of hair off her damp forehead. "And even if she still lived, I just couldn't move in on her again. After all, she did her share of raising kids. If we don't pay our rent, we'll be evicted. You already know how hard it is to find a place to live." The thought of living out in the tents where rats and roaches roamed at will gave her the shudders.

"Yeah, yeah, I know," he said, fidgeting. "But I don't have time for this right now." He gave her a quick peck on the cheek and reached around for his lunch bucket and patted her behind in the process. "I hope you didn't put in those same old cold sandwiches like you've been doing," he said, hustling out the door and off to his job at the shipyard.

Bea tried to save the money Hal brought home every week, and Hal tried to spend it. Most of the time, Hal won. A regular stream of bill collectors forever knocked on their door. She hated it, hated the way it made her feel inferior, unworthy. At times, she wished she were more like Hal, easy-going, able to make casual conversation with people, never meeting a stranger. But when she tried, her tongue stuck to the roof of her mouth.

More than anything, she wanted to go back to bed for a little more sleep before the baby awoke, but responsibility hung around her neck like a lead weight. So, instead, she filled the sink with hot soapy water and plunged in the dirty dishes. While she scrubbed off the dried eggs and sticky syrup, she thought about the thousands of Depression-desperate families from the backwoods of Texas and Louisiana who had poured into town to take the new jobs at the shipyard. The supervisors, Hal complained, hired the untrained workers on the spot, never mind they didn't know a rivet gun from a welding torch.

She breathed a sigh of relief that she didn't have to work at the shipyard with all those men like so many other women did these days. They liked it, she'd heard, but Mama always said it cheapened a woman, that a woman's place was in the home taking care of her husband and baby. Wash and iron his clothes in the daytime and yield to his demands at night. She did what Mama said the good Lord put women on this earth to do.

But the days sure got long. And the nights were the worst.

She always looked forward to Saturdays, the one short day of her week. Hal drove them downtown where everyone gathered to visit. He and his friends usually walked down to Cherry's Club, a little hole-in-the-wall across the street from the shipyard. She'd stuck her head in the door once when she needed to get Hal's paycheck to buy food. The place smelled of stale beer, missed urinals, damp old men, and cigarette smoke. No one had to tell her not to go in again. She refused to even touch the doorknob.

Hal and the other men played pool and drank beer while the wives sat outside in the cars, watched the kids, and chatted. The bad part of the trip came when they drove past whole families in tents or makeshift shelters of wood scraps and cardboard—no water, no electricity, and not even outdoor toilets. The people had money, but there just weren't enough houses for people to live in, regardless of how much money they made.

Someone knocked on the front door, rousing Bea from her thoughts. She dried her hands on a dishrag and opened the door to Masil, her friend who lived down the court. Bea breathed a sigh, thankful not to see the man from the rental office looking for money she didn't have.

Masil flounced the tail of her print dress, stood on tiptoe, and peeked around Bea. "Good morning. Hal gone to work yet?"

"You just missed him." Bea smirked as she swung the door open. "Come on in and have a cup of coffee."

"I'd love a cup. We're out."

Bea knew Masil had come to share the latest town gossip. Without a malicious bone in her body, gregarious Masil kept Bea and many others in the neighborhood up to date with current events. Keeping track of the war effort and all the people who'd moved to town kept her busy.

"You got enough coffee for a second pot?" Masil asked. "Ernie complains about how weak I make ours, but we're almost out. Soon as I get my ration coupons, I gotta go stand in line for more." Masil hustled through a living room exactly like hers to the equally exact kitchen. "Baby still asleep?"

"So far, yeah. I hope the rainy weather keeps him down for a little while. What's on your mind?"

"I gotta tell you something, but . . . but . . ." Masil helped herself to the coffee and flopped into a kitchen chair.

"Tell me what?"

"I know sometimes I repeat things I shouldn't, but . . ."

No conversation that started that way ever ended good. "Do I want to hear it?" Bea knew when Masil looked the way she did now, concern written all over her face, she couldn't keep silent, even if someone threatened to tie her to a stake and put hot coals on her tongue if she did tell.

"Now remember, I don't know if there's any truth in this or not, but since I heard it, I figured maybe, you know, where there's smoke—"

"There's fire. Okay Masil, I get your point. What did you hear?"

"Yesterday at the beauty shop, I overheard Peg tell Wanda that she saw Hal . . ."

Bea's heart skipped in her throat. She dreaded what came next. It wasn't good, not by the expression on Masil's face. "What? Peg said what?"

"Looks like Hal's the latest man . . . caught in the . . . goings-on at the shipyard."

"What do you mean?" Bea knew what she meant.

"You know how it is these days with all those women who work right alongside the men. By the time some of 'em have worked at the shipyard three or four months, they've fallen in love with someone. Next thing you know, the men quit their wives, and the women leave their husbands, if they had one in the first place, to get remarried. Or sometimes they just shack up together."

"And Hal's one of them?"

"He's been seen playing around with one of the women, yeah. Ernie said he saw her up in the cab of Hal's gantry the other day. I don't know what's going on between them, but thought you might want to put a stop to it—that is, if you can."

A wail from the bedroom dropped Bea's heart back into her chest. Her day—the same one that had just crashed to earth—started anew.

She darted down the short hallway to a screaming Percy, his face as red as his hair. His hands were clenched into fists and snot ran down into his mouth.

"Hey, hey, little guy, you're okay. Mama's here. Shh, hush now. You don't have to scream. I've got your breakfast all ready for you." She scooped him up, held him and the ammonia-smelling diaper at arm's length, and headed to the bathroom.

By the time she got to the kitchen with Percy on her hip and the smelly diapers in her hand, Masil had poured another cup of coffee and sat at the table dunking a cold biscuit into the hot liquid.

"I feel just awful being the one to tell you this, sweetheart," Masil yelled over cries of the hungry baby, "but you're my best friend. I couldn't keep that from you, not when everybody in the whole town knows but you."

Bea got out a dish and spooned in leftover scrambled eggs. She plopped Percy, still screaming, in the high chair built by her grandfather, the one used by all of her siblings and now Percy. Between his screams, Bea spooned food into his mouth. At first he looked startled, then swallowed the mouthful and grabbed for more.

The plate scraped clean and Percy happy once again, Bea spread a quilt on the living room floor, plopped the baby in the middle of it and handed him a rattle whittled from a scrap of hardwood and sanded smooth. With effort, Percy finally got his eyes, hands, and feet coordinated, and the rattle went straight to his mouth. Masil sat on the pallet beside him and tickled the bottom of a pink, bare foot stuck up in the air.

"Wha' cha thinking?" She looked at Percy, but spoke to Bea.

Bea didn't answer. Despite the steamy morning, a block of ice had formed in her chest.

Masil ignored Bea for a few minutes, playing kitchicoo with Percy while he chuckled, eyes sparkling and drool running down the side of his face.

A loud knock on the door rescued Bea from her frozen state. Relieved to have something to do other than think, she hurtled toward the door. The same man who dunned her for the rent the week before stood on the other side of the screen.

Bea took a step back too late. He'd seen her. "Ma'am, sorry to bother you again . . ." He took off his hat and twirled it between his hands, ". . . but I really need to collect the rent."

"I can't give you what I don't have." Bea knew she sounded bitter, but for the life of her, she could do no other.

"Ma'am, you're behind. You know lots of people beg us to move into these places. If you don't pay soon we'll be forced to evict you." With that warning, the man turned and walked off the porch.

Bea lifted her head, turned from the door and pushed her spine as straight as Mrs. Stark's—the richest woman in town. Only the quiver of her chin gave indication of the effort expended.

"I wish I could help, honey," Masil said as she rose to her feet, her eyebrows knit together.

Bea collapsed in the rocker and fought the tears that threatened to overtake her. "It's not like Hal doesn't make enough money, but he spends it on any and everything else but our bills. I hardly get enough to keep food on the table, much less pay the rent. Now he wants to buy a shrimp boat. Swears he can make lots of money selling shrimp."

Then, slamming a lock on her emotions, she pulled her thin lips into a tight line. Dammit, she might cry in the middle of the night, but not in the daytime where anyone could see her. "I've got laundry to do, Masil, so if you don't mind . . ." Percy had dropped his rattle so she bent over, collected it, and put it in his hands. Her lips twitched when he rewarded her with a big smile. Oh, for problems so easily fixed.

"I get your drift," Masil said. "Okay, honey, I know you need some time alone. I'll go home. But you come get me if you need me or you get ready to talk, okay?"

Bea gave a slight nod as she accompanied Masil to the door and latched the screen behind her.

Alone at last, the death-sentence-of-a-day loomed before Bea. The baby seemed content for the moment, so she stumbled to the kitchen, stood like a zombie, and faced the diapers she'd brought from the bathroom. She pulled out the new rub board, filled the sink with scalding hot water and Swan soap, and dumped in yesterday's pile of dirty stinky diapers. But the strong smell of ammonia made her rush to the backdoor for a quick breath of fresh air. Then she returned to the sink and plunged her hands down into the hot sudsy liquid. Mindless, she scrubbed.

"I am thankful, dammit," she said, stubbornly. "What I'm thankful for is this blasted rub board to scrub my clothes on." It had taken her weeks to save enough pennies to buy it at Farmers Mercantile.

The diapers clean, she drained the dirty water out of the sink and refilled it with fresh, clean. After she rinsed the soap from the diapers, she wrung them tight, wishing with each twist Hal's neck lay in the palms of her hands.

All the while, rain fell in buckets. She was trapped inside the place she hated—the ugliest house she'd ever seen. Desperate for dry diapers, she rummaged through a drawer until she found a ball of twine, strung it across the living room and tied it on nails Hal had hammered into the walls for just such days. That done, she clothes-pinned the diapers and rags to the twine. Hopefully the diapers would dry before she ran out of the few she had left, but with weather like this, the air felt as wet as the clothes.

Throughout the day, she struggled with whether to confront Hal. If she did, she'd be forced to do something about it. She wasn't completely surprised by his actions. She'd known the tall, red-headed, greener-pastures kind of guy would never be content for long, regardless of where he went or who he married. She had known that, and married him anyway—she, a stiff young woman who tied any emotion into the corner of a handkerchief and beat it into submission with a baseball bat.

Maybe she'd just act like she didn't know anything about the affair. After all, she had Percy to think of, and tomorrow they might be evicted.

Chapter 3

Oskar Eichel trudged down Highway 90 for an hour or so when an old flatbed truck pulled alongside him and a heavily wrinkled, gray-haired woman with snuff running out the side of her mouth leaned out the truck window and offered him a ride. He preferred walking, rather than taking a chance someone would guess his relationship with the enemy, but she insisted. Oskar hoped he wouldn't have to talk much, fearful his speech might give him away. Contractions gave him the most difficulty. He must remember to use them more often when he spoke English.

Most of the way, the woman talked on and on about the war, taking an occasional break to spit out the window. "I can always tell where a man's from by the way he talks," she said. "Like you, for instance. I can tell you're a Yankee."

Oskar didn't correct her. By the time she reached her turn and dropped him off, he silently thanked his stepfather for making him take all those English lessons before they immigrated to America. At least he'd done that much for Oskar.

He continued on foot down the side of the highway, which, according to the map he'd memorized, led to the German POW camp located on land owned by a Lutcher Moore Lumber Company. The prisoners—some 140 of them—detailed in from a U.S. Army base near the town of Huntsville, worked the rice fields.

Rounding a bend, he saw row after row of tents. A column of Army trucks sat nearby with prisoners climbing onboard, none of whom looked like his younger brother, Wilhelm. The trucks rattled off and headed down the road. The guards looked relaxed and content in their jobs and so did the prisoners. Oskar doubted his brother would be in a POW camp, but with him born a German, and not taking his papers when he ran away, no telling what might have happened.

Oskar headed off behind the last truck, keeping an eye open for cars on the road, hiding in the ditch when one approached. By the time he reached the rice fields, he found himself on the opposite side of the parked trucks, making it difficult to get a glimpse of the prisoners without getting closer. He dare not attract attention to himself.

He noticed a black DeSoto pull off the road and head across the field toward the clump of trees where he hid. When it slowed and stopped a mere ten meters from him, he held his breath, fearing his own demise.

A movement across the field forced his eyes off the car and to a German prisoner crouched low, headed his way. Every inch of Oskar's body cried *flee*. Only one part of him said wait, watch. He slowed his breathing and stilled his muscles as the door of the vehicle opened. Out stepped a woman with hair as dark as midnight. A smile of eager anticipation played across her face. She exited, closed the door and hurried to the front of the automobile. All the while, she watched the prisoner head toward her.

The German, obviously trying to look invisible, hurried his steps.

Even from a distance, Oskar knew where this scene headed and how it would play out. He tried to turn away, wished for escape from a private moment between others, but try as he might, he could not peel his eyes off of them. Mesmerized, he watched them draw closer, each eager for what lay ahead, driven by an unrelenting need to copulate, willing to risk everything.

The German looked over his shoulder as he drew closer and stepped under what little cover the tree branches offered this early in the day. He must know he took the greater risk. But maybe he didn't. It must not be easy facing a hostile community who knew you were not only a loose woman, but also one who cavorted with the enemy.

The fleeting question of how the rendezvous had been arranged raced though Oskar's mind. Perhaps she delivered food from a local eatery and they'd made eye contact, agreeing to the clandestine meeting. If the guards caught him, his days wouldn't be as pleasant as they had been working outdoors in the rice fields.

That fact likely made their rendezvous even more exciting for both of them.

The woman slipped off her undergarments, tucked her print skirt between her thighs, crawled onto the backseat of the black DeSoto and waited.

Despite himself, Oskar's unquenched passion welled up, a passion only dreamed about since leaving a childhood sweetheart behind in Germany. Guilt slammed his eyes shut, hoping to erase the image, yet the uncontrollable desire to join them forced his eyes open again.

Unable to do other, Oskar unbuttoned his fly.

The prisoner, now at the car's front fender, fumbled in his trousers as he ducked his head and headed to the open door.

Oskar watched as the man crawled in on top of her. His greedy mouth searching, he licked, nipped, and kissed her bare skin like he had no other chance to ever touch a woman. He inched around until he had easy access, slid one hand up her skirt and found her.

She groaned.

Oskar matched his breath to theirs and found his own release.

Later, the two crawled from the backseat, straightened and rearranged their clothes while the woman nudged her dark hair away from her face, laughing.

Oskar waited until the car drove off and the guy turned in the direction of his work crew.

"Psst, psst," Oskar called.

The man stopped, listened. "Who's that?"

"Over here." Oskar whispered.

"What do you want?" the man asked, moving a step closer.

"Heil Hitler." Oskar breathed the ugly words into the moist air, hoping to throw the man off. The words bounced back at him from the voice of the other.

The prisoner hustled over as Oskar stepped from behind the tree.

"I'm trying to find my brother," he explained. "I wonder if he might have been picked up and . . ."

"Who is it? What's his name? There's not very many of us here, maybe a hundred or so. Tell me, tell me quick." He glanced over at a guard heading his way, yelling.

"Eichel, Wilhelm Eichel."

"Never heard of him."

"Hey, get over here," the guard yelled. "What do you think you're doing?"

The POW zipped his pants, turned and headed toward the guard, arms in the air. "Just taking a piss. Just taking a piss."

Oskar plastered himself against the tree, forcing his body into paralysis, waiting until both men were far enough away. Then, relieved, he crawled to a nearby clump of bushes that offered a little more cover. Exhausted, he slept.

When darkness fell he headed off again. He passed a tomato garden, its bushes laden with deep red fruit. He plucked several, stuffed a few in his bag, and went on to fulfill the next step of the quest—to locate an old abandoned barn where he could sleep safe and dry.

Chapter 4

A day spent with a teething, fussy baby and wet clothes hanging all over the house left Bea exhausted and not in the best of humor. By the time she got Percy down, hopefully for the night, the Westclox pointed to straight up eight. Hal still hadn't come home. She looked outside, listening for his rattletrap car. All she heard were frogs begging for more rain. She closed the screen and turned inside, sick over the rumor about Hal. A vague ache in her bones confirmed her suspicion.

For a lifetime she'd lived by the answers given to her by others. She never questioned, never modified. Now, it seemed the more she embraced those answers, the less they fit life's questions. She walked around with this cloud of confusion over her head because Mama taught her that women lived in a world of certainties. Do this, get that. And when life didn't pan out the way she expected, she'd redoubled her efforts. For surely the problem didn't lie in the answers she'd been given, but the effort she put forth.

Now she'd dug one hell of a deep hole for herself.

She'd worked really hard to be a good wife to Hal, fulfill her wifely duties. At first, the sex had been good. Hal knew she was a virgin, and took his time with her, tried to make her feel good about her ability to please him. Then, later, it seemed he'd grown weary of the effort and only wanted to satisfy his own needs. Hop on, hop off. She'd taken to using Vaseline every night to make it easier for him and more comfortable for her. After all, Mama taught her to never refuse her husband or he'd go looking for it elsewhere. So much for that advice.

She kept herself looking nice for him. She showered every day, wore clean, freshly ironed clothes, and brushed her hair until it shone. Sadness overwhelmed her nights, but she refused to let it ruin her days. She cooked his meals, cared for Percy. What else could she do to make the man happy?

Clueless, she wandered into the kitchen, flipped on the light and saw Hal's supper on the stove, now as cold as her heart. She snatched the plate, walked to the backyard, and scraped the food into the neighbor's dog dish. If Hal ever did come home, he could damn well eat his supper out back with the other dogs.

Back inside, she dropped the plate and fork in the sink, turned around and leaned against the edge of the cabinet and stared at nothing until a blob of dried food on a chrome table leg caught her eye. She flicked it off with her fingernail, then sat at the table and aimlessly switched on the radio. In what had been Red Skelton's time slot, before his draft number came up, the station now filled with Ozzie and Harriet Nelson singing *Mairzy Doats*. Despite her mood, the catchy beat caused Bea's fingers to drum on the yellow Formica table. After the show ended, she headed to bed only to lay awake thinking about Hal and the other woman.

It must have been after midnight when the front door opened and closed with barely a click. Next, the bathroom door squeaked shut, and soon a strip of light gleamed from underneath. A couple of minutes later the toilet flushed and she heard him brushing his teeth. When the bathroom light went off, Bea held her breath.

The door opened and soon the springs on the bed groaned as the mattress sagged under the extra weight.

If she didn't say anything, didn't move, maybe he'd think she slept.

He shook her shoulder. "I need to come clean. Bea, I've met this woman . . ."

She tried to speak, but her chest felt like the house had caved in and she lay under a pile of rubble.

He waited, then spoke again, hesitantly. "You're not going to say anything?"

SYLVIA DICKEY SMITH

A million words charged through her brain, but not one formed well enough to exit her mouth.

"Say something, damn it," he yelled.

"Shh, you'll wake the baby." Bea sat up and looked at his bare rigid back. The skies had cleared and now the full moon hung just outside their open bedroom window. Shadows danced across his shoulders.

She sank back down. "What the hell do you expect me to say? I already knew about it. I wondered if you'd have the guts to tell me yourself."

"How'd you hear?"

"Masil came by this morning."

"I should've known."

"It seems everyone else in town already knew—everyone but me, that is."

"She's got a big mouth and puts it in everybody else's business."

Bea slung herself across the bed toward him, unable to hold the tears that had threatened to fall all day. He half-turned and grabbed her, pulled her down on the bed with him. She lay against his smooth, bare chest, his arms around her. "I'm sorry, Bea, I didn't expect this to happen. I don't know what to do, but . . . but . . ."

She jerked away. "What's her name? I want to know what her name is."

"Bea, don't do this. I don't want to hurt you."

"Hurt me? It seems a little late for that." She huffed to Percy's door and closed it, pulled down the blackout shades then flipped on the light in their bedroom. Through clenched teeth, she demanded, "Tell me, you bastard. What's her damn name? I have a right to know."

"It's Violet."

"Violet?" The name tasted bitter on her tongue—bitter as quinine. "And just how do you expect me to take care of the baby—this baby—*our* baby while you're screwing around with her? Don't we count for something?"

"She's a real nice woman, Bea. You'd like her if you gave yourself half a chance."

"Like her? My God, Hal, our rent is overdue and you're out screwing around with some woman? You must be crazy if you think . . ." Bea fled into the dark bathroom, tears streaming down her cheeks and into her mouth. She swiped her nose and wiped her hand on the muslin nightgown. Oh, how she wanted to slam the door, but she didn't need Percy bawling along with her.

The icebox opened and shut. Hal had gone to the kitchen looking for his supper. Well, he could look in the neighbor's damn dog dish in the backyard. She stood in the middle of the tiny bathroom and waited for her world to change back to what it had been before it collapsed, trapping her, sucking her down into thick bottomless quicksand. She'd done everything she could to make Hal happy—done her best to take care of his needs, never said no—not even once—even though he never gave her time enough to even get ready.

She flung open the medicine cabinet, grabbed the Vaseline and slung it across the room, breaking the jar and smearing thick petroleum jelly across the linoleum floor.

Overcome with it all, she lowered the toilet seat, sat and buried her face in her hands.

Morning after morning, she had staggered to the damn kitchen, even through weeks of morning sickness, cooked him hot biscuits and eggs, fixed his lunch, and fried fresh fruit pies. He took the pies to work and ate them in front of the other men just to make them jealous.

She was pretty, she knew it. All the men told her so with their eyes. But she'd been faithful.

And for what? This?

Why did Hal sleep with that other woman—that *Violet*? What did she have that Bea didn't? Money, maybe? Masil said Violet came from one of the timber families. But money never had meant much to Hal. He could take it or leave it—and leave the bill collectors on their front porch while he gallivanted around, leaving her behind to keep a roof over their heads. Sometimes he called her wooden. Maybe she was—but in times like these it served her well.

After the house grew quiet, Bea stood, splashed cold water on her face and tiptoed into the baby's room. When they got married, she'd tried to get Hal to use condoms, but he didn't like the feel, so she hadn't insisted. Nine months later, along came Percy. She'd never been around children much, and didn't think she could change nasty diapers and clean spit-up, but she did the best she could, and she'd fallen in love with the little guy.

Now Percy lay in his bed fast asleep, innocent and helpless. All he had was her—all she had was responsibility.

* * *

The next morning, as Bea slipped out of the bedroom, she grabbed Hal's khaki pants and took them into the bathroom with her. Rummaging through his pockets until she came up with a wad of bills, she unfurled enough to cover the rent and returned the remainder. Quiet as a mouse, she tiptoed back into the bedroom, put the pants where they were and headed to the kitchen, relieved Hal didn't stir.

Despite the sweltering temperature, Bea shivered when he walked into the kitchen a little while later. When he came to where she stood pouring hot gravy into a bowl and planted a kiss on her cheek, an even colder chill ran down her spine.

"Don't," she said. "And don't *baby* me." She slammed the bowl of gravy on the table beside the biscuits, fled to the bathroom and locked the door in case he followed.

Not that he ever followed her anywhere.

She opened the medicine cabinet, took out a tube of Tangee lipstick and smeared it on, marveling at how the orange color changed as soon as it touched her lips. She'd read it had something to do with a woman's own chemistry. She grabbed a brush and swept her hair into the latest Rita Hayworth style, parting it on the side and letting it fall to her shoulders. She stalled a little longer and plucked a lone gray hair from her head and dropped it in the waste basket.

The front door opened and closed. Good, he'd left for work.

In her bedroom, she slipped out of her nightgown and pulled on a flower print dress just as babbling sounds came from across the hall. She stepped into Percy's room where the smell of ammonia almost bowled her over. He rolled onto his stomach and pushed up on his hands, arched his back, his eyes seeking hers. Successful at last, his face broke into a happy grin.

The block of ice stored in her chest melted. "Morning, Sweetie. Let's get you cleaned up and fed. Mama needs to get away for a while today, okay?"

After changing his clothes and shoveling oatmeal in his mouth, she swung him to her hip and headed to the neighbor's place on the other side of the duplex.

"Mrs. Woods, would you mind watching Percy for a few hours? I need some time to myself—to get away and think about things."

"Ah, honey, no problem. What's one more?"

What's one more? Bea barely managed her one. She couldn't imagine *one more* adding little to an already overloaded brood of children.

"I have a pallet ready. My kids love the little guy. Here, give him to me."

The large woman took Percy from Bea's arms. "We're going to have us a good time today, aren't we, sweetheart? Look, kids, here's Percy." She put him on the floor in the middle of her three youngest, each clamoring for his attention. Her older children had walked the short distance to summer school. "I hate to say so, Bea, but you look like you really need a break. You take your time. Percy and me will do just fine. Last night I cooked a big pot of fresh green beans. I'll mash some for his lunch."

"Oh, that'd be great. Thanks so much, I really do appreciate it. I won't be late."

"Wait a second. I almost forgot again. Let me give you this." Mrs. Woods reached in her apron pocket and pulled out the bottle of

Mercurochrome she'd borrowed, and handed it to Bea. "The kids love the bright red color. They call it monkey blood, and beg me to put it on every little scratch they get. If I don't return it, they'll use up the whole dang bottle."

Bea tightened the lid before she tucked it in her pocket, fearful even the tiniest leak would ruin her dress.

She kissed Percy on the cheek and headed through Riverside Addition—government war housing. The endless rows of frail gray duplexes squatting atop river sand looked like the long lines of homeless people she'd seen in front of a soup kitchen. No trees, no grass, no flowers—no nothing, except maybe an occasional tuft of a sickly-yellow weed. It was the ugliest place she'd ever seen. No wonder she struggled with feeling thankful for where she lived—but then she reminded herself of the alternative, living in a tent.

A constant stream of muddy cars splashed by, forcing vigilance less she get soaked with the wet stench. She passed by Tilley Elementary, one of three government-built primary schools constructed in Riverside and named to honor the first local young men killed in the war. The other two, Manley and Coburn, were located on opposite sides of the addition.

After a brief stop at the rental office to cover her past-due rent, she continued on to the bus stop where a line of people waited—men, women and children heading to or from work. It still startled her to see so many women wearing pants. The war had changed the world, as she knew it. Where would it end? Where would *she* end?

The bus driver, a middle-aged man dressed in the usual khaki uniform seemed in a big hurry to keep on schedule. He barely grunted when she climbed aboard and dropped her ration coupon through the slot, and then he took off before she had time to find a seat.

At the next stop, the grizzled man who sat behind the driver scooted over to the window seat and motioned her to sit in the space he'd vacated. With scarcely a glance her way, he continued reading a newspaper that screamed the latest war headlines.

Bea pulled a cloak of invisibility around her and stared through the front window, thankful the man kept his head buried in the newspaper.

The bus passed large plots of land where tents squatted, stake-to-stake. Even in broad daylight, big rats scampered from one tent to the next. Orange had changed so much since the war started that she hardly recognized it any more. At least Riverside Addition provided some housing relief. Lots of folks who had been living in tents moved into the new duplexes as soon as they were completed. Should she be evicted, which lucky family from which tent would move into her home the same day she moved out?

She lost track of how long she rode the bus, but when it reached the edge of town, Bea stood and headed down the aisle.

"You got family around here or something, ma'am?" The driver looked her up and down, from her swollen eyes to her run-over brown oxfords. "Ain't nothing much around these parts 'cepting the prisoner camp up the road yonder. Sure you wanna be left here? I ain't coming back this way till late today."

Desperation drove bravery. More than anything, she needed a few hours alone—without any interruption. "I'll be okay," she said to the driver. "My grandfather's old farm is just down the road."

Without looking back, she stepped off the bus and headed down a long, tree-lined dirt road, desperate for time away from the world. Time to think.

Walk, just walk, she told herself. *Walk 'til you drop, walk 'til you make some kind of sense out of . . .*

The sun hung high in the sky. Her damp dress stuck to her clammy skin by the time she spotted the dilapidated barn squatting in the middle of a big field full of brush and prickly-pear cactus.

Her grandfather's barn looked like Bea felt. Abandoned. Forsaken.

At least it provided a shady place to stop and rest. Perhaps pleasant memories from her childhood might crowd out, if even for the moment, what she faced in the coming months.

Just the thought of her childhood sent a pleasant shiver through

SYLVIA DICKEY SMITH

her. She hastened her step, eager now to get inside, eager to sit and recall days on her grandfather's farm when she'd followed Edith around and spied on her. Both her older sisters, Edith and Marie, seemed to attract good-for-nothing boys, and both ended up marrying the same kind of men. Marie, already gone from the house when Bea was little, trailed along behind that self-centered pretty-boy Sol for years, until he finally married her, Bea figured, out of pity. Edith had gone through a series of marriages, getting divorced and remarried over and over. Then again, there was no telling how many more men she'd slept with that she hadn't married.

You'd have thought Bea would have learned something from watching them. But no, she'd married the first man who'd asked—Hal, whose Aunt Irene was the same Irene Sol had chased unsuccessfully before he gave up and "settled" for Marie. But that was typical of Orange, at least before the war started, when it had been a small town. Everybody knew everybody—sometimes, too well. Now, Bea found herself in the same pickle. Why did the women in her family forever attract no-good men? Or maybe there weren't enough good men to go around.

The closer she got to the barn, the more abandoned it looked. Determined shrubs that once sprouted around the doorway and windows were now dead branches blowing in the warm wind. Any life that might have once filled the barn, abandoned it long ago. Left behind were only sprigs of weed punching their way through a forgotten path. The remnants of a lone fireplace stood exposed not far beyond the barn, the only evidence a house had once been there.

Bea stumbled to the barn and entered the wide door.

A sense she'd just entered the shell of herself so overwhelmed her she dropped to the earthen floor. The dry, husky smell of hay and dust coated her throat, sending her into a coughing fit. She collapsed alongside a rusty pitchfork, flinching when a field mouse skittered up the wall and over the window frame away from her, just like she flinched away from Hal earlier that morning.

She pulled her knees up to her chest, wrapped her arms around her legs and surrendered to self-pity. What did she do now, a woman with a baby but no husband? If Mama hadn't passed last year, she could move in with her again, but . . . Mama was no longer an option.

Overwhelmed by desperation and helplessness, the tears came and didn't stop until she reached the point of exhaustion. Drained, she struggled to her feet, knowing she must return and wait for the bus. She wiped her face with her skirt tail, glad no one saw the mess she'd made of herself.

Outside, she stared at a deep blue sky that went on forever. Huge puffs of white, cottony clouds drifted by as though they, too, had no one who cared if they came or went. Halfway across the brittle-grass field, though, a movement caught her eye. She pulled up short, her heart in her throat, thinking she'd been the only human around. But now a tall blond-haired man in dark clothing darted from behind the barn and ran toward the barbed-wire fence. Had he been inside with her, heard her crying? The thought embarrassed her.

He took one quick glance at her, then bent over and tried to step through the wire. But the back of his shirt caught on one of the barbs and, in haste to free himself, pulled the rusty staples from the fence post. The barbed wire recoiled around him like a snake. The more he struggled, the more entrapped he became. Blood soon stained his shirt, as he tried to free himself from the tangled wire around his feet and ankles.

Bea couldn't stand to see the man so helpless, trapped. She knew what that felt like. Against her better judgment, she called as she ran towards him. "Be still. You'll just make it worse. Wait, I'll come help you."

"Do not bother yourself. I can get myself loose." He moved, and another wire clawed around his ankle.

By the time she reached him, he looked more like a snared rabbit.

"Don't be silly. Here, I'll hold this wire while you hold that one, then when we get them both up, ease under here. Careful or you'll tear off another hunk of skin."

"It is okay, really."

"Stop arguing. Duck under while I hold this one up."

It took several minutes before they worked him free.

"Thanks," the man said. "This wire is vicious, is it not?"

"Very unforgiving. It's like stepping in a bed of water moccasins. Once you're in, every move just makes it worse. You're pretty cut up."

She remembered the bottle of Mercurochrome in her pocket. "You're in luck. I have antiseptic and a handkerchief here. Come, let me help you to the barn, and I'll clean up the wounds."

"That is very kind of you, madam, but I don't want to cause you inconvenience."

"No problem. I'm just worried about a couple of those nasty cuts. They look deep, and with this heat and humidity, you don't want to take a chance on infection. Here, let's go sit you down." She took him by the arm and led him into the barn away from the hot sun, where he could sit and put his feet up while she doctored his wounds.

"My name is Bea," she said, guiding him to a musty pile of hay.

"Nice to meet you, madam. My name is Oskar Eichel."

"Sit down here."

He slid his arm from around her shoulder and eased down on the hay. "You're far too kind, madam. I can attend to this."

"It won't take me but a minute, and you can be on your way." Her thoughts went to Percy. She really must get home to him, but Mama always taught her to do like Jesus said and be a Good Samaritan. It wouldn't take but a minute to treat the man's wounds, and then she could head to the bus stop. She knelt on the floor in front of him and propped his foot in her lap.

Glad that she had tucked an extra handkerchief in her pocket earlier that morning, she pulled it out with the bottle of antiseptic and soon had the wounds doctored and wrapped. "The cuts should be okay until you get home and clean them better."

She looked up at the young man, surprised to see he stared into her eyes with an intensity she'd not experienced before now. Their eyes held for an instant, until, uncomfortable, she broke her gaze. A small half-moon-shaped scar in the right corner of his lip caught her attention. A scar he might have gotten as a boy when he fell on a piece of glass from a broken Coca Cola, or maybe a beer bottle.

An overwhelming urge to caress the scar forced Bea to cram her hands down inside her pockets else she reach up, run her finger down the scar and ask what happened. She had no right to ask such questions, or to touch him in such an intimate way.

"You are most kind." His words were soft and low, as if he were surprised, awed even, by her kindness. "Do you live nearby?"

His question startled her, for until now, she hadn't thought about the vulnerability of her situation, on an abandoned farm, all alone with a stranger who talked a little funny. Then again, since the war started, lots of people from other places lived here, and they all talked funny.

"Yes, not far. I must be going or my family will be looking for me." She hustled to her feet, collected her bag and stepped back, not understanding why more than anything she wanted to step forward.

"I've kept you way too long," he said. "I know you must be on your way. Please forgive me for taking your time."

Oskar collected his duffel bag and bid her farewell. She watched the strange, good-looking man head across the field. His leaving left her sad, as if she'd lost a chance for something she never knew existed.

She wondered about the man as she boarded the bus. Who was he? Where did he come from? And why had she behaved so out of character?

Chapter 5

Oskar watched the woman with the pretty blonde hair walk down the road. Keeping out of sight, he made sure she boarded the bus before he followed on foot in the same direction. He hoped the highway led to Orange and the famous Consolidated Shipbuilding. It sounded like a good place to get a job. He heard they hired anyone who stood on two legs and breathed. If that were the case, he fit the bill.

He wondered if his brother really had fled to this area with the band of gypsies who had passed through Seguin. The wagon driver sure looked like he was telling the truth when he whispered that Wilhelm had hid inside, and that they had headed to Orange County where work was plentiful.

After he found Wilhelm and got him enlisted in the Army, he might settle here himself, put down roots. But first, he must accomplish that goal, or he'd have hell to pay. He wasn't ever going home again, anyway, so whether he found Wilhelm or not might not matter—but he'd promised his mother . . .

Branches of an orange tree, laden with fruit, hung over the road. Half-starved and thirsty, he plucked one, peeled it and gobbled it down, reveling in the warm sweet juice on his parched throat. If sunshine had a taste, this would be it, he decided. He picked a couple more and tucked them in his bag for later.

"Which way do I go now?" he asked, standing in the middle of a crossroads. Before he decided, a butterfly flitted over his head and landed on his chest. Stunned by its beauty, he stood motionless, not wanting it to leave. He slowed his breathing and, in the dimming light, stared down at the creature. Its colors were each outlined in black, and the lower half of its wings were solid black except for a dollop of reddish-orange smack in the middle of each. The upper wings glowed brilliant turquoise. All except the top tips. They looked like a brush stroke of paint scooped off the sun right before it slipped below the horizon.

The butterfly looked stunned, unsure which way to go, or how long it took to get there. Oskar remembered reading how, when they first exited the cocoon, they were disoriented for a brief while. He felt sympathy for the small creature.

It fluttered its wings and took flight, only to light on the branch of an overhanging pine tree. Fragile, spindly legs grasped the needles. The butterfly fought to get its bearing, then flittered off into the growing darkness.

When he'd first said he'd look for Wilhelm—not as if he'd had a choice and keep his mother happy—he hadn't realized how far the trail went. And he knew that for a German to travel across a land at war with his mother country held its own unique risks. For anyone might easily doubt the Eichel brothers' loyalty to their new country. Little did they realize the risks were greater for Wilhelm or Oskar over there in Germany, than they were here in America.

He stepped from the growing shadows into the roadway, and an old flatbed pick-up truck screeched to a halt alongside the shoulder. The driver leaned across the seat and called out the passenger window, "I thought I saw someone standing there. What way you headin', sonny? I be glad to give you a lift if you want one."

Oskar hesitated. He'd only been in the states for a year or so before the war started and knew he still hadn't lost all his Germanic accent, although he had managed to fool most of those he had met so far. By and large, they just thought he was from some other part of the country.

"That bag looks mighty heavy, fellow, and I reckon you're a soldier home for a spell. I be glad to take you as far as I'm going, couple ten miles down the road."

Oskar looked both ways and leapt across a ditch of murky

water.

"You sure?" he asked, mumbling a little. Maybe he'd take the old man up on the ride. He'd walked too many miles since leaving Seguin, and his new boots had already rubbed a blister on his left heel, with another starting on the right.

"Thanks, I appreciate it." Oskar tossed his duffel bag in the back of the truck, grabbed the door handle and pulled. It creaked and popped as it swung out on rusty hinges. He climbed in only to be assaulted with the smell of sweat and oily rags on the floorboard, topped off with the distinctive odor of wet dog.

"Name's Lem Weeks, sonny. It's sure been a hot'n' today, ain't it?"

"Yes sir, it sure has been. You live around this area?"

"Me and my wife and a passel of dogs and cats do, just a mile or two off the road up yonder."

That explained the dog smell.

"Can't see the place less'n you walk into the woods a ways. We keep to ourselves mostly. Once a week, I head in to town with our ration coupons and try to get gas for old Bessie here."

He patted the dash with affection.

"'Course, the wife makes sure she gets her sugar and butter, that sort a thing. She likes to cook for all the grandkids living with us since our daughter got killed in the war and whilst their daddy is somewhere in the South Pacific in some submarine."

"I'm sorry about your daughter. Was she a nurse?"

"Nah, she weren't content to do the job of a woman. She went off flying them planes—a WASP, she called herself." Grief coated his words, but the old man's chest swelled with pride. "She planned to join up with a friend. At the last minute the friend backed out, so my daughter ended up traveling all by herself over to Sweetwater, Texas, where she took her training."

"You must have been proud of her."

"I was, but her mama weren't. Kept begging her not to go, said she was afraid for her, but my daughter said she just had to."

"If you don't mind my asking, what happened?" Oskar asked.

"I don't mind. I'm proud of my gal's gumption, just sorry to've lost her so young and with all them kids. She towed targets for Air Force pilots' shooting practice. One day over Shreveport, Louisiana, this blistering storm came up and got her."

He grew quiet, as if remembering the day they received word of the accident. After the long pause, he picked up where he left off. "It's been a few months now, so the pain ain't quite so bad as at first, but them kids miss their mammy something awful. Wife thinks if she keeps enough food cooked up, it'll keep their minds off of their loss."

"Your wife sounds like my mother."

"Then you must have a good 'n. Wouldn't trade mine for no amount of money. You from these parts, son? You don't talk much like it."

Oskar laughed nervously. He expected people to ask, but he wondered if every time they did, he could expect the same amount of sweat to pop out on his top lip. With this heat and humidity, he could always blame the weather. He guessed there wasn't a good way to hide his nationality. One day he hoped he'd feel more like an American, but right now, he felt like the enemy.

"No, sir, I'm from over near Seguin, actually. My ancestors came over from Europe many years ago."

That seemed vague enough. If he told the old man of his German heritage, the man might die of a heart attack right there in the middle of the road.

"Seguin, huh? Then I guess that makes you Lutheran."

"Well, yes, that's right. You must know something about that part of the state."

"Little bit. My wife's folks are from that area and that's what they are. Man, did they get mad at me, a Hardshell Baptist, for marrying her and taking her away."

"Hardshell? I have heard of Baptists, but not that kind."

"It's a church what believes the good Lord chooses folks He

wants saved and saves 'em. And if He ain't picked you, ain't a lick of sense in my trying to convince you to get saved, 'cause you ain't getting to heaven. And if God does pick you, ain't nothing you can do to stop it, neither."

Oskar waited politely for that conversation to die a natural death.

"How long have you lived here?" Oskar asked, holding on to the dashboard as the old man made a sharp turn to the left.

"Oh, I's born and raised here. Always did have wanderlust about me though. Course that's afore I married my wife, Mabel. After that, we bought a few horses and settled in here."

"Oh, so you raise horses?" Oskar's favorite topic.

"That and farming. Keeps food on the table for all them young'uns, don't ya know? Got this one horse, man, she's a beauty. A real spitfire she is, too. I call her Lightnin' even though Mabel says that name sounds more like a stallion. But this gal? She ain't gonna let no man ride her. If you try, she'll reach back and bite your foot right out of the stirrup. Sassy she is, too. I done 'bout give up on her."

The old man stopped the truck at a row of mailboxes. "This here's where I turn. My house is just yonder up the road a ways."

Oskar pulled on the broken door handle and swung the door wide. "Thank you. I appreciate the ride. Nice meeting you." He grabbed the duffle bag from the back of the truck where he'd piled it earlier.

Just as he closed the door, the old man called out, "Say, I could tell you had a thing for horses when I mentioned Lightnin'. Would you like to come see her? Won't take but a minute, then I'll bring you right back here to the main road."

"I'd like that very much. Back home I owned a horse and folks always said I had a special way with them." He climbed back in and the old man turned onto the rutted dirt road leading to his house.

A couple minutes later, Lem pulled into the yard of a gray clapboard house with a dog-run down the middle and not a drop of paint anywhere on it. Four stair-step children ran around odd pieces of junk piled in the yard. They played some kind of game Oskar didn't recognize. Chickens clucked, and in their usual manner, ignored the world around them as they pecked the few blades of grass that survived active feet and a rooting pig. A mangy cur rounded the corner of the house yelping as if his best friend, once lost, had now been found. Guess he wasn't a Hardshell Baptist like his owner, Oskar thought, and chuckled to himself.

The mutt put on his brakes right before he reached the old man, but not fast enough to stop his forward momentum, and tumbled into the old guy's legs. Oskar grabbed Lem and steadied him.

"Gosh darn mutt," Lem swore.

After the dog, came the kids. They yelled something Oskar couldn't make out.

"Now you kids just run off and play." Lem slammed the truck door and made off toward a small corral. "This way." He motioned over his shoulder.

A barn door stood open, and a big defiant Gray stood in the doorway looking as if she knew they were coming to see her, and she was neither interested nor impressed.

They walked up to the fence and leaned on the rail.

The Gray ducked her head and snorted, pawing at the ground.

"See, what'd I tell ya. She's already pissed, just seeing me walk up. She's the boss mare, ain't no denying that."

Lightning eyed Oskar, dropped her head and looked up at him through long black eyelashes. Slow, hesitant, she put one foot in front of the other, easing toward the fence. She stopped six feet away.

Back home in Germany, folks knew of Oskar's skill with horses. He didn't believe in cruelty to animals and never used a whip on a horse regardless of the situation. He trained them in a way most men wouldn't have the patience to do.

Oskar held out his hand for her to smell. "Come on, girl, I'm not going to hurt you. And I promise I will not get on your back and try to break you. Come on, come on."

One step at the time, the horse moved closer until she stretched her neck far enough to smell the tips of Oskar's outstretched fingers. She sniffed, turned her head to the side and snorted, then came and sniffed again. She took another step forward.

"Well, I swan, I never seen her do nothin' like that before. Son, you do have a way with 'em, that's for sure."

"She's a beauty, Lem. Just a little suspicious." Oskar laughed, and Lightning reared her head at the joke.

He thought of his older brother, Dolph. He had stayed behind in Germany when the family left for America, and was now one of Hitler's storm troopers. It broke Oskar's heart to think how the war had ripped his family apart, much like America's Civil War had once divided North from South. It was complicated in the Eichel family because Oskar knew his father—stepfather, actually—had sympathized with his older son, mostly because *he* was his flesh and blood son. Oskar, however, had been sired by a secret affair of his mother's.

After moving to America, Wilhelm, the baby of the family, screwed up and got himself in trouble with the law. Thank goodness the leader of a gypsy band traveling through town told Oskar how Wilhelm had headed this way with them. If Oskar didn't find him soon, and get the boy enlisted in the Army, there'd be hell to pay.

Oskar wouldn't ever live at home again, but he couldn't abandon his mother. She'd put up with a lot living with her husband, Karl, all to keep her children clothed and fed. No, he had to find Wilhelm.

He glanced over at Lem, who stood reveling in the touch of his horse's nose as it nudged the carrot in his hand.

According to the propaganda of both countries, the enemy was some sort of crazed monster. On the contrary, people he'd met since arriving in America seemed to Oskar much like folks back home. Just people trying to make a living, who want to offer help to others, while at the same time find joy where they could.

"Say, son, I know you're anxious to get home to your family, but it's 'bout dark now. If'n you want, you can bed down here in the barn, then strike out first light. I get up early. What say I wake you at sunup, and take you down to the main road like I promised?"

"Thank you, sir. That offer sounds too good to refuse."

"Great. I'll get the missus to put together a plate of grub and bring it out. We can't do too much for our boys who defend our country."

Oskar smiled. "That would be great, sir. Again, thank you."

After he finished a plate of beans and rice and a hunk of cornbread, Oskar spread a horse blanket and settled down to spend another night with hay and horses. But he lay awake for a long time, his mind wandering from this to that—to the blonde-haired woman who showed him such kindness, to the old man and his wife, and to Lightning. That horse didn't care that he had been born a German and still had family there who fought with Hitler's troops.

As promised, at sunup the next morning, Lem opened the barn door, ready to go. Oskar folded the blanket, tossed his duffel bag in the truck bed again and climbed into the passenger seat. The truck rumbled down the road to the cutoff.

"Tell your mama she's got a great guy," Lem called out as Oskar headed off, turning to wave thank you.

Back to a trudge toward town, bag over his shoulder, Oskar again questioned why he'd decided to chase after his spoiled little brother. If the boy wanted to go to jail, let him. Lightning didn't like to be dominated and Wilhelm didn't either.

By the time he reached town, he decided he needed to stop thinking so much. He'd let the smell of that woman in the barn get to him, he chided himself. After all, it was only natural to find the woman attractive, to want to follow her, smelling around like a dog after a bitch in heat. But he was stronger than his emotions. He would find Wilhelm, and get the hell home—or wherever the trail took him after that.

SYLVIA DICKEY SMITH

Chapter 6

Hal adjusted his hard hat and started the climb up the tall ladder of the giant gantry crane. He felt like he hadn't accomplished much in his life, but it sure made him feel good to know his job at the shipyard aided the war effort. His skill as a crane operator working on dreadnaughts and other war ships meant he'd escaped the draft, which suited him just fine. He didn't have the guts for that kind of thing anyway.

Breathless by the time he reached the top of the crane, he stepped inside the cab, straddled the metal seat, and checked below. When no one signaled for a pickup, he pulled out a Camel, lit it, and waved the smoke rings away from around his face.

The din of the shipyard never stopped. Night and day, day and night, the pound of sledge hammers on the hulls of ships, the staccato rhythm of riveters peening one section of metal after another. Further offshore, the dismal wail of fog horns sounded a low wail for the thousands of men who had died on the battlefront and for those yet to die before this damn war ended.

A shrill whistle announced the end of one lunch and the beginning of another. For some, it signaled the end of a workday; for others, the start of theirs. Many of those leaving hastened out the gate, eager to clean up and head across the Louisiana Bridge to Showboat Ruby's. He wondered how many of them would get knocked in the head and rolled for cash, and which ones would drink their paychecks before they got home to their wife and kids. He'd done the latter himself more than once.

He felt bad about sleeping around on his wife, but hell, he had needs, and with the women here working alongside the men . . . well, resisting temptation never had been his strong suit. Besides, he'd never worked alongside women every day, their soft, round bodies a call he couldn't refuse. After all, a man could only stand so much. Especially when his wife had to use petroleum jelly before she went to bed at night to do her wifely duty. A warm, willing woman in his arms—hell, what man resisted that? Besides, what with the war and all, who knew what tomorrow might bring. Others used that excuse. He guessed he could, too.

He hadn't expected Violet to get pregnant. He felt guilty leaving Bea and Percy, and it hurt like hell when he told Bea about Violet, but the thought of bringing a bastard child into the world broke his heart, too. Mama and Papa—what would they do when he told them? Mama wouldn't say much, but Papa sure would.

Far below, the foreman signaled up to Hal. He shifted gears and headed the boom toward a load of pipe.

Just before the five o'clock whistle blew to signal the end of Hal's normal work day, his foreman called up to ask if he'd work a double shift. Since going home wasn't such a good idea, Hal agreed to do so. He shut off the crane and headed down the ladder to grab supper from one of the many vendors who sold food just outside the gate.

Starved, he wolfed the first sandwich down fast, like he did everything—at least to hear Bea tell it.

"So, did you tell her?" a voice from behind asked.

Hal squinted in the bright sun as Rufus walked his way. "Hey, Rufus, what's going on?"

Big-boned, tenderhearted Rufus couldn't squash a bug about to bite him in the butt. He leaned against the wall beside Hal, took off his hard hat, and plopped it on the ground beside him.

"How'd it go last night with Bea? You tell her?"

"Yeah, I told her alright, but it seems her friend beat me to it—except for the fact that I got Violet knocked up. I still have to break that news to her. I feel like shit, Rufus. I don't know what to do."

"Well, you know things ain't going too well for Violet, neither. Men around the yard talk about the woman in personnel whose belly's getting bigger and she ain't got a ring on her finger. Folks won't look kindly to her having a kid and not married, especially them brothers of hers. They found out yet?"

"Nah, she hadn't told them. She can't hide it much longer, though."

"Best thing to do is come clean, I say." Rufus opened his lunch pail and pulled out a couple of biscuits and ham. "By the way, I rode the bus to work this morning and guess who I saw on it, all by herself."

"No clue." Hal said, his mouth full of food.

"Bea."

Hal choked. He pounded his chest with his fist until the spasm subsided. "Bea? By herself?"

"In the flesh and all by her lonesome. She's a mighty good looker, you know."

"Yeah, yeah, don't give me that. What the hell's she doing on a bus all by herself? And where was my son?"

"Maybe she looked for Violet."

"Nah, that don't sound like Bea. She don't go nowhere without that baby." He pulled wax paper off one of Bea's fried apple pies he'd saved from lunch. She made them fresh for him every morning. He relished the first bite. This might well be the last pie she cooked for him. Truth be known, he couldn't blame her.

Rufus drooled. "Man, you gonna give up that good cooking? I'll bet you Violet ain't used to cooking like that, what with them servants and all."

Hal chuckled. "You're not getting any of this, ol' buddy. I might not get any more myself, and I'm not giving you none of this pie." The joke lightened Hal's mood and by the time the whistle blew, he felt eager to go back to work.

* * *

When Hal's swing shift ended, he crossed the street and walked into Cherry's Pool Hall to down a couple of beers before he headed home to face Bea.

Illuminated signs on the walls advertised different brands of beer, but did little to light the room well enough for Hal to see, until his eyes adjusted to the dim interior of the joint.

Several men sat at tables on the right holding dominos, playing Shoot The Moon. Behind them, pairs of jaunty, wisecracking fellows played pool while others waited their turn at the tables. Green-shaded lights suspended from the ceiling highlighted the balls in various patterns of play while the sweaty men, still wearing their dirty work clothes, hunkered over them like loose women ready for a good time.

The vinegary smell of pickled boiled eggs tickled Hal's nose.

Soon as the bartender saw Hal, he popped the top on Hal's favorite brew and plopped it in front of him before Hal could take his usual seat at the end of the bar. A buddy who smelled like he'd had more than his share of the brew scooted up next to him.

"So, you got the Spanish Inquisition yet?" He lifted a beer bottle to his lips, took a big swig and ordered another, wiping his hand across the circle of condensation on top of the bar. "Any time you go sticking it in a woman that ain't yours, you gotta expect it, man. What surprises me is she ain't already kicked you out."

"How do you know she hasn't?"

"My wife told me she ain't—not yet, at least. She keeps up with the goings on around town."

"Well, your wife's right. She hasn't yet."

"The old lady also said the woman you knocked up works across the street at the shipyard." He snickered and tilted his beer bottle towards Hal. "That, I'd worry about, sir. It's just a bunch of two-bit whores what work at the shipyard anyway, you know. My old lady said so, said no decent respectable woman did that sort of thing."

Another man spoke up. "Wait a minute. We gotta get them ships built. Women are all we got now since the able-bodied men are off fighting the war. If the women didn't pick up the slack, all we'd have is old men like me to build 'em. 'Course the Army left a few here who know how to operate them big cranes." He raised his bottle to Hal and staggered through the door to the toilet. When he did, the smell of urine wafting through the open door almost knocked Hal off the barstool.

Calm as all get out, Hal sat his beer on the counter. He turned to the man who had insulted Violet, pulled his fist back and punched him in the jaw. The hard blow knocked the tipsy fellow clean off the barstool.

While the man collected himself and crawled back up, Hal flipped a couple of coins to the bartender and headed out.

"Way to go, Hal," someone yelled from the back of the room.

He stepped outside and almost tumbled into Violet, dressed in a tan suit and platform shoes. Her brown pageboy glistened under the gigantic streetlights from the shipyard across the street.

"Was looking for you, Hal." She ducked her chin and looked up at him through thick, dark eyelashes. "Doctor says the baby will be born around Thanksgiving."

She hesitated. "Did you tell Bea about us?"

Hal's fingers toyed with a strand of her hair. "Yeah, I told her. She's not too happy. Says she don't know how she'll take care of Percy all by herself."

"Didn't you tell her what I said? That you and me could take Percy, and that I'd raise him like my own?"

The knot in his stomach grew heavier. "Not yet. I don't know how she'll take that news."

"But you have to tell her, Hal. Otherwise, she might not let you go, and ..." Violet's words trailed off, her chin quivered. She dabbed at her eyes with a lace-edged hanky. "I can't have a bastard, Hal. Promise me I won't. My folks won't be able to lift their heads in this town."

"It's okay, baby, don't cry. It'll be all right." He pushed a sprig of hair off her face just as two guys headed toward them.

Shit, it was Bernard and Horace, Violet's two younger brothers. But where was Johnny, the oldest—and the meanest—of the three?

The need to flee pounded inside Hal's chest. He grabbed Violet's arm and hustled her down the alley. "It's your brothers. Hurry, my car's parked down the street."

Hal had feared they'd be after him soon as they found out about the baby. He guessed they had. Bernard, the youngest, had a reputation of being as spoiled as a piece of meat left out over night in the middle of July. Things had to be his way or no way. Talk around town was he'd been involved in several fights across the Louisiana Bridge over at Showboat Ruby's. Some even said he'd killed a man one night, just because the man called him out on how he talked to the waitress. Horace, the middle of the three, wasn't so bad, but didn't have backbone enough to stand up to the other two. He did just what the other told him to do.

Hal and Violet didn't get far down the alley before a rough hand grabbed his arm from behind, jerked him around and shoved him against the side of the building.

It was Bernard, with his hot, foul-smelling breath. Horace was a step behind him.

Violet flailed at their backs with her fists. "Leave him alone. If you don't stop right this minute, I'm telling Daddy."

Bernard spoke first. His scrunched face in half shadow made him look like a monster. "What's this about you and my sister? I hear you violated her and now she's carrying your bastard kid. What you gonna do about it, that's what we want to know."

"Okay, guys, settle down. I didn't do anything to Violet that she didn't want me to."

Soon as those words left his mouth, Hal knew he'd said the wrong thing. Bernard's arm came up fast and before Hal could retract what he'd said, Bernard's fist slammed his head against the brick wall.

"You sonofabitch. You're a married man. You've already got a kid."

"Stop it," Violet screamed from behind her brothers. "Quit hitting him. This isn't his fault."

"Don't you worry none," Hal yelled, trying to dodge the blows.

"I'm going to marry her."

"Come on, Bernard," Horace begged. "That's enough. Let him go."

"You damn right you're going to marry her." Bernard pulled his fist back again and in one swift motion, slammed it into Hal's chin, ramming his head against the wall one more time. "If you don't, you're going to wish you were never born. And just to make sure you don't forget ..."

Another quick, sharp blow followed, and Hal slumped to the ground.

Chapter 7

Bea stood just inside the screen door and looked out. Had Hal worked a double shift or was he with *that woman* and not even coming home? Finally, a car pulled into the parking lot, the top half of the headlights blackened due to the war. She pushed the door open a little and watched until she recognized his silhouette walking slowly up the sidewalk. Just as he reached for the screen door, she swung it open, startling him.

"You work this late or you been with that whore?"

He kept his face down and crammed his pay envelope in her hand. "Now you've got money to pay the rent," he said, nudging past her and into the dimly lit living room.

She didn't tell him she didn't need it now, that she'd taken it out of his pants pockets earlier. No matter, next month's rent would come soon enough.

Then she saw his busted lip and a left eye almost swollen shut. "What happened to you?"

"Not now, Bea. Not now."

When he limped straight to the bathroom and shut the door, reality slapped her in the face. She had hoped all that about another woman would blow over and things would return to normal—whatever that was. Evidently, something else was going on besides him sleeping around.

When he didn't come out of the bathroom after several minutes, she stormed to the bedroom and flopped down on the edge of the bed and waited.

Hal came in a few minutes later and slumped beside her, his left eye now swollen totally shut. She didn't say a word, only sat with her hands in her lap and her heart frozen over.

"Violet's carrying my kid. I've got to marry her, Bea."

"Marry her? You're already married . . . to *me*."

Percy cried out in the other room. The bed rattled as he flipped over, and things grew quiet again—except for the blood rush in Bea's ears. "So what does that mean?" she asked. "You're leaving me and Percy for her and her bastard?"

"She said she'd take Percy and raise him as her own, Bea. That way you won't be stuck with a kid to raise all by yourself."

"Like hell she will. Over my cold dead body."

"I don't know what else to do. I can't just let a baby of mine be born without a name, Bea, you know that. Besides, her family has standing in town. I . . . I . . ."

For the first time since she'd known him, Hal had run out of something to say.

"Is that what happened to your eye and lip? She hit you?"

He shook his head. "Nah, me and these guys at the yard got in a tussling match. It's nothing."

She snorted. "Looks like they got the best of you—that's for dang sure."

"I don't guess we have a beef steak in the icebox."

Bea said nothing. She never did. When she died, that's probably what her family would engrave on her tombstone. *Here lies the woman who never said nothing.*

She stood, walked around the bed and crawled between the covers. At least tonight she had something to cry about.

Chapter 8

Images of herself and Percy living in a rat-infested tent on Green Avenue haunted Bea all night long. It reminded her how ashamed she'd been as a child carrying a syrup bucket to school packed with only a cold biscuit.

Soon as Hal left for work the next morning, she grabbed Percy, fussy as he was, and headed down the court to see Masil, who sat on the front steps with a coffee cup in her hand.

"I kind of thought you two might drop by today." Masil scooted over to make room.

Percy chuckled when he saw her and flapped his hands.

"Come here, you sweet thing." She sat her cup on the porch and grabbed the baby's outstretched arms.

"If you don't take him, I think he'll jump," Bea said, relieved of the load. She eased her sleepless, weary body to the step beside them.

"You sure are a happy little guy today." Masil bounced him a few times, then straightened his shirt and smoothed his flyaway red hair. "Want a cup of black joe? I've got some left. I can heat it up for you."

"No, thanks, I'm not going to drink up yours."

"That's okay, I can get more ration stamps in a day or so."

Bea stared off down the court.

"You told him you knew, didn't you?"

"I didn't have to." Bea sniffled and swiped her hand across her top lip. "*He* told *me*. And get this. Now she's with child and he plans to marry her."

"He can't marry her, he's married to you." Masil's voice went up an octave. "You mean he'll leave a wife and a kid because the other woman's pregnant? Trade two for two? That don't make sense."

"That's what he told me last night after we went to bed."

Masil sucked through her teeth. "Good Lord, what's this war doing to all of us?" She shook her head. "Here you are with a baby and a husband with a dangling dick looking for another place to stick it. And if that ain't bad enough . . ." She pitched away the little coffee left in her cup. It splattered and left a dark stain on the pumped-in river sand.

"What're you going to do?"

"That's what I came to ask you." Bea stuck her cotton print skirt down between her legs, leaned her forearms on her thighs and stared at the brown spot in the sand. After a minute, she reached over and wiggled Percy's toes. "I love this little guy, but sometimes I feel like he's this weight around my neck and I'm in deep water. And then I feel so ashamed for feeling that way."

Masil ignored the last comment. "You've got to get a job, Bea." Masil jiggled the baby who had grown fussy again. When that didn't work, she stood, swung him to one hip and swayed back and forth. A look of glee spread across her face.

"That's it. Go to work and support yourself. Lots of women work these days. It's no big deal. You'll do just fine."

Fear crawled inside Bea's stomach and tied it in a knot. She shook her head. "No, I can't do that. What would people say? Besides, I've got Percy to take care of."

The screen door of the neighboring duplex opened and a young girl, maybe fourteen or fifteen years old, came out, crossed the porch, and bounced down the steps shared by both units. Only a banister separated the front doors of the duplexes in Riverside, allowing for little privacy during the hot, humid summers.

A big smile spread across the girl's face when she spied the baby.

"Hi, Nelda," Masil said, as Percy almost leapt from Masil's arms into the outstretched ones offered by the neighbor girl.

SYLVIA DICKEY SMITH

"Nelda and her family just moved here from Lumberton." Masil scooted over again to make room. "Nelda, this is my best friend, Mrs. Meade."

"Hi," Nelda said, glancing from Percy to Bea and back to Percy. Her smile revealed a slight gap between her two front teeth, and a cluster of freckles sprinkled across her nose.

The two young ones played while Bea and Masil returned to their earlier conversation. Or rather, Masil returned to the topic. Bea clamped her mouth tight and crossed her arms over her chest.

Masil reached over and put her hands on Bea's crossed arms. "You can't let what other people say bother you, honey. Do what you have to. I don't really see you have much choice, not if Hal moves out. You struggle now to get him to bring his paycheck home before he stops by the pool hall and spends it on beer and bets. With him gone, you gotta go to work and take care of yourself. You can work the night shift at the shipyard. The baby will be asleep while you work. Then you can sleep while he takes his naps during the daytime."

"Wait, whoa, this is moving way too fast."

"I'll bet Nelda here could watch the baby." Masil turned to the young girl. "You've taken care of babies before, haven't you, sweetheart?"

"Oh yes'm. I've taken care of babies my whole life. I'm the oldest of eight. I love 'em when they're little like this." She tickled Percy's tummy and he giggled, pushed her hand back. Percy wound his fingers into her mass of light brown curls.

"Ouch, that hurts," she said, and unwound the tiny fingers from her hair. "What's his name?"

"It's Percy." Bea looked from Nelda to Masil. "You really think they'd hire me at the shipyard? I don't know how to do anything but be a housewife and mother."

"I hear they're desperate for workers, what with all the men off to war. They don't care if you know the job or not, they'll teach it to you. Just go see."

"How would I get there? I don't drive and even if I did, Hal won't leave the car behind."

"One step at the time. Come on, I'll take you right now. You can at least see if you can get on. Nelda, can you watch Percy for an hour or so?"

"Just show me where his diapers are and tell me what he eats. I can take care of the rest. Piece of cake."

"Cake?" Bea asked.

Masil chuckled. "It's the latest phrase. My younger brother says that all the time. It means something's as easy as eating a piece of . . . well, you know."

"Wait, you're moving too fast, I said. I'm not sure I want to get a job."

"Honey, you don't have a choice."

"Yeah. I've got to do something." Bea's shoulders slumped in submission.

Without another word, Masil went inside and gathered her purse. By the time she returned, Nelda had asked her mother if she could babysit for an hour or so. Before Bea knew what happened, Nelda headed back to Bea's house with Percy, and Masil led Bea down the sidewalk to the parking lot. It felt to Bea like a march to the gallows.

The black two-door Ford sat parked next to the curb. A sudden downpour of rain the night before had left the lot flooded up to the curb's top. Masil leaned over and opened the driver door. "Stay there, Bea, and I'll back out to the middle where the water's not so deep. Else wise, you'll soak your shoes."

After Bea got in the car, Masil drove out to Avenue C, plowing into water so deep it seeped in the doors and started running across the floorboard.

"Whatever stupid engineer designed these streets as drains ought to be forced to live here in this mess," Masil said as both women lifted their feet off the wet floor. "The rain just stands and waits for the next car to drive by."

She steered straight for the curb and drove both right wheels up on it, lifting the bulk of the car high enough above the water to keep it from flooding.

Soon they turned onto Front Street, where the shipyards and all related activity went on twenty-four hours a day. The only empty parking place was directly across the street from Cherry's Club, Hal's favorite hangout.

Resentment crept between the edges of Bea's anger. She shoved her shoulders back and opened the car door.

"Good luck," Masil called. "Don't hurry. If I get hot, I'll go inside Cherry's and get a beer."

Bea looked daggers at her.

"Just kidding, honey, lighten up."

"If I go, you go." Bea yanked Masil from the car, laughing, and the two marched together across the street and past all the catcalls and wolf whistles from men who hung around outside the gate.

Pissed as hell at every one of them, Bea lifted her chin and refused to look their way, while Masil swung her hips and winked.

"You're just making it worse, Masil. Quit it." Bea's cheeks felt on fire.

Throngs of men and women hustled in and out like a busy bee colony with way too many worker bees. Once inside, the deafening sounds of riveting, clanking steel, and pounding sledgehammers competed with cries from sea gulls overhead. The hot metallic stench of acetylene torches melding metal to metal coated the air. Bea pulled a handkerchief from her pocket and covered her nose.

Alongside the dredged-out Sabine River, hulls of half-finished war ships waited—destroyers, destroyer escorts, landing craft, each impatient to enter the war. Gantry cranes hoisted heavy loads from one place to another. Bea wondered which one of the gantry cranes Hal operated, and if at this very moment Violet sat inside the cab astraddle his lap.

She followed Masil through the shipyard and the throngs of gawking, whistling men. Bea cringed with every catcall, but Masil thrived on the attention. She reminded Bea of a prancing peacock.

They stepped inside the office marked Personnel, which smelled like sweaty people. A lone desk piled high with papers and a Royal typewriter occupied a spot near the window. An attractive woman wearing a shoulder-length pageboy hair cut sat behind the desk, worry lines creasing her forehead. When Masil cleared her throat and greeted the woman, she stood quickly, pulling on the bottom of her tan jacket that fit a little too tight around the middle. "Can I help you?" she asked.

"My friend here wants a job, but she needs to work on the night shift."

Fear pounded in Bea's ears and almost drowned out the woman's reply.

"We're hiring for that shift right now. If you can start tonight, I can probably get you an interview while you're here."

"Yes'm, she can start tonight," Masil said. "What does she need to wear?"

"Pants for sure." The woman looked from Masil to Bea. "And you'll have to wear your hair tied up in a scarf for safety reasons. Durable shoes are a must. You have a pair?"

Masil punched Bea in the ribs before she could say no.

"Yes, she has a pair," Masil answered for her.

Bea didn't, but one look at Masil's stern expression told her to keep quiet about it. Quietly, Bea took the pencil and the application offered her, crossed to the chairs against the wall, and filled it out while Masil kept vigil over Bea's shoulder.

When it was done, Bea handed the completed paperwork to the young woman, returned to her chair and sat with her legs crossed, swinging one foot faster and faster.

"I don't know why I let you talk me into this," Bea whispered in Masil's ear. "They'll take one look at my application and then store it in moth balls."

"No, they won't either," Masil whispered back. "They need workers, bad. They can't get these ships out fast enough. You just watch what I tell you."

Bea watched all right. She watched the white-faced clock on the wall, watched the minute hand tick off her future, watched the doorway the receptionist had walked through with her application in hand. Still, the clock ticked.

Unable to bear another rejection, Bea grabbed Masil's elbow. "Let's get out of here. This is a waste of time, they'll never—"

"Mrs. Meade, will you come this way please?" A burly man dressed in a white shirt and tie led her to a small office down the hall.

The interview didn't take long. Bea needed a job and the man needed a materials handler. Before she knew what had happened, the man had tossed her application on his desk with the order, "Report to work tonight at midnight. We'll train you, then you'll get to work."

Bea staggered back to the reception area while the world spun faster than her grip on reality. The secretary stood with her back to Bea and dug through files in a drawer in the back corner. Masil sat against the opposite wall, looking like she'd die if she didn't say something important real quick. Her eyes cut to Bea, then at the woman at the filing cabinet, then over toward the desk.

"What's wrong?" Bea mouthed.

Masil sent her gaze back to the desk and to the nameplate on it, not visible when they'd entered a few minutes earlier. Now, the stack of papers was gone and the woman's name broadcast itself to the room.

Violet Winters.

Oh god, oh god. A sharp pain stabbed Bea. Hal had called the woman Violet, said she came from a well-to-do family. Well, Winters was one of the town's richest. The woman in the tan, too-tight suit must be the woman who carried Hal's baby, the bastard child, the same woman who threatened to take Percy away and raise him like her own.

Over her cold dead body. Bea battled the urge to attack the woman like a mama bear protecting her cub. Instead, she fled out the door, down the hall and outside, vaguely aware that Masil trailed behind.

"I'm sorry, honey, I had no idea . . ." Masil called out.

Blinded by rage and tears, Bea fled through the yard, elbowing her way through throngs of workers coming in, then through a group of men who stood outside the gate. This time, she ignored their cat calls and wolf whistles, refused to look their way, pissed as hell at every damn one of them.

All the way home, Bea cried. Masil sat wordless—the first time Bea had ever seen her without something to say. Finally, as they approached the parking lot, Bea wiped her face, stuck out her chin, and rammed a rod down her back.

Relieved when they walked into Bea's and found that Percy had been bathed, fed and put down for his afternoon nap, Bea smiled at the babysitter. "Hope he didn't give you any trouble?"

"That's the sweetest baby." Nelda laid down a well-worn copy of *Song Hits Magazine* she'd brought with her. "He got all tired and fussy so I put him in the kitchen sink full of nice cool water. He loved it. Heck, I wish I fit in the sink. We never had indoor plumbing before and I still ain't got used to it. Bathing kids is a piece of cake when you don't have to haul water from the well."

Bea smiled at Nelda. "Percy's going to love having you here. I can tell already."

Masil chimed in. "They want her to start work tonight."

Bea nodded, still a little stunned by it all. "Nelda, if your mama will let you stay, you can sleep here, then when I get home in the morning, you can go back to your house. It'll be daylight by then, so . . ."

Excitement lit Nelda's eyes. "Let me run go ask her, but I'm sure she'll say it's okay. If I work for you, I can buy me some clothes. I need so many things that Mama and Daddy ain't been able to afford, like brassieres and under drawers."

Eyes wide, Masil looked at the girl's bosom. "You don't need a brassiere, honey. You're flat as a pancake. Save your money and get a pretty skirt."

SYLVIA DICKEY SMITH

A mischievous smile crossed Nelda's face. She pulled her blouse high enough to unpin a large safety pin and started to unwind a tight band of flour sacks sewn together. "Mama wraps this every morning," she said, snickering.

"Good Lord," Bea and Masil said in unison, laughing at the girl's lack of modesty and the large breasts under her now way-too-tight blouse.

"You do need a brassiere, don't you?" Bea felt a little ashamed of her own complaints. "And here I felt like I needed clothes. At least I got bras and panties."

"Oh, living here in Orange is heaven. The first thing Mama said after Papa got a job here was now we could both have a pair of shoes instead of us sharing that one pair handed down from somebody else."

Nelda's eyes grew larger. "The first time me and Mama walked into one of the stores here in town, we didn't know how to buy clothes, 'cause they were hanging on these racks and all. We didn't know what size we wore or nothing."

"I guess that means you like living here," Masil said, her voice full of laughter.

"You can say that again. We don't have to pick cotton, chop cotton, milk cows. Heck, taking care of Percy ain't no job a'tall."

Bea peeked through the bedroom door at Percy, who lay fast asleep with a sweet smile on his face. When she returned to the living room, Masil had rewrapped Nelda's chest and was attaching the safety pin.

"Run home now," Bea said, "and see if it's okay for you to stay overnight."

"Oh, it'll be okay, but I'll check just in case." The girl darted out the door humming a tune. Bea was pretty sure it was the start to *My Dreams Are Getting Better All the Time.*

"While she's doing that, Bea," Masil had a big smile on her face, "I'll run over to my house and get you that pair of slacks and shoes. You've got a headscarf, eh?"

Chapter 9

Oskar walked into the security office at the shipyard and stuck his hand out to the man behind the desk.

"My name is Oskar Eichel and I am German."

The man jumped up so fast his chair shot across the room. He reached into the holster under his arm for a weapon.

Oskar held both hands up. "I am not armed."

"Then what do you want, and why the hell are you telling me this?"

"I tell you this because, although I am a German, I am not a Nazi."

The security officer slowly removed his hand from his revolver, then sat down again in his chair.

"That's a relief. Have a seat. I'm Daniel Baxter, Chief of Security." His eyes stayed alert, fixed on Oskar.

Daniel had dark hair, and eyes the same color. When he had been standing, he had been tall, six feet if an inch. Oskar figured the man's chiseled chin and regal-looking nose must drive women wild.

Oskar sat in the chair indicated. "I wanted to be up front with you. I just got hired on here at the shipyard as an oiler. My family came over from Germany shortly before America got embroiled in the war. We saw the handwriting on the wall and wanted no part of Hitler and his sort."

"So you settled here?"

"No, just east of San Antonio, in a town called Seguin. There are many others of German descent in the area. My father—stepfather, actually—had family there.

"So what can I do for you?"

"I came to this area hoping to find my younger brother. I figure he may show up here at the shipyard looking for a job, and I wanted to ask you to let me know if he does.

"What's his name?" Daniel pulled out a pad and started writing.

"Wilhelm. Of course he may change it to William, who knows?"

"Know why he ran away?"

"Stupid kid stuff. He just turned seventeen when two other kids talked him into driving the getaway car for a minor robbery. He hadn't been in trouble before, so the judge ordered him to join the Army instead of jail time. He agreed, but then he bolted. My mom begged me to go find him and make him enlist."

"What makes you think he might be in this area?" Daniel fiddled the pencil on the desk.

"Because I heard he took off with a band of gypsies headed this way, hiding in one of the wagons."

"That's a good reason. There's a band of them that passes through here often. They have a place they stay on the edge of town, you know, but I wouldn't suggest you go near them if they're around. They're weird folks—they don't welcome strangers to their camp. By the way, have you talked to Personnel? They might keep an eye out for him, too."

Oskar nodded. "Yeah, but all they could tell me is that his name isn't on the employee list. I'll try to find a way to check the campsite. Someone must have connections, and can get in there and talk to them."

"I'll keep an eye out." The officer stood up. "I'd like to help the boy. Truth is, I did something foolish when I was that age."

Oskar thanked Daniel and left the office feeling like he had met someone he could trust.

He located the crane he'd been assigned and found a tall red-head fellow in khaki pants and a long sleeve shirt leaning against the crane's ladder, one foot propped behind him, smoking a cigarette.

Oskar approached. "Are you Hal Meade?"

"Sure am, what can I do for you."

"I'm your new oiler. Personnel told me to report here and you'd show me the job."

Chapter 10

Bea spent the rest of the afternoon asking herself what she'd let Masil talk her into, and what Hal would say when he heard she had a job. When he walked in the door not long after quitting time, Bea's belly cramped. Would this be the day he packed up his things and moved out? At least her rent wasn't due for a couple of weeks, and she already had next month's rent tucked away.

But he didn't mention the topic. Instead, he tossed his hard hat on the table, and dropped another bomb.

"The foreman fired my oiler today. No matter how much we trained that kid, he couldn't learn the difference between a grease gun and a can of worms." He leaned down and pecked Bea on the cheek.

She stiffened, shifted Percy to her other hip.

"Come to find out, the foreman hired a replacement by the end of the day." Hal checked the coffeepot on the stove, struck a match and lit the burner underneath the pot. "And the new guy needed a place to stay, so I told him he could bunk here. He's getting his bag out of the car right now. He'll be in directly."

Bea stared at Hal, dumbfounded.

A movement out the front window caught her eye, and she saw a tall blond man carrying a duffle bag over his shoulder, come up the sidewalk toward their front door. Panic squeezed her chest when she realized it was the same man she'd helped untangle from the barbed-wire fence out at her grandfather's farm.

Hal shoved the screen door open. "Come in, buddy. You can put your bag down anywhere. I just told my wife here that you'll bunk with us for a while. Bea, why don't you see if that coffee's hot?"

She didn't move. Her legs wouldn't let her.

"This here is Oskar Eichel, Bea. Here, my friend, have a seat." Hal indicated the end of the couch.

"Nice to meet you, madam." Oskar's eyes said he recognized her. His words didn't.

"My wife'll have supper ready in a few minutes, won't you honey?" Hal glanced at Bea for reassurance of that fact.

"We'll just move Percy's crib into our bedroom," Hal added. "You can have his room. Bea can make you a pallet on the floor till you can get yourself a bed."

"Hope this is not too much of an imposition, madam." The stranger gave a slight bow towards Bea, who turned to the kitchen to fetch the coffee.

"Oh, she don't mind, do you baby?" He crossed his legs and leaned his right arm on the back of the couch.

"Hal, can you help me in the kitchen?" she asked.

He got up and followed her.

"So he'll be paying room and board?" Bea whispered to Hal, who stood in the middle of the room looking around as if he didn't know which cabinet held the coffee cups. The knot in her stomach clenched tighter.

"Shh, he'll hear you," he whispered.

She seldom questioned him, but her new job gave her a mite more courage. She wondered how submissive Miss Violet was. She looked like a spoiled brat, but Hal never spoiled or indulged anyone—except maybe himself.

"For your information, he's agreed to pay us a few bucks a week, yes. The poor guy didn't have any place else to live. He's my oiler, for God's sake. I couldn't just let him live on the streets."

With Percy still on her hip, she pointed at the cabinet. "There's the cups."

Annoyance coated the act, but Hal collected cups and saucers and sat them on the drain board.

Percy started fussing. She jiggled him, weary of pacifying

anyone.

She pulled down another plate and plopped it on the table. Out of the corner of her eye, she saw Oskar peek into the kitchen.

"Me and Oskar both have to pull a double tonight," Hal said. "Soon as we eat, we head to the shipyard." He motioned to their new boarder. "I'll show you where you can wash up." He led Oskar to the bathroom.

Percy had fallen asleep in Bea's arms. Thankful she'd left the pallet on the floor in the living room, she eased him out of her arms and laid him down on it. He stirred. She leaned over, patted his butt and hummed the beginning of a lullaby. When he settled down, she tiptoed back to the kitchen and took a pan of cornbread out of the oven.

Hal and Oskar came into the kitchen just as she flipped the hot bread onto a plate and set it on the table.

"Bea makes the best cornbread this side of my mama," Hal bragged.

"It sure smells good." Oskar pulled Bea's chair out and held it for her.

Hal waved his hand. "Oh, don't bother about that, man, she can handle that chair better'n you and me put together."

"Madam." Oskar ignored the comment, motioning Bea to sit.

Heat rose to her cheeks. She hesitated a moment and glanced at Hal, who said, "Suit yourself," as he reached for the bowl of beans.

"Thank you," Bea said while Oskar scooted her chair under her.

Half way through the meal, Percy started yelling to high heaven. Bea rushed to get him, eager to escape the discomfort she felt every time Oskar looked at her.

Her own Papa had been tender, had always spoken kindly to her mother. Each evening, he'd come wrap his bear-arms around Mama and tell her how much he loved her and how pretty she looked. Mama might have been pretty once, but by that time, she'd lost all her teeth, and the dentures Papa saved up to buy never did fit right, so they stayed in a Mason jar filled with water.

She never thought marriage would be like it was with Hal. She was starved for affection, for attention, for respect as Hal's wife. Instead, she felt like a slave. Oh, he loved her all right, same as he loved everybody else in the world. But he didn't love *her*, particularly.

Then she remembered with fear that at midnight she started a job at the shipyard. Good thing the place was big and busy enough she didn't have to worry about running into Hal. She didn't dare tell him about the job. Not just yet. Both he and Oskar would be long gone back to their double shift before Nelda showed up to take care of Percy.

Chapter 11

Nelda walked in the front door right on the dot. For the next few minutes, Bea explained Percy's routine and what to feed him should he awaken before she got home. In the back of her mind, however, she wondered who she might be when she came home, and if she'd feel any differently than she did right now.

Nelda misread Bea's nervousness. "Don't worry, Mrs. Meade, Mama said to tell you she'd keep an eye on us. And if we need anything she'll help out."

"That's great, sweetheart. Tell her thank you for me. No, I'm not worried about that. I know you'll do fine. Besides, he's already asleep and should stay that way 'til morning." She collected one of Hal's old lunch pails she'd packed for herself and headed to the front door. "What I'm nervous about is the job. I've never had one before, and I've sure never worked around so many men."

Truthfully, she'd never been this nervous before about anything. Not even the night she went into labor with Percy. She and her sister Edith had been home alone. A freak ice storm had blown in earlier that day and the roads were frozen. After a short labor, Edith helped deliver Percy like she knew just how to do it. The doctor arrived the next morning and said there wasn't anything left for him to do. Both mother and baby were fine.

"Show 'em who's boss, Mrs. Meade. You can do it." Nelda called out as Bea mustered every ounce of courage possible, stepped out the door and into a foreign world.

Self-doubt feasted off of her every step. "I don't have to do this," she argued into the warm, moist night air. She could turn around and go back home.

Oh, yes you do, something argued back.

She pushed on, one foot after the other, heading in the direction of a night sky that looked like morning. The night air and the brisk walk began to ease the knot in her chest, but did nothing to relieve the queasiness in her stomach. Masil's boots were too big so she'd pulled on two pairs of Hal's socks. Still, the boots rubbed up and down against her heels with every step. She adjusted the socks, hoping she didn't have blisters by the time she got home.

And the pants—humiliation made her cheeks hot just walking down the street wearing them. Mama, a devout Holy Roller, would have hidden her face in shame if she'd seen her daughter wearing men's clothes. Of course, Mama was old—and old-fashioned old.

Earlier that day, when Bea tried on the pants and complained about them being men's clothes, Masil laughed, reassuring Bea they were made for women to wear and not men.

Bea wasn't convinced. Thank goodness Papa hadn't lived to see her in those pants. Now if Jesus just held off His second coming until she got back home and in a dress . . .

The polka-dot scarf tied around her head slid to one side. She tugged it back in place and shoved a sprig of hair underneath. She hoped she didn't look as silly as she felt.

Before the war, soon as dark fell, the streets looked like they'd rolled up the sidewalks—empty, everything closed. But after the Japanese bombed Pearl Harbor, you saw people all hours of the day and night. Even gasoline rationing didn't keep cars parked long.

One car pulled over and the woman behind the wheel offered Bea a ride but, uncomfortable with strangers, she declined. Besides, the cooler night air felt better than being cooped up in a hot car. That, or cooped up inside her house crying her eyes out. She still didn't understand what the nighttime did to her emotions, why she felt so incredibly lonely while everyone else slept. The graveyard shift might improve that situation.

A slight breeze blew in and cooled the thin layer of perspiration on her face.

SYLVIA DICKEY SMITH

Masil had told her the unions were the ones responsible for women working at the shipyard getting a decent wage. When the war started and all the men went off to fight, the yards were so short-handed the bosses were forced to hire untrained and mostly uneducated women like her. They wanted to pay them as little as possible, of course. The unions got involved and said if women were going to do the same work as men, they had to pay them the same. Thank goodness for the unions.

Long before she got halfway there, the sounds of the hollow booming of hammered hulls reverberated across the night air, almost hypnotizing her, drawing her toward the sounds.

A few minutes before midnight, Bea turned onto Front Street, where thousands and thousands of shipbuilders walked shoulder to shoulder, heading in or out of the various shipyards. The whole area, lit up like the sun at noon, made it possible to read newspapers outdoors in the middle of the night. She wondered why the air raid wardens insisted people paint the top half of car headlights black. If the enemy came, they shouldn't have any problem locating the shipyards, or the dreadnaughts under construction. Like the Japanese did at Pearl Harbor. She tried to shake off that scary thought.

She approached the gate of Consolidated and felt like she'd stepped into the middle of a 4th of July parade. Wolf whistles came at her from small groups of men around the gate, some leaving, others coming. They also whistled down at her from the tall gantries. Even the newspaper boy crying the latest war headlines stopped to look her up and down.

"You're way too young, kid," she admonished.

"Lady, I ain't as young, and you ain't as grown," he said, laughing, pocketing the change handed him by an old codger as he left the yard.

It took a few minutes to locate where she'd been told to report, and it took most the night to get her bearings. Another woman materials handler showed her how to take orders, where to collect the materials, and then how to request jeep transport to the job site for delivery. At first, she felt overwhelmed, but when she saw other women doing the same job, she dug in her heels. They didn't look any more capable than she did. If they could do the job, so could she.

By the middle of her shift, she too had caught the contagious spirit of the yard. She was surprised how excited she felt about the opportunity to do something for the war effort. Often, though, she thought of Percy, and worried. She hoped he slept through the night and didn't give Nelda any trouble.

Order in hand, she slid out of the jeep's passenger seat. While the driver waited, she delivered the parts to the correct department. At one point she took shelter from a brief shower inside one of the warehouses, then took off on the next delivery.

Absorbed in learning the job, she lost all track of time. Soon, the night had passed and her shift ended. Exhilarated and exhausted, she bustled out the gate alongside hundreds of other tired, dirty, greasy men and women carrying helmets and empty lunch boxes.

She wondered how many of them had a bed to sleep in. Some of those were even rented by the hour—*hotbeds,* folks called them—still warm from the stranger who just got up and went back to work. Hal said sometimes, instead of sleeping, the work-weary people staggered across the river to Showboat Ruby's, and if they didn't get knocked in the head or stabbed, came back across the Louisiana bridge a few hours later and went straight to work.

It seemed like the whole town had gone crazy. All people wanted to do was make money and spend it on a *high-heel good time.* Right now, the only thing she wanted to do was go home, take a nice warm shower and get into bed.

A bright orange sun glowed above the horizon as Bea trudged home bone-weary, knowing she must stay awake until Percy took his morning nap. She had hoped he'd slept all night, now she hoped he'd sleep all day, too. What a pathetic mother.

The early morning world looked so different than it did the night before. Beautiful sprawling oaks covered in Spanish moss, towering pine trees, and green grass everywhere looked more beautiful than she'd ever seen them—until she reached Riverside. Not a single tree or blade of grass dared stick its head above the inhospitable sand. Rain from the night before left huge puddles down the middle of the streets. Flooded-out cars, stranded by their owners, waited for the water to go down and their distributor wires to dry out.

By the time she got home, the heat and humidity had added to the stench of a night's labor. She even smelled herself. Weary, she stepped through the front door, ready to hop into the shower before Percy and Nelda awoke.

Instead, to her shocked surprise, the tall blond-haired, blue-eyed Oskar sat in the living room jiggling Percy on his knee. Nelda wasn't anywhere in sight. Neither was Hal.

"Excuse me, madam, we got off early—"

Bea jerked the bandana off her head and ran her fingers through her matted hair while she looked around the room.

"If you search for the girl, she isn't here. Your husband sent her home."

"My husband? Hal? When did he get home? Where is he?"

"We got in about an hour ago. He left me here with the baby. I promise I took good care of him. See, he is happy."

Percy laughed up at her, delighted in his horsey ride, drool running down the sides of his mouth.

"The girl said she fed him, so he and I just played . . . how do you say it? Horse?"

"Where's Hal?"

"I'm not certain, madam. He mumbled something about *finding her and bringing her back where she belongs.* Your husband and I got off early and came straight home."

"I don't know about you," she said, trying to regain her composure, "but straight home? That sets a record for him."

"Yes, madam."

"Sorry. I know it's not your fault. By the way, how're your wounds from the barbed wire?"

"Oh, they're getting well, thank you. I didn't say anything about your help bandaging them. I was uncertain whether to or not, and took the path of discretion. When you did the same, I felt much relief."

"Thank you." The man might be good-looking, but he wasn't from around here. He talked funny.

"I owe you a debt of gratitude," he continued. "I didn't have a place to sleep, until your husband said I might bunk here for a while. I know it must be difficult to have a stranger in the house. But it is almost impossible to find somewhere to sleep. Last couple of nights I slept down at tent city with rats running over my feet. And before that I slept in a barn with a horse named Lightning."

He laughed a soft pleasant laugh. She couldn't blame him for not wanting to sleep with rats.

"That's okay, we'll get by," she said, smiling. "Thank you for taking such good care of Percy. He loves horsey rides. Your leg will get tired before he's ready to stop."

Oskar looked at Percy, then to her. "Please forgive me, but I have not had a chance to unpack my things. After payday, I will purchase a small bed." His prancing knee didn't miss a stride.

She waved her hand at him. "I'm heading to the kitchen to get something to eat. Have you had breakfast?"

"No, I have not. Here, let me help you." He scooped the baby up and plopped him on his hip.

"You talk different than most folks around here." Bea opened the icebox and pulled out a basket of fresh eggs. "You must be new in town. I suppose you came looking for a job, like everybody else."

"Yes, I did."

"What about your family? Have any around here?"

"I have a younger brother I'm trying to find. I believe he might be somewhere in the area." He walked over to the screen door and stared out back while Percy, still in his arms, patted the wire mesh.

Bea glanced at him, then brought her attention to the eggs, as Oskar, who looked like his mind had taken him a million miles away, watched the next-door neighbor pin wet clothes on a clothesline.

"I'm going to level with you, Mrs. Meade—" He turned to face her.

"Bea, please."

"Okay, Bea. I must be honest with you, but I ask that you keep this between the two of us, please. I don't want to cause alarm. There is no reason for it."

"Why? What's going on?" She spooned the eggs onto plates, then poured coffee for each of them.

"My brother, Wilhelm, couldn't stand the thought of fighting on opposite sides of the war . . . fighting his brother . . . his *other* brother."

"I don't understand."

"Wilhelm is . . . German."

"Your brother is . . . Then you're . . ."

"Yes, I am German. I don't tell people because I don't want them to be afraid of me."

She added toast to their plates and put them on the table. "Let's have breakfast."

He followed her request, balancing Percy on his knee.

"I haven't frightened you?"

Bea ignored the question and instead, asked her own, surprised she felt so calm about the whole thing. "So does that mean you're a Nazi spy?"

Oskar choked, trying not to spew coffee across the table. When he could finally speak, he said, "No, Bea, I am not a spy."

"Whew, I thought I might have to shoot you," she said, then wondered where that came from. She'd never been known to have a sense of humor. At least Oskar had the courtesy to laugh.

"So I haven't frightened you?"

"What's to be scared of? So you have a brother in Germany and one here you're trying to find. Is there something else I'm missing?"

"No, that's about it."

"The one in Germany, is he in the German army."

Oskar paused, then said quietly, "Yes, he fights for Hitler."

They both sat there for a while in silence.

"This infernal war has made everyone unsure about so many things," said Bea, finally. "About tomorrow, or family, or . . ." She wanted to say *husbands*, but didn't.

She took his empty plate, stacked it on hers and went to the sink. "I'm sorry about your brother—both of them. I hope it all works out. Maybe you'll hear from the one you're looking for soon. What did you say his name was?"

"Wilhelm."

"Like William, I suppose."

She started to fill the sink with hot, soapy water.

A knock at the front door drew Bea away from the most interesting conversation she'd had in days. Young Nelda stood on the other side of the screen, fidgeting. "Mrs. Meade, I had to come back and check on Percy. I hated to leave when I did, but Mr. Meade asked where you were and I told him—"

"I know, Nelda. Mr. Eichel here explained. That's okay. You didn't know I hadn't told Mr. Meade."

She opened the door so Nelda could step inside. Bea smiled at her as if all was well, though she wasn't so sure herself. "Percy's just fine. Mr. Eichel took good care of him until I got home. I'm sorry you got caught in the whole thing. Are you okay?"

"Oh, yes, I just hated to leave before you got home."

"It's okay, but I do have to go to work tonight. You can stay again, huh?"

"You think your husband will mind? He looked pretty mad earlier this morning."

"It'll be okay. I really need you here to take care of the baby. I'll have a talk with Mr. Meade."

"So, same time as last night?"

"Yes, that worked perfect." Bea rubbed Nelda's shoulder. "And don't you worry. Everything will be okay."

"So, do you want some help now with Percy?" Nelda glanced from Bea to Oskar, who had come to stand in the doorway to the kitchen, as if unsure how comfortable Bea might be in the house alone with the stranger.

But something about Oskar made Bea trust him, made her not mind what others might say about a married woman alone in a house with another man. "Sure. You go on." She nudged Nelda out the door and waved. "I'll see you tonight."

She returned to the kitchen where Oskar was again sitting at the table, entertaining Percy with a shiny teaspoon she'd left on the table. The man sure had a knack with kids. "I guess you heard all that."

"Yes, madam, I heard."

"I got a job at the shipyard yesterday, but I didn't tell Hal because I knew he'd be mad. I thought I'd be home before him, and he wouldn't have to know. Nelda's staying here with Percy while I'm gone."

"You were correct. Indeed he was angry when he heard."

"I got the job before I knew you were going to be boarding here. Now I'm worried it won't look right for you to be here while Nelda's here by herself. Her mama might not like that. You think you could stay out a little later?"

"Certainly, but what about your husband?"

She hadn't thought about how it might look with Hal home alone with Nelda. That wouldn't work either. Now what did she do? She couldn't make her husband stay out of his own home. Then again, maybe she could.

Chapter 12

Oskar went to his room, stretched out on the mattress and thought about Bea. He hadn't told her the whole truth. For one thing, he hadn't described the abuse he'd endured from his father—his stepfather, he reminded himself. Or the grudge the man held for him. It wasn't his fault his mother had an affair with a gypsy, which resulted in Oskar's birth.

He hadn't spoken of the favoritism his stepfather showed towards Wilhelm, the baby of the family. Or of his real father's hatred for Hitler and everything he stood for.

Then, there was the whole thing with the oldest brother who refused to immigrate to America and now fought with Hitler's storm troopers.

Oskar rode the fence between loyalties to two countries. Not that he believed in Hitler and his henchmen; he shuddered at the destruction they caused the world, and he'd been eager to come to America. He longed to see everything that this country had to offer, its music, freedom, the opportunity. . . .

Of course most Germans suffered from *fernwah*, that urge to travel, to leave Europe and see the world, but *heimat* was still homeland.

Did Americans suffer from *fernwah*? It looked to him like they seemed perfectly content here in their own small world, doing their part to help a country at war. Of course, so many had been eager to leave their small communities or farms to come to Orange to get jobs. It seemed to Oskar like many of them were enjoying their new surroundings, with its nightlife and juke joints and lots of money and girls and . . .

Restless, he flipped over on his side and rested his head on his elbow.

Would he ever feel content, or would he always have this call to high adventure, where the rush of adrenalin kept him charged?

A woman like Bea was on the other end of that spectrum. She looked like someone who wanted stability, to settle down and stay in one place.

He looked at the clock. If he didn't go to sleep soon, he'd never get to work on time. He needed his rest if he was going to help build the war ships that would battle his native land.

It looked more evident every day from the news that Germany would be on the opposite side of a win. Thank goodness.

SYLVIA DICKEY SMITH

Chapter 13

Soft taps on the pane of Violet's second-story bedroom window awakened her. She threw off the floral coverlet and raced over to the window where a soft breeze ruffled her nightgown.

Hal stood on the lawn, below. Something about him looked different, though. His naturally ruddy complexion looked even redder than usual and he had a scowl on his face.

"Good morning," she whispered down to him. "What's wrong?"

"Meet me in the rose garden," he mouthed, pointing to the rear of the house.

The garden sat behind the potting shed, safe from prying eyes.

Violet threw on a house dress, ran a comb through her hair and smeared on pink lipstick. By the time she got outside, Hal's jaw twitched, as he paced back and forth, skimming rocks down the gravel path. One skittered into the rose bushes and the flowers released a sweet fragrance.

Wary that Hal's anger might be directed at her, Violet held her breath. The last thing she needed was for this whole thing with him to fall through. If it did, she had no idea where to turn. "What's happened? You okay?"

"It's Bea, dammit. When I got home from work, I found her gone. A neighbor girl I didn't even know had stayed overnight with my boy. She told me Bea had gotten a job at the shipyard."

"I know she did," she said, tentative, fearful of changing the path of his anger from Bea to her. Not that she feared getting hit. She'd faced worse than that. She just didn't want him to get so mad he'd change his mind. Then she'd have to start all over with another man.

He stood with his mouth agape. "You knew?"

"She came to the shipyard yesterday and got hired on the spot. My boss put her on as a materials handler. She started last night on the midnight shift. I figured you knew."

He cursed, paced back and forth across the path, gravel crunching under his feet. "No wife of mine will work outside the home. What will the other guys think? That I can't provide for her."

"Think about it, Hal. Her with a job means she can support herself and the baby. This way, we can be free to get married."

He stopped pacing. A slow grin spread across his face as he grabbed her by both arms. "You're right, Violet. I hadn't thought about that. You're a genius, sweetheart. Why am I so upset? That takes the pressure off of me." He pecked her on the lips. After a few more passionate kisses, he took off, inspired by the new twist of events.

Relieved, she headed up to the house, slipped through the back door and into the kitchen, hoping Mama and Daddy hadn't missed her at breakfast. Daddy left early for work every day and Mama wrapped bandages at the USO so, hopefully, they thought she'd slept late and the coast was clear.

Her three brothers must have eaten and left early, too. The dishes had all been washed and put away except for a plate of food on a sideboard—evidently saved for her. The help had moved on to clean other parts of the big two-story house.

Morning sickness still dominated her mornings, especially until she ate solid food. Thank goodness she hadn't thrown up in front of Hal. She tiptoed to the sideboard and lifted the cloth. Cold, soft-scrambled, sickly-yellow eggs stared back at her.

She barely made it outside before the retching started.

At last, drained from the exertion, she swiped her hand across her mouth as she straightened and waited to see whether or not the wave had passed.

It seemed it had, at least for the time being. She headed to the kitchen, sat at the table and nibbled on a dry piece of toast.

Maybe something was wrong with her or the baby. She'd never

SYLVIA DICKEY SMITH

considered the possibility of miscarriage, but if she lost the baby, Mother and Daddy would never have to know, wouldn't have to live with the shame. Next time, she'd know what to do to not let this happen again. She'd shove him off, scream, lock her door. But for now, she had to get out of the situation the best way she could with as little shame as possible.

Soon, everyone in town would know her secret because her stomach grew bigger every day. The household maid and her long-time nanny, Sadie, had looked at her suspiciously the last few weeks. She knew Violet better than did her own aristocratic, proud mother, Gladys, who stayed forever caught in a social whirlwind.

Since the war started, a growing number of social get-togethers involved the assembly of bandages for the boys who fought overseas. After the news of the first local casualties arrived, Gladys and her influential friends were the ones who persuaded the city to name the three Riverside elementary schools Tilley, Colburn, and Manley, after the first three boys from Orange who had been killed in the war

Footsteps slapped on the hardwood floor outside the kitchen. Violet held her breath. She hoped it wasn't Mother. The door swung open and Sadie filled the passageway, her hips almost wide enough to touch both sides of the doorframe.

Violet sighed with relief and put her head down on the table. Sadie had always been there for her, ready to take care of whatever Violet needed. How she wished Sadie could take care of this problem, but she knew no one could and she had only herself to blame. She'd also known it was wrong, bad wrong.

"Wha'cha doing, child, coming in here this hour of the morning? If you folks knew what you been up to they'd skin you hide. I gots a good mine to do it me self." Sadie's dark skin glistened in the lights.

"You scared the life out of me, Sadie. Where is everyone, and why are you at work so early?"

"Ah, child, you know I ain't one to sleep late. I gots work to do. Besides, I gots to get up them blackout shades. Don't you go questioning me, kid. It ain't me done something I don't want nobody to knows. You look guilty as sin, child. What you been up to?"

The stress of the last few days broke over Violet and she fell into the arms of her nanny, the one place she'd be safe.

"What, child? You have been up to something." She gently pushed Violet from her ample bosom and looked into her eyes. "Don't tell me—you with child. I can see it . . . I can see it in you eyes, so don't even try to deny it. Who's the boy?"

"He's . . . he's . . . not a boy, he's . . ."

"Well, he shore ain't a woman." Her black eyes peered into Violet's soul, sought the unvarnished truth.

Violet squeezed her eyes shut. "It's . . . he's a man and he's married."

Sadie squeezed her tighter. "Child, you mama and daddy gonna kill us both. I's supposed to take care of you, but I can't stays awake twenty foe hours a day. You slipping away afta I shuts my own eyes gonna be the end of you and me. Now, tell me what you gonna do 'bout this situation."

"He promised we'd get married, Sadie, that he loves me, but . . . but . . ."

"What? How he gonna marry you if he has one wife already? And don't tell me you got pride. That's a luxury a woman with a baby in her belly can't afford."

"But . . ."

"What? What you not tell me?" Sadie pushed back and looked Violet in the eye.

"He already has a son, a baby less than a year old."

Sadie glanced to heaven. "Lord, deliver me. I never . . . Not only you break up dat marriage, but you take the baby's daddy away from him. And how you expect that wife a his to take care of herself and that child?" Sadie walked to the sink, picked up a bar of lye soap, turned on the tap and scrubbed. "I wash my hands from you, young lady. I never thought any child a mine would do this. You mama and daddy got a good reputation in this town—did. Now, what's this gonna do to them?"

"I told him I'd take the boy and raise him as my own."

"Land sakes, child, that baby got a mama. How you think she feel, you take her man and her baby?"

"I feel so bad, Sadie. It just happened one time."

"Yeah, you done go jump off that Port Arthur bridge one time—see what happen. You dead, child, you dead. I told your mama the day you was born, them violet eyes was gonna get you—gets us all. Same ole' story, same ole' verse. That Satan done got the best of us."

The air raid siren went off at that moment, which saved Violet from any further rumination about her condition, saved her from admitting the truth—that she wasn't the one who sinned.

Chapter 14

Hal felt better when he left Violet's house. Bea had lifted a weight off his shoulders with the job. He didn't want to leave her and Percy, but he had no choice. He couldn't leave Violet to face all this alone. Besides, she'd been so eager that day. It had been a long time since he'd had a woman that willing. Poor Bea did her best, but . . . He wouldn't confront Bea about her new job. He'd just go home and pack his clothes when he knew she wasn't at home.

He arrived at the shipyard just in time for his shift to begin, clocked in and climbed sixty feet up the ladder to his crane. At the top, he stepped into the engine room at the rear of the operator's cabin, checked the oil and water and found it all in good condition, thanks to Oskar.

Next, he cranked the engine and the familiar sound exploded in his ears, along with the heavy smell of burning fuel. Inside the operator's cabin, he straddled the metal seat and pushed and pulled levers, twisted others, worked the crane cables up and down.

He shoved his problems as far back in his thoughts as possible, for the job required every ounce of his attention. The gantry creaked and groaned down the tracks to where another load of parts waited. When he reached them, he moved levers until he secured the load in the jaws of the machine, then read the weight scale to make sure he hadn't overloaded the gantry. If he had, the whole thing could topple down on top of everyone beneath it. He'd seen a number of people hurt or killed on the job and he sure didn't want to be the cause of another accident. His nerves felt stretched to the limit.

Confident of the weight, he blew a warning and swung the load over to the ship under construction, checking both ways as he moved.

The foreman signaled and Hal released the material. The ground crew waved that it would be a few minutes before they would be ready for the next load so he parked the gears and pulled out a cigarette. Anxious for a breath of fresh air, he stepped outside the cabin, lit up, took a drag, and blew the smoke above his head.

He felt bad about Bea, bad about what he'd done to Violet, too. There just didn't seem a good way out of the situation. He planned to leave a wife and child to marry another woman who carried his second child. Was it worse to be divorced or to have a bastard child?

Violet had said her brothers were looking for him again. He didn't know what to expect after the last time, but he did know it wouldn't be pretty. Frank said they were out to kill him. He doubted that. They'd rather their sister marry him than live in shame. Maybe he should go to her house and try to talk to her dad. Yeah, that's what he'd do. He'd go after work.

The foreman signaled from below. Hal dropped his cigarette and ground it out on the metal floor, then headed inside the cab.

Chapter 15

Bea grew more confident each night she worked. So far, she hadn't run into the woman from Personnel—the woman who stole her husband. But finally the night came when Bea entered the break room and nearly collided with a tall, violet-eyed girl. It was the same woman she'd seen in the personnel office the first day she came to apply for a job.

The woman with Hal's baby in her belly sidestepped Bea and hustled out of the room as though she hadn't recognized her.

"You know that girl?" one of the women at the corner table whispered to the other.

"Yeah, that's Violet Winters," the other woman said. "I hear she got herself knocked up. Looks like another casualty of war. Wonder who the daddy is."

Bea went over to the trashcan, opened her lunch box and dumped in the leftovers she'd brought from home. Without a cent to her name until payday, that meant she'd go without until she got home, but she'd suddenly lost all desire for food.

She knew where Hal's gantry was and went to find him, thinking about that first night she'd gone to work. When Hal had learned about it, he'd been furious that she had taken a job without asking him first.

Now, the way she saw it, he had lost the right to any say about what she did or didn't do. If he tried to, she'd remind him of that fact.

But instead of finding Hal, she found a young man hiding in a dark corner behind the ladder at Hal's gantry. They saw each other at the exact same minute, and both of them froze, eyes locked onto the other like two startled cats. A yelp slipped out of her mouth.

He grabbed her around the waist with one arm and covered her mouth with his other hand. "Shh," he whispered, his eyes still locked on hers. "I won't hurt you."

She nodded and he eased his hand off her mouth, but kept his arm around her waist.

They stood and looked at each other, like neither one knew what to do next. She knew she wasn't supposed to be there herself, she did not have permission to be in this section of the shipyard—and since he didn't wear an employee badge, he didn't either.

"Routine check," he mumbled. Bea wasn't sure if he was from Security, or why he was checking on Hal.

That's when they heard Hal, back from a smoke break probably, and the man's eyes went from hot to cold.

"Hide back here," she whispered, and pushed him into a gap under the gantry's ladder. "Before long he'll go for another smoke. You can leave then." For the first time in her life, Bea gave thanks Hal smoked. Still, she hadn't a clue why she'd protected the young man.

She stepped from the shadows, startling Hal as he stepped on the ladder up to his crane.

"Oh," he said, and bristled at her. "What do you want?"

"Routine check."

Hal looked puzzled.

Reminded why she'd come, she shoved the young man out of her mind. "Actually, I just wanted to tell you I saw your little plaything in the break room. Nice work, Hal. I hope you enjoy your new life with her. And I hope you'll enjoy your place in hell when you get there."

He kicked at the ground. The muscle in his jaw twitched. "You're no saint either. You took a job here at the shipyard and you didn't even ask me first, let alone tell me. Do you know how humiliated I felt when some of the men told me they saw you here?"

"Funny—that thought never crossed my mind." She tried to keep the smirk off her face, but doubted her success. "Seems to me you gave up all rights over me when you slept with that woman." She spun on her heels and stomped back to her jobsite.

She stewed over the sight of Violet and the encounter with Hal the rest of her shift. Bumfuzzled that he'd think he had any say over what she did, the more she thought about it, the madder she got.

Without realizing it, she delivered the wrong part to the wrong job site. She looked around her, desperately hoping no one saw the mistake. She hailed the jeep driver right before he left to pick up another handler. When he asked what happened, she shook her head, but he must have known she'd made a mistake when she returned with the part. By the time she found the correct part and delivered it, the foreman yelled what the hell took her so long.

Relieved when the whistle blew, she walked out the gate past a kid dressed in grungy overalls. Tobacco juice ran out the side of his mouth.

"Knife sharpeners, get your *genuine* knife sharpeners," he called out, as he sharpened a pocketknife on a wet rock and wiped it on a faded *Bull Durham* sack filled with something. "Hurry, get your magical knife sharpeners here." Several men stopped, laughed, and tossed a couple of bills to the boy and collected one of the bags.

Bea stopped, picked up a bag, curious as to the magic. All the while, the boy kept a steady pace with his vocal advertising.

"What's in the bag?" she asked.

The kid shrugged and grinned up at her. "Sand."

"Sand? You're selling sand? I got a whole neighborhood full of the stuff, why should I buy this? What's magical about it?"

"It's magical 'cause *I'm* selling it," he said, and hailed his next customer.

Bea tossed him the bag.

"Don't you want one, ma'am?" the boy called out.

"No thanks," she said, and walked on. The rate at which people walked by the kid and snatched up the Magic Knife Sharpener showed how things around town changed since the war started. Used to be, no one in town had money, especially for something as foolish as a *Magic* Knife Sharpener made out of sand. Now their pockets bulged with money and nothing to spend it on.

For years, she fantasized about falling in love. She'd marry a wonderful man. They'd raise a house full of kids. He'd be faithful, provide for her, and come straight home from work every night. She never expected it to turn out like this.

Yes, things had sure changed, but not for the better, at least not for her.

Lost in the past, Bea didn't see the black sedan pull alongside her, slowing down, until the horn blew. She jumped, then recognized the vehicle. Bea peered through the window at her sister, sitting behind the wheel.

"Hey, Toots," Edith called.

Edith's raspy voice made Bea smile. A number of years older than Bea, Edith was the one person always ready to rescue her, especially after Mama died. Their other sister, Marie, a little more than two years older than Edith, seldom came to town anymore. It seemed that Marie thought herself too good for the folks in Orange, too good for her own family. On the occasions when she did come to town, it had usually just been to see Mama after Papa died. Even then, she didn't stay long. But after Mama died, she never came at all.

Edith acted like it didn't hurt that Marie didn't visit her, but Bea knew better.

Bea and Edith were good friends, but Bea was not as close to Marie. Bea blamed it on the age difference between them, and Marie's husband. Sol. Even when they did come to town these days, Sol never visited his wife's family. He preferred to sit on the front porch with his own mama.

Bea opened the car door and slid in. "Where've you been, dumping that no-good fourth husband of yours? I don't know how you do it, Sis. I can't live with the one I've got and you keep taking in a new one." She laughed, but only slightly. Edith had indeed gone through a number of husbands, and others had described her as a "loose" woman.

"No, Bea I've decided to take a break from marriage. Just play the field, you know what I mean? How about you? Still stuck with Hal?"

"Looks like I might not be for long."

"What?" Edith slammed on the brakes, swerved onto Turret Road and pulled to the curb while Bea grabbed the door handle and held on. When the car stopped and Bea's heart took up its beat again, she turned away and stared out the passenger window. Two boys and a dog raced down the sidewalk. One boy grabbed a stick and threw it into a vacant lot. The dog raced after it.

Edith grabbed her arm. "Toots, look at me. What's going on between you and Hal. And why've you dressed like that? I almost didn't recognize you."

When Bea was a child, Edith had always been the most patient with Bea's frequent crying jags. Edith would roll over and spoon Bea with her own body and hold her until exhaustion brought blessed relief to both of them. Neither of them understood why Bea cried.

"Hal's sleeping around on me."

"I knew it." Edith banged her fist on the steering wheel.

"No, you didn't know any such thing. You just never liked him."

"That's true," Edith said, chuckling. "Now, tell me why you're dressed like that. Did you go to work at the shipyard?"

"I did. I took a job after I learned about Hal and the other woman. I figured I'd better get ready to support myself."

Edith pulled a Lucky Strike from her pocket, lit it and inhaled. The smell of the tobacco intermingled with soft circles of smoke. "Good for you. I guess you found someone to stay with Percy."

"A neighborhood girl, yes." Bea hesitated, sucked in a gut-full of air and on the exhale said, "She's pregnant."

"The neighbor girl?"

"No, no. The other woman," Bea said.

"You mean the woman Hal shacks up with—she the one pregnant? His baby?"

"That's about it."

"I always knew that man wouldn't keep his talleywhacker

buttoned in his pants. So, what next?"

"He says he's got to marry her because . . . Oh, hell, Edith, I have no idea what he plans to do."

"What he plans to do? What about you, Toots?" She put her hand on Bea's. "Maybe you and Percy could move down to Galveston Island and live with Marie and Sol. They have a big house right there on the beach, you know. Besides, it's time she helped . . ." Edith stopped and shook her head. "No, I don't suppose that would be a good idea."

"Probably not. In the first place, my own sister wouldn't have me. And she sure wouldn't want a baby to mess up that spotless house."

"That's for sure." Edith sat silent for minute. "You know what? I think it might be a good time for you to have your fortune read."

"My fortune? Are you crazy?" Bea laughed with the absurd idea.

"Not at all. I've got this gypsy fortune-teller friend who reads palms, tarot cards, that sort of thing. Maybe she has a crystal ball. Maybe she can help you learn what you do wrong and what you need to do to make your life run better."

Sudden laughter made Bea sputter all over herself. "Is she the one who helped you get your life straight? That's why everything is going so good for you right now?"

"Oh, hush laughing. I'm serious," Edith said, chuckling at herself.

"So how in the world did you meet a gypsy? I hear they're filthy people living in that wagon camp outside of town. Don't they live off of stealing from other people?"

"They're different than we are, yes. But they're people just like you and me," Edith said. "I met them the other day when I was at this guy's house. One of the gypsy men from the camp came over as we stood in their front yard talking. He asked if he could buy a couple of my friend's nice little pigs, that they were the perfect size to roast for a wedding celebration. The guy said no, that he needed the pigs to feed his own family. The gypsy begged and begged, told him how important weddings were to gypsies, and could they please buy them. My friend gave in. He figured if he didn't, they'd come in the middle of the night and steal them."

"And the moral to that story is . . ."

"The gypsy could have just stolen the pigs, but he didn't. He bought and paid for them."

Edith restarted the car. The conversation lagged. Bea rolled down the window for fresh air and then held her hair as the wind whipped it in her eyes. A child on a bicycle rode by and waved. Bea waved back and thought of Percy. What would he look like at that age?

Edith broke the silence as they pulled into Bea's parking lot. "So you're working at the shipyard now? Good for you."

"Just started. I felt so scared I must have gone to the toilet twenty times in the first hour."

Both women headed up the sidewalk, the summer sun already hot this early in the day. As they walked inside, Bea called out, "It's me, Nelda, I'm home. My sister's here with me."

"Okay, Mrs. Meade, we'll be right there. I'm in the bedroom changing Percy's diaper."

Bea went straight to the icebox to fix them each a glass of ice water. She pulled out an ice tray and found it empty. Turning on the tap, she let the water run into the metal compartments of the tray.

She slid the refilled tray inside the icebox and removed the other, but found it in the same condition. "Nelda, how come we don't have any ice? Both trays are flat empty."

"The icebox is broke," Nelda called as she approached the kitchen without Percy. "I forgot to tell you about it. I tried to get some last night, but it quit making ice. Down here's cool, but . . ." She put her hand on the inside wall of the appliance. "I keep going and looking, but ain't no more ice made. The one at our house don't work neither."

Bea turned the tray upside down. "It's bone dry, Nelda. It can't make ice if the trays don't have water."

"You mean you have to fill 'em up with water?" Nelda's mouth dropped open.

"Well, how else would it make ice?"

"I weren't too sure. I'm not used to all this fancy stuff. We come from the country—didn't even have lights and running water, much less an icebox."

The two laughed as Bea showed Nelda how to fill the trays and tuck them into the freezer section.

"Just wait till I tell Mama." Nelda giggled. "She's going to be so happy to make her own ice. We've been buying it from the man at the ice house."

Edith had walked in on the conversation and snickered with them, but then the whole thing seemed to grow funnier to her, for she wrapped her arms around her stomach and dropped to the floor, hysterical.

Nelda giggled.

Bea snorted. "It's not that funny, Edith."

"It is, too," she said between sobs of laughter.

"It is not. You just got your giggle box turned over."

But the laughter *was* contagious. Soon, all three were sitting on the floor holding their bellies and laughing so hard they could hardly breathe.

"Shh," Nelda said, trying to stop. "I just put Percy down."

"Okay," she said, "that's enough."

That just caused them all to laugh harder.

Finally, Bea headed from the kitchen, Nelda following close behind, chatting like a magpie gone berserk.

"Papa heard about jobs down here, so we all just piled in the car and came. Mama don't drive you know, so after Papa got a job, while he worked, me and her and my little brothers and sisters walked around town all day, looking for a place to live. When it got dark and Papa found us, we parked the car someplace and slept all piled on top of each other. When Papa finally found us a place here in Riverside, we all cheered."

Hal would love to hear that. At least someone was thankful for what they had.

Bea walked into the bedroom to strip off her work clothes, but when she opened the closet, the only clothes inside were hers. Without a word, she headed to the bathroom. Hal's razor, shaving cup, toothbrush and *Brylcreem* were also gone.

Bea stepped into the living room.

"Nelda? Did Hal come by?"

Nelda stood looking at Edith, her face an expression of helplessness.

"It looks like he came and took everything. Did he say anything or just pack his things and walk out the door?"

Nelda nodded reluctantly. "Pretty much packed and left without saying anything."

Bea plopped on the couch, her elbows propped on her knees and her eyes staring straight ahead.

"Okay, honey," Edith said, dismissing Nelda. "You can go on home now. Thanks. You know when she needs you again, huh?"

"Yes, I'll be here tonight at the regular time. Sorry, Mrs. Meade, that you had to come home to all this." Nelda slipped out, taking care not to let the screen door slam behind her.

"Well," Bea said, "he did it. I expected as much."

Edith sat beside her and wrapped an arm around her shoulders. "Good riddance is what I say. Now you can start over. You've got your job, and Nelda helps with Percy. You'll be fine."

"I'm not so sure. I'm not as strong as you." She stared off into space until realization hit her. "What will I do about Oskar?"

"Who's Oskar?"

"A male boarder Hal brought home a few days ago. With just me living here, I can't let him stay. That just wouldn't look right. Folks will talk something awful."

"A boarder? Where is he now?"

"I don't know, but he'll probably be here soon. I asked him not to come home while Nelda was here by herself with the baby. He oils for Hal."

"Oils?"

"He keeps Hal's crane in working condition—makes sure the working parts are oiled. Hal says he's the best he's ever had."

"Well, it seems to me a man in the house could be a big help to you."

"But what will the neighbors say?"

Before Edith could answer, footsteps sounded on the porch, the door opened, and Oskar stepped inside carrying a small mattress over his shoulder.

When he saw Edith, a blush colored his face. "Excuse me . . ." He stuttered, stepped backwards. I didn't know you had company, Mrs. Meade." The mattress slid to the floor.

"No, Oskar, come on in. You might as well be a part of this conversation. This is my sister, Edith."

"How do you do, Edith," he said, his voice full of courtesy and kindness. "My name is Oskar Eichel."

He shook her hand then looked from her to Bea. "I came home soon as I heard Mr. Meade had moved out. I saw him on the street right after I bought this." He indicated the mattress on the floor. "I tried to get him to come home and talk with you first, but he said no, it'd be okay. I figured you would want me to move out, but I'll need a few days. . . ."

Bea felt flustered. She wasn't accustomed to a man considering her feelings like that.

"Got any place in mind?" Edith asked, lighting a cigarette.

"I don't know, but I'll find something. Meanwhile, ma'am, can I sleep here until I find another place? I promise I won't be here when you and the girl are here alone, but at least I can pay you a few dollars every payday. That way you can buy some fresh vegetables for the boy."

Bea's heart warmed toward the polite man. "I know you're good with babies. Yes, you can stay here until you find someplace else."

Oskar smiled gratefully. "You need help with anything, you just let me know. I do not want to be a burden on you. This war is hard on everybody. I can take your coupons and stand in the sugar line for you."

"Oh, that would be great if you could. I've got our rations for this week, but next time would be great." Hal never stood in the ration line, said it was a wife's job.

After dinner, while Bea and Edith cleaned the dishes and chatted in the kitchen, Oskar got his room set with flour-sack sheets on his mattress in the middle of the room.

The two women came in to inspect. Oskar stood up. "I'm lucky I found this bed when I did. It was the last one in the store and the shipment just got in this afternoon. People are desperate for bedding. At least this one is new—not slept on by God knows who. My buddy at work said he got crabs from the room where he slept."

The morning continued pleasantly enough. They all had breakfast, then Oskar went to bed. Edith left shortly afterward, but agreed to return that evening to help Nelda with Percy, who was teething and fussy. Bea rather suspected Edith's return had more to do with Oskar not working the swing or the midnight shift that night. A twinge of jealously crept in. Bea shoved it off as quickly as she identified it. She had no right to be interested in another man.

Chapter 16

Marie pulled on her housecoat and tiptoed to the big fancy kitchen before Sol arose. He'd be furious if he knew she started with the booze this early in the day. Of course he suspected, but there wasn't any need in confirming the fact for him. She filled her cup half full of tap water and topped it off with Four Roses.

Alcohol fed Marie's courage. Without it, she didn't stand a chance with Sol. He'd say one little thing and she'd scurry inside her shell, fearful to stick her head out until he walked off in disgust.

Hands shaking, she lifted the cup to her lips and sipped. By the time Sol walked in a little while later, she felt brave enough to broach the subject she'd been wrestling with for weeks. "It's been a long time since I've been to Orange, Sol. I'd like to go see my sisters."

"Who do you plan to stay with, Edith, that whore of a sister? She's probably between husbands now anyway." He stared at the cup in Marie's hand and tossed her a disgusted look. "I see you're boozing again," he said, his voice as hard as an ice cube on a winter day. He turned away, lit the burner under a teakettle of water and tossed the spent match into the trash.

"What do you mean? It's just water."

"Don't start that crap again with me."

She took a sip of her drink. "Maybe we need some time away from each other anyway. Don't you think if I went back to Orange for a few days it would be good for both of us?"

"There's nothing wrong with this marriage except your drinking. But if you want to go, go right ahead. I won't stop you. Just don't come back."

"Oh, Sol, don't talk that way, you—"

"I can talk any way I damn well please." He sauntered out and headed to the front door for the morning newspaper.

I hate him, I hate him, she thought, glaring at his retreating back. The depth of her hatred gnawed at her like a rat trapped in an empty corn bin. She fled out the kitchen door and down to the edge of their property that ended in the waters of the Gulf of Mexico. A breeze toyed with her limp blonde hair. Maybe Sol would have loved her better if she'd been a redhead like Irene Meade. The ultimate insult came when Bea had married Hal, Irene's nephew.

Sol fussed all the time about how she'd let herself go to pot. Humph, Irene was older than she was, and probably didn't look a bit better, especially after having nine kids. Marie had given birth to none, as least as far as most people knew, and still kept her figure. Of course, there was the baby she had given up for adoption, but she never counted that one. When folks asked if she had kids she always said no.

A cool breeze blew off the water. She shivered and pulled her housecoat tighter, aware for the umpteenth time how miserable she was—had always been. Maybe she got what she deserved—a vengeful God who refused to forgive her.

Not a day went by that she didn't replay the whole thing in her mind. How she'd lain in bed the next morning, those many years ago at Blind Aunt Gertie's house, wanting so badly to look at her new daughter, knowing if she did, she'd never be able to let her go—and let go she must. If she didn't, she'd lose Sol. At that time, she thought she'd die without him.

What a fool she'd been. As it turned out, he hadn't been worth the sacrifice. She'd never known a man so mean, and old age certainly hadn't mellowed the bastard. If anything, it made him worse.

It had been years since Sol had returned to Orange. He said he hated the town. That he was above the likes of the people who lived there. She didn't know where he got off with that idea. He'd been born and raised there too, by parents with no more money than hers.

She could pack a bag and leave, and Sol likely wouldn't even miss her for a while. Wouldn't notice she'd gone—that is, until mealtime.

She could—if she had Edith's guts. How many times in her life had she wished she could be more like her younger sister and say to hell with all the men in her life—particularly Sol. What would he do if she up and left? Probably track her down and kill her.

Marie listened to the waves pound against the shoreline. She looked down at her cup. Empty—just like her life. She turned away from the ocean, walked inside and poured herself another drink.

SYLVIA DICKEY SMITH

Chapter 17

Bea left for work a little later than usual. The oppressive heat slowed her steps. By the time she reached the shipyard, she barely had enough time to clock in, and only if no one got in her way. She pushed through the throng of workers, out of breath, breathing hard.

"Hey, Bea, over here," someone called out.

Frustrated, she stopped to see a friend of her oldest brother Ivan standing over in the corner between two buildings.

"What is it, Ike? I need to get to work or the foreman will fire me."

"Tom ain't gonna fire you, baby. Say, I hear your old man done left you for that ritzy girl who works in the office—and a Winters to boot. That so?"

Bristling, Bea turned and headed toward her station, ignoring him and his question.

Ike stepped up close and, as she stopped to punch in, rubbed his crotch against her behind. "Come on, sweetheart. Daddy'll take care of you if you treat him nice."

Bea spun around, heat rising to her cheeks. "Ike, you and your family go to the Baptist church every time the door opens. You're a deacon. You even teach Sunday School. Why are you acting like that?" She stepped off to the side. Ike followed, sidling up to her again.

"Just having a little fun, baby. Everybody's doing it these days. With this war and all, times are changing. Don't be so old-fashioned. A little piece of ass won't hurt nobody."

"What about your wife? What about her?"

"She won't never find out. And you ain't even got a man right now to cheat on, so what's the harm in a little nookie?" He wrapped his arms around her waist and pulled her tight. His greasy lips pressed hers hard. Bile came up in her throat. Unable to stop herself, she gagged.

"What the hell's wrong with you, gal?"

She wiped her lips and broke free of his grasp. "I'll tell the foreman."

"Don't make me no never mind," he laughed. "You go tell him. He ain't gonna do nothing to me. Can't. Don't have enough good welders as it is and we gotta get these ships built."

She simply turned and took off toward the foreman's office

He called after her. "Even tell my wife if you want to. She won't never believe you. She already knows you can't keep a man. That he has to go someplace else 'cause you don't put out. Go on, run."

Bea bounded into the foreman's office, but it was empty. She stopped in the middle of the room to catch her breath. She couldn't do this. She couldn't work with these men snatching and grabbing at her, thinking she'd be easy just because her husband left her. The last thing she needed right now was another man.

Besides, the risk of another baby, and she'd . . . The thought of another mouth to feed made her clench her legs together to ensure no man got between them. A chill ran down her back. How'd she get herself in such a mess?

She turned to go and ran into Tom Witherspoon, the foreman, standing in the doorway. His face registered shock when he saw her. "My God, Bea, what happened?"

"Ike happened."

"Say no more. What a jerk."

"I thought I could do this, Tom, but I can't work around men like him—and I can't quit either."

"We can try you somewhere else. How about riveting? You're little, and your hands are tiny. You'd be good at close work, and riveters need to work in tight places at times. What say I talk with the foreman over that section and see if he can use you? I know he's always yelling for more riveters."

"Riveters? Isn't that a man's job?"

"A few men complain about women taking away men's jobs but they're behind the times. These days, more and more women are proving themselves. We don't have enough able-bodied men around to do all the jobs. They're off fighting the war. Heck, we've learned women can do a lot of these jobs better than men. What do you say, want to give it a shot?"

Bea stood, not sure what to say, thinking about what he said.

Tom walked around her to the doorway. "Hey, Norm, come here a minute," he called to someone down the hall.

A moment later, a short, stocky man with thinning hair stepped into the office.

"Bea here is looking for a riveting job," Tom said. "Got any openings?"

"I always have openings for riveters. Especially for people with training."

"That's just the thing. She doesn't have training in that. She hasn't even been on my crew for long, but she's a hard worker and learns fast. I don't want to lose her, but I also don't want to hold her back."

"Needing more money, is she?" Norm looked from Tom Witherspoon to Bea. "You work nights, huh? Tell you what, since you've already been working here for a while and are familiar with things, I can team you up with one of my best riveters and get him to teach you the job. That's the best way to learn it. But it'll be a day job. Can you be here by eight o'clock?"

"How about day after tomorrow?" Tom suggested. "She can work tonight, take off tomorrow, and then come to work the next day. By the time she gets her first paycheck, it'll make up for the hours she's missing, and she'll have time to get a pair of coveralls."

Bea's head swam. "What do I need to bring?"

"A pair of coveralls," Norm said. "You already have your boots.

Other than that I'll take care of everything. Just show up at eight o'clock. You'll be working with Tony. He'll teach you what to do. Now he's kind of a lecher, so watch yourself, but he's good at his job."

"God, not another one."

Norm looked at Tom. "What's that about?"

"Ike's been bugging her."

Norm shook his head. "We do the best we can to make these guys behave. You have a problem, come see me. But Tony here—he's not a jerk, just a charmer. Whatever he tells you, take it with a grain of salt. He's a smooth-talking son of a gun. He's turned many a gal's head, got more than one of them in love with him. Follow me, I'll introduce you."

Tony had dark eyes, dark hair, one curl hanging down on his forehead, and arms like those of a steamship worker. He looked her in the eye. Bea's stomach flip-flopped.

"Tony. Bea Meade. She'll be working with you tomorrow. She knows nothing about riveting so you'll have to teach her from scratch. Tom says she's a hard worker and needs the money."

Norm looked at Bea, then at Tony.

"She's a lady. You treat her like one, okay?"

"Aye, aye, sir," he said, giving Norm a sharp salute. Satisfied, the foreman walked away.

Tony tipped his helmet to Bea and wiped his face with the sleeve of his blue work shirt. "Evening, ma'am, pleased to make your acquaintance. I can always use a hard worker. Guess your husband's off fighting the war, eh?"

"My husband creates his own wars, thank you very much."

"Ma'am?"

"He works here on one of the gantries."

Underneath the sweat and grime, Tony turned several shades of red. "Oh, right, you said your name was Meade. Guess he's Hal, eh? I'm sorry, ma'am. Didn't mean to pry. You come here tomorrow and I'll teach you everything you need to know. And I'll behave, okay?"

Bea smiled in thanks.

Norm nodded. "Fact is, I'm glad you're getting a chance to learn riveting. A good riveter is harder to find than a materials handler. A few years ago, I never would have suspected women could do that job. As it turns out, most women rivet better than many of the men do around here."

Bea headed back to her work area. She took the next materials order, filled it and hurried back, her mind preoccupied with the new job offer, wondering how in the world she'd ever learn how to rivet. She turned a corner and ran smack into a man she'd never seen before. Startled, she stepped back and tripped over a ladder.

The tall, dark haired man reached out and grabbed her before she hit the ground. "Whoa, careful," he said.

She grabbed his arms for support, finding her balance as she steadied herself. "I'm sorry. I didn't see you coming around the corner."

"I don't suspect you did."

"Where you looking for me?"

"No, ma'am. You're Bea Meade though, aren't you?"

"Why? Who are you?"

"I'm Dan. Daniel Baxter."

"Okay, now I know your name, but that doesn't tell me who you are or what you're doing."

She thought to herself, and you're the second person I've seen sneaking around this area, but she didn't say it.

"Just checking things out. Security. That's my job." He stepped in a little closer. "I just heard they're making you a riveter."

"How'd you know that? I just found out myself."

He changed the subject. "I also heard you took in a boarder recently?"

"What? There's nothing wrong with that, is there. What's this all about?"

"Just curious." He reached over and tucked a loose curl underneath her bandana. "Don't forget, I'm watching." He turned and stepped into the shadows.

Another jerk, she thought.

* * *

Bea finished her shift, eager to have a day off before coming back to train with Tony. A tow-headed kid stood outside the gate selling the two local papers. "Get your *Orange Leader* here, read what's happening on the battlefield." Then, "*Beaumont Enterprise*," he called out, with a heavy emphasis on the second syllable in Enterprise. Bea smiled at the lilting melody as he sang and sold.

Bea handed him a quarter. "The *Orange Leader*, please," she said.

He returned her change and handed her a paper.

"You get up bright and early, don't you?" She glanced at the headlines.

"Yes'm, I do. Gotta get these papers sold before I can go home, Otherwise, Mama won't let me in the front door. Won't be no beds empty till later, no way."

"Everyone has a house full these days, huh?"

"Yes'm. You been out to tent city? Seen what's going on there?" The boy shook his head. "Ain't never seen nothing like it, ma'am. Kids and more kids, rats, trash piled high, no running water. Head lice ever where. Even saw a whole family asleep on pieces of cardboard. Folks are desperate. My mama put up a wall down one side of our house, rented out the other side to three different families, and they was thrilled to death to get a roof over they's head."

The boy's words caused Bea to think about her own housing situation. She'd finally caught up on the rent, and felt fortunate not to live in Tent City, but what would happen to her now? The duplex was rented in Hal's name. If he married Violet, would he decide to move into the Winters mansion or kick Bea out of the house and move into it with Violet? If he did, there wasn't anything to stop him—then where would she live?

When she arrived home, weary and hot, she took a quick shower and crawled into bed beside Nelda, still sound asleep. Bone-weary, she questioned why in the world she let them talk her into riveting. Oh, yeah, she'd make more money, but it sure wouldn't stop the harassment from the men. Their jealousy over her taking that kind of job would only make it worse.

She drifted into a weary sleep.

Bea and Nelda both woke before Percy. She sent the young girl home to let her mother know Bea's shift would be changing to days and ask if Nelda could still take care of Percy. Then Bea staggered to the bathroom and looked in the mirror. Her hair, so long and hot on her neck, drove her crazy. Hal never would let her cut it in the summer, and he didn't like her to wear it up. Even more reason to cut it.

She fetched a pair of scissors and waited. By the time Masil arrived for her usual chat, Bea stood at the front door with the scissors.

"Okay, I want you to cut my hair. I'm sick of this long stuff. Hal never would let me cut it, but by God, he can't say a thing now."

Masil's eyes grew big as coffee cups. You're gonna cut it? Really?"

"No, I'm not. You are."

"I cut my own hair, but that thick, curly crop on your head scares the life out of me."

"Mama never would let me cut my hair when I was little. Then I married Hal and he wouldn't either. Now you cut it, and hurry. I don't have long."

Masil took the scissors, wrapped a towel around Bea's shoulders and after a couple of breaks to change dirty diapers, to feed the baby, and put him down to play, Masil finished whacking off Bea's thick mop.

"I'm no beautician," Masil said with some satisfaction, "but . . . wow!" She leaned back to assess her work, taking a deep drag on a cigarette before running off to collect ration coupons.

Bea scooted into the bathroom and stared at herself in the mirror. What she saw stunned her, for the cropped hair lay in soft curls just like she'd always wanted. "Jesus, Mary and Joseph," she said. She adjusted the style, tucked the comb in the cabinet, then slipped out of her gown, turned on the shower and stepped in. Reveling in the hot running water, she adjusted the shower temperature and began to rub her body with the bar of Lifebuoy soap.

Mama always taught that her body was the only thing she had to offer. She also told Bea that any male over the age of ten was not to be trusted—the same day Mama caught Bea's oldest brother Ivan with his hands down Bea's clothes. "Don't ever let them touch you anywhere underneath your clothes," she said. "If they do, you run fast and scream loud."

Way back then, Bea didn't understand what Mama meant. Since Mama dressed her in feed-sack dresses up to her neck and down to her toes, there wasn't any part of her body not covered with clothes. Once, when Bea sat with her legs on each arm of an over-stuffed chair, her mother came in and told Bea if she didn't put her legs down, she'd squirt her crotch with cold water from a water gun.

No wonder she had a problem opening up to Hal. But right now, the warm water and soap felt mighty good—everywhere she rubbed.

Later, she stepped out of the shower thinking, *so that's what it's all about.*

SYLVIA DICKEY SMITH

Chapter 18

Hal's day started bad and got worse. First, his mama didn't wake him up on time, and then by the time she fried his eggs and a big slice of ham, he was already full—of listening to her tell him what a no-good bum he'd turned out to be. Go back to his wife and son.

He shoved back his chair and stalked out the door to the shipyard.

He climbed the ladder, went through his daily checklist, blew the warning whistle, and headed the crane over to collect a load of pipe. When he swung the load around, he watched, horrified, at some kid looking the other way, heading straight into the path of his crane.

"No, no! Watch out!" He yelled, panic filling his chest with a swelling pain. He double-checked his warning bell, despite the fact he could hear it going off with his own ears. Even if he reversed the crane, that wouldn't stop the momentum of the swing. He leaned out the cab window and shouted down. "Watch out! Stop!" But his voice was lost in all the noises of the yard.

He was helpless to stop the impending collision. Hal's world crashed, as the load slammed into the guy, knocked him clean over the edge of the half-built destroyer and into the Sabine River several stories below.

He'd killed a man. . . .

He couldn't believe it. . . . He'd actually . . .

Hal shut off the engine, scrambled down the ladder, and rushed over to the gathering crowd along the edge of the ship.

"I sounded the alarm, I know I did! You heard the whistle, didn't you?" he asked anyone who would listen.

When they brought the victim up, relief flooded Hal when he

saw the young man move slightly. The kid was in a lot of pain, and the medics feared his back was broken, but Hal hadn't killed someone.

After transporting the man to the hospital, the safety officer came over to Hal.

"Several men saw the whole thing, Hal. You weren't at fault, and I don't want you to think you are."

"What the hell was the kid doing? Why the hell wasn't he paying attention?"

"I don't know, Hal, but several people signed a statement saying the accident victim wasn't where he should've been, and that you followed proper safety procedures."

Relieved, especially since he had second-guessed his every action from the moment he had seen the inevitable coming, his hands still shook and his knees felt weak.

By the end of his shift, he was in no mood to listen to Mom and Pop preach to him again.

But he did, and as expected, his parents bitched about his behavior. How he ought to go back where he belonged with his wife and baby. How Violet would be fine. Violet's family would take care of her, and he should take care of his.

By the time he'd been home a couple of hours, his head swam in parent-induced guilt. When he could take no more, he stood, adjusted his khaki pants, and said, "I'm heading out for a while. I'll be home before bedtime."

He stopped by Rufus' house. He and his wife were just sitting down to supper and invited Hal to join them. The fried chicken and pinto beans were good, but nothing compared to Bea's. The biscuits? Not even close.

He guessed Violet didn't even know how to cook, having household help to do everything. He really had gotten himself in a pickle. Out of the frying pan into the fire. He should've known better than to mess around. It made no difference that everyone else out at the shipyard was screwing other men's wives. He had to get caught. Dammit, this war was messing up everything. If only Violet hadn't gotten pregnant. He should've used a rubber but, hell, that felt like washing his feet with his socks on.

He said goodbye to Rufus and thanked his wife for supper, then built his courage and drove to the Winters house to talk to Violet's father.

The long curving sidewalk of the Victorian-style house went on forever. By the time Hal reached the end of it, his underarms felt wet and his hands were sweating. He wiped his palms on his pants, crossed the wide porch and knocked.

A young girl answered.

"Evening," he said, tilting his khaki hat to the back of his head. "Is Mr. Winters in?"

The child turned and yelled, "Grandpa, some man wants to talk to you?"

"Who is it?" a gruff voice called out. Soon a giant of a man with a handlebar mustache and long sideburns filled the doorway.

"Yes, can I help you?"

Hal pulled off his hat, twirled it in his hands, stuttering. "My name is Hal Meade, I wondered if we could . . ."

The man turned red-faced. "Get back inside, Margaret," he ordered the girl, then stepped outside and closed the door behind him.

"So, it's you." His voice sounded bitter, sarcastic.

Hal swore he could see steam exiting the man's ears.

Hal put his hat back on, then took it off again and spun it in his hands. "I know you're mad, sir, but I can explain."

"Explain? Explain? Do you realize it's all I can do to keep my boys from coming after you? I had to lock the gun cabinet and hide the key to keep them from getting in a heap of trouble. You aren't worth jail time. I told that girl not to go work down at that shipyard with all that philandering going on, but no, she wouldn't listen."

Suddenly the door popped open. There stood Violet. Despite the odd expression on her face, Hal had never been so glad to see anyone in his life. He wiped sweat off his brow and took a step back, the beat of his heart moving down out of his throat and back into his chest.

"Daddy . . . Hal . . . what's going on?"

"I wanted to tell your folks I'd marry you, but your daddy here—"

"How the hell do you plan to marry my daughter when you already have a wife and a baby? You going to just let them starve to death?"

"Daddy, I told Hal we could raise his baby, too, like our own. We already decided that."

Hal spoke up. "Well, that was the plan, but Bea said no, we couldn't."

"I don't know what you two will work out, but I wash my hands of the whole affair." Mr. Winters stomped inside and slammed the door.

Violet grabbed Hal's hand and led him to the porch swing where they sat, thighs touching.

"What is it, Hal? You look terrible."

"I almost killed a man today. A kid really. Knocked him clean off the deck of a destroyer and into the river. If it hadn't been for the crew close by, he'd a drowned. As it is, he's in the hospital. I can't live like this. We need to get something settled before I do kill someone. I can't keep my mind on the job and worry about you."

"I'm okay, baby." Violet ran her hand down the back of his head.

"I just love your red hair," she said. "I hope our baby's is just like yours."

"I don't care about the baby's hair color. I just hope it's a girl." Hal took her hand. "I need to talk to your brothers. Otherwise, they'll break into that gun cabinet and shoot us both."

No sooner had the words left his mouth than two young men swaggered up the sidewalk, their eyes locked on Hal and their sister.

"There's Horace and Bernard. What do you think they expect from me, Violet? I've already told them I'm going to marry you."

"Who knows, but if they come up here and start making trouble,

I'm going inside and get Daddy. He'll put a stop to it."

"You really think so? He's pretty mad at both of us."

"He's mad, but he won't put up with violence."

"Where's Johnny? I never see him hanging out with these two."

Violet didn't answer, but Hal felt a shiver run through her, as if the mention of Johnny's name caused a chill.

Chapter 19

Bea donned a pair of coveralls she'd borrowed from a neighbor and, soon as Nelda arrived, left for the shipyard. Never had she dressed like this before, and the fabric felt as hot and heavy as a quilt on a summer day. The buses ran, of course, but the walk gave her time to build her courage. Eager to learn her new job, by the time she arrived, her discomfort with the clothes didn't exist.

Consolidated Western Steel expected a busy day—the official "laydown" of yet another dreadnaught destroyer, the DD878. Since working there, she'd learned that Weaver, one of the other shipyards in town, built minesweepers, and Levingston, ocean-going tugs. Consolidated's contracts were for the dreadnaughts, destroyer escorts and landing craft.

When she walked through the gate, local dignitaries, supervisors and contractors were converging with a stack of drawings for each stage of the build-out, starting with the basic bottom hull of the dreadnaught. A few months later and the ship would be ready for launch.

She found Tony in front of a group of women, clipboard in hand. Soon as Bea arrived, he started calling out names, checked them off a list, and handed the clipboard to his assistant.

"Good morning, ladies, and welcome." His smile showed off a mouth full of pearly whites. "Today is the first day of an exciting new job for you. Today you become a lady riveter," he said, emphasizing the last word, as if proud of the title. "The men around here may tease and taunt you, but pay them no mind. That's just jealousy talking. Our lady riveters do a much better, neater, faster job than any man out here. So hold your head high and give 'em hell."

An experienced lady riveter joined the class to explain the nature of the task. "A rivet," she said, "is a permanent mechanical fastener. Before you install it, it has a smooth cylinder-like shaft with a head on one end. You place the rivet in a pre-drilled hole then deform the tail so that it expands to about 1.5 times the original diameter of the shaft. That's what holds the rivet in place. So you can tell one end from the other, we call the original head the factory, and the deformed end we call the buck-tail." She held up an example of a rivet as she talked, demonstrating with a piece of metal with pre-drilled holes.

"After the rivet is installed, it has a head on each end. This makes it much more capable of supporting a shear load. Plus, it can also support tension loads." She glanced up. "Anyone here know what a tension load is?"

A woman near the rear of the crowd raised her hand. "Isn't a tension load one that runs alongside the axis of the shaft?"

"That's right. Good for you. See," the instructor said, a grin spread the width of her face, "that's why we do our job so well. We're a smart bunch of gals. Don't ever put yourself down for being a woman.

"Now, what's a shear load? Anyone?"

No one said anything.

"Okay, I'll give you this one. A shear load runs vertical—at a 90-degree angle—to the axis of the shaft. Bolts and screws are better for tension applications."

Each of them were assigned rivet guns, safety glasses, helmets, heavy-duty gloves and other gear, along with further instruction on the whole process of riveting, including the dangers involved. The group then toured work under construction. Men they passed teased and taunted them, calling them lady riveters. Apparently, no one told them the women considered the title a compliment.

Bea flew through the class, loving every minute of it, feeling like she made a contribution to something bigger than her. Before, she never liked to sweat, but now, the hard physical labor intoxicated her. After they finished the initial instruction, each woman received assignment to work alongside an experienced riveter.

Tony, Bea's trainer, led her through the yard to the current destroyer under construction. The day passed before she felt ready for it to end.

She headed out the gate only to run into the one person she hoped she never saw again—none other than Daniel Baxter. As before, something about him made her feel like she'd broken the law.

"How'd the new job go?" he smiled, looking her in the eye.

She looked away.

"Let me ask you something, Mrs. Meade. Do I make you uncomfortable?"

"Absolutely not. What makes you think so?"

"It could be because you refuse to look me in the eye."

"I do not." She forced herself to hold his gaze as long as possible, then looked down at the dirt under her fingernails. "And don't call me Mrs. Meade. Since you seem to know everything else, I'm sure you know my husband and I are separated."

"Actually, I do, and I saw you walking to work last night. I know it must be difficult for you, caring for a baby all day, then having to walk to work at night." He smiled. "Let me ask you something, Bea. Can I call you Bea?"

"You can ask me anything you want. I reserve the right not to answer. And yes, my name is Bea."

"Fair enough."

She waited, expecting another question about her boarder.

"Do you know how to drive?"

"What? Why?"

"Now that you have this big promotion and live in a household without a car, or a . . . Well, you qualify for gas ration coupons, and . . ." He stopped mid-sentence, turned away, then back to her. "Why don't you drive? All the women these days are learning how, what with the war and all."

"What difference does it make to you?" She lifted her chin,

frustrated at the man butting into her business.

"None. I thought it might matter to you."

It did. For months Bea had begged Hal to teach her to drive, but he had given the same answer every time she asked. "You don't need to drive, baby. I'll take you anywhere you need to go."

"I'd like to learn to drive. But without a car, it wouldn't do me much good."

Daniel's face brightened. "Well, as a matter of fact, I have an idea. I know just the guy that can help you. His name's Tank and he owns this junkyard. He salvages parts from cars, puts them together and comes up with one that runs. Cost you a little or nothing. He'd probably let you pay a little down and a few dollars each payday."

"Why should I buy a car? I told you I don't drive."

"Stick with me, and you will by the end of the day." Before she could object, he took her by the arm, ushered her across the street to a black sedan.

She'd never in her life gotten in a car with a man she barely knew. What would Hal say?

Then she realized what Hal said didn't matter a hill of beans. She hopped into the passenger seat.

After a quick stop by the house to see if Nelda and Percy were okay, and ask if Nelda could stay a couple more hours, Daniel drove her to West Orange.

She kept a sharp eye on Daniel, who now and then took his eyes off the road long enough to glance back at her.

"You look nervous. Don't be."

"I've never done anything like this before. I'm not sure I'm ready to learn to drive."

Daniel swerved to avoid a mangy dog sauntering across the road. "It's a new day, Bea."

New day or not, little Bea, the woman who never took a risk in her life, had vanished. Another woman now occupied her body, and sat calmly in the seat next to a man she barely knew.

They pulled up in front of a junkyard and a burly man who,

without a doubt, spent most of every day with his head under the hood of a car and washed his hands in motor oil instead of soap and water stepped out of a small one-room shack. He wore a tee shirt stained with sweat and dirt. Bea imagined what it smelled like and hoped she didn't have to get that close.

Tank, evidently.

Daniel did most of the talking, explaining they were looking for a reliable car Bea could afford. Then, the three of them walked between rows of cars that looked like mismatched soldiers standing at attention.

"Now this one here is mostly a '37 Ford." Tank pointed to one. "I think it's the best deal for the money."

"Can we drive her?" Daniel asked.

"Be my guest," Tank said, and opened the driver's door for Bea. "Climb in little lady, start her up and listen how she purrs like a kitten."

Bea slid behind the steering wheel, her heart pounding as loud as the jackhammers at the shipyard. Dan stood beside her with the driver's door open, pointing out the gear, the clutch, the brake and most important of all in this town, the windshield wiper. After she convinced him she knew the name of each and their location, he closed her door, headed around to the other side and got in.

"Okay, now, be sure it's out of gear. Here, where I showed you."

Bea checked. "Is that it?"

Daniel jiggled the gear. "That's it. Okay."

She turned the key and the engine started, but it sounded more like a woman in labor than a purring kitten.

"Now, remember what I said? What do you do next?"

"Press on the gas?"

"The clutch, Bea, the clutch."

"Oh." Bea stepped her left foot on the clutch, pushed it to the floor, and held the other foot on the brake.

"Now, take your right foot off the brake and slowly press down on the gas pedal with the right foot while letting up on the clutch with your left."

The instructions sounded easy, but when Bea tried to make the car move forward, the whole car jumped, sputtered and died—six more times.

"That's okay. It takes a while to get the hang of it. My dad said I almost broke his neck when he taught me. You're getting frustrated, Bea. Be patient. You'll get it. The key is to get the feel of the timing — releasing the one while you apply pressure on the other. Think of it as a balance scale. You don't want one end to fall below the other. Now, try again."

After more attempts than Bea cared to count, the car inched out the junkyard gate. Unique, to say the least, the car's beauty so awed Bea she had difficulty focusing on the task at hand. She kept thinking how independent she could be with her own car, and now knew why Hal never wanted her to learn how to drive.

Two hours later, Bea had the process down pretty darn well. By then, night had fallen and they steered off the back roads where there was no traffic at all, to the main roadway where her first encounter with an oncoming car sent her veering off the road and into a dry, shallow ditch.

Shaken, Bea sat there wondering if she'd survived, while Daniel roared with laughter. "That's my fault, Bea. I should have explained how to handle oncoming cars—how you share the road by staying to the right of the imaginary line down the middle. But not too far to the right! But I know it's tough to see with everyone's headlights half-covered."

A car passed them, then backed up, and called out his window. "Need a hand?"

In short order they were on the road again and headed back to the junkyard. Daniel then taught Bea how to haggle over the price, and they agreed on payments.

Afterward, Daniel followed Bea home.

She turned into the parking lot and parked the '37 Ford like her name was Miss Astor, rather than Meade.

SYLVIA DICKEY SMITH

At Nelda's, they found Percy plopped on his back in the middle of Nelda's bed, fast asleep.

"Why don't you just let him spend the night here, and Nelda can bring him home in the morning before you leave for work," Nelda's mother suggested.

Bea agreed, thanked them, and she and Daniel stepped out into a fine mist. Late summer was not her favorite season. She wished for the smell of pine trees, but she'd have to settle for the nip in the air brought by the impending rain. The mist turned into a light rain as the two ran down the sidewalk and up the steps to her front door.

Oskar ran up on the porch from the opposite direction and stepped on the porch just as they did.

"Hey, Bea, I expected you to be working tonight. Aren't you on the graveyard shift?"

"No, I started days. I'm a riveter now."

"Well, congratulations." He looked behind her at Daniel.

"Hello, Daniel. Nice seeing you again."

Bea looked at the two of them. "Oh, so you've met. Daniel taught me to drive and helped me buy a car."

"Really?" Oskar raised one eyebrow, but extended his hand.

"So you're the German I heard lives here," Daniel said with a little laugh. "If I'd known it was you I wouldn't have been worried." He shook the proffered hand, then they all stepped inside.

"German, yes, but don't say that too loud around here. Folks get kind of scared. They think all Germans are like *The Madman*. I don't blame them. I'm scared of him, too. But I can assure you, I'm not your enemy. Or a spy."

"Thanks for clearing that up," Daniel grinned.

Bea excused herself to the kitchen to put out the leftovers, but kept an ear on the conversation between the two men.

"So, you haven't found your brother Wilhelm yet?"

"Not yet."

Bea glanced around the door. Daniel had moved over to the sofa and had pulled a pack of cigarettes from his pocket. He offered one to Oskar, who declined.

"Don't smoke?" Daniel took one and lit it, then tossed the match in a nearby ashtray.

"Never picked up the habit," Oskar said.

Neither man said anything for several minutes.

"Bea?" Daniel walked into the kitchen. "I think I'll head home, now that the rain has stopped."

"You don't want to eat a bite before you go?"

"Maybe next time. Smells good though.

"Thanks for the driving lessons, and I'm in love with the car." Bea walked him to the door.

"Too bad it isn't me you fell for," he said, laughing and waving over his shoulder as he left.

Chapter 20

Oskar got up from the sofa, frowning. "What did he mean by that?"

"I have no idea. Food will be ready in just a minute." Bea headed back to the kitchen.

Oskar went to his room and changed into a dry shirt, then joined Bea as she bustled about to warm up some food for them.

"Want me to put on a pot of coffee?" he asked.

She nodded, and he filled up the kettle and put it on the burner.

"How's the riveting going?"

"It's hot, dirty work. But I think I've got the hang of it." Bea reached behind him and pulled the shade down before the block warden stopped to remind them of the blackout. "Thank goodness, cool weather's coming."

"The pay's better though, isn't it?"

Bea loved the way he talked. He didn't say ain't or other slang like most folks around here. The hint of an accent crept in from time to time, but then he hadn't been in America very long. Mama always taught her to use good English, to not stoop to speaking like her brothers, who sounded like they'd been raised by hobos riding the rails instead of strict Pentecostal parents.

Bea filled their plates, and together they sat down to eat.

"Is Orange your home?"

"I've lived here all my life," Bea said. "Hal always wanted us to move away somewhere, but I wouldn't hear of it. Orange is home. I don't like strange places."

"Some people don't handle change very well. Me? I like to

travel."

She picked up the cellophane pack of oleomargarine she'd put on the table, and began to massage the yellow food coloring into the white mixture. "Hold on a minute and we'll have oleo to put on our bread. That's the one thing I miss with this war, butter. That and silk stockings."

"If you don't mind me saying so, you don't need stockings to look nice." He glanced at her and smiled until she ducked her head.

When they finished, She grabbed the plates and headed to the sink.

Oskar stood. "You wash, I'll dry."

Hal had never done a dish in his life, joking he didn't think dishwater hands looked good on a man.

"That's okay, you don't have to . . ."

"I insist. Where's a dishtowel?"

Bea opened the drawer to her left, pulled out a homemade tea towel and handed it to him.

Oskar moved in next to Bea and reached into the sink for a plate. "My mama always taught me, you eat, you help clean up."

"Tell me about your mama. What's she like?"

"She has kind eyes. You remind me of her. One thing different, though, my mama always speaks her mind. You seem to keep things bottled up."

Bea suppressed a laugh. "I don't *do* emotion." She'd learned not to trust them, to keep them crammed down inside, away from public view.

"What kind of work does your daddy do?" Bea asked, hoping to get the subject back to him.

"He owns a clothing store in Seguin. And my mother—well, to tell you the truth, she's a fortuneteller. And my stepfather hates it."

"I thought only gypsies told fortunes."

He smiled. "She learned from one."

"Folks around here don't trust gypsies. They think they're all crooks."

Oskar chuckled. "Well, they're not too far wrong—but they don't mean any harm, it's just how they live. That's how they survive."

"Wilhelm is younger than you?"

"Correct. We came to America because my step-father had the foresight to see where Germany was headed."

"And your older brother stayed behind?"

"He's made the German military his career, and has worked his way up in the ranks. Plus, his wife didn't want to leave her family."

"But why didn't you get drafted by our Army after the war started? I didn't think they let able-bodied men out these days."

"I have flat feet."

The air in the room shifted. Concern drew Oskar's eyebrows together. "This Daniel fellow who brought you home . . . I don't mean to pry, but I'm curious why he's friendly to me. And to you. Because of me, perhaps? There's little I can do to harm anyone."

Bea shook her head. "He works in security, that's all I know."

"He's chasing the wrong man, then. Word is there's someone else hanging around the yard that security can't catch or identify."

A flash of the young man she'd run into underneath Hal's crane came to Bea's mind, and she started to mention it as she eased the sticky skillet down into hot soapy water.

But Oskar picked that moment to put away a dish and his arm brushed against hers. A warmth spread from the touch all the way down to—well, all the way down.

Before she recovered, a knock sounded, followed by the front door opening.

"Hey, Toots!"

Bea's sister Edith came into the kitchen.

"Say, I was about to go over to the USO to see *Double Indemnity* . . . this couple begins an affair and then plot to kill her husband. Either one of you want to go? We could take a pallet for Percy and put him on the floor. He'd sleep fine."

Bea and Oskar dried their hands and put away the hand towels.

Edith flashed her winning smile at the two of them. "Let's all go. It'll be fun."

"Sure," Oskar said, "I'm up for a show. What about you, Bea?"

Bea shook her head. "Percy is staying at Nelda's, but I'm too bushed. You two night owls go ahead."

After they left, Bea changed into a nightgown, pulled her mother-of pearl brooch out of the cigar box, crawled in bed and tucked it under her pillow.

She cried herself to sleep again that night, but for a change, she wasn't really sure why.

Chapter 21

When Bea awakened and glanced out the window, she saw a day as gray as she felt. Instinctively she reached across the bed for Hal but felt only an empty pillow. She groaned and turned over, wanting nothing more than to go back to sleep and never wake. The memory of Hal's affair, and now the challenge of learning to rivet, made her want to shut out the world a while longer.

Then she remembered. "It's Saturday. I don't have to work today."

She stretched long and hard, then lay thinking about Percy, who had spent the night at Nelda's house. She loved the little guy, babbling with the new discoveries he made every day.

It didn't make sense.

What drove Hal away? Is Percy why he'd sought another woman? The war changed everything. The men at the shipyard only thought about one thing—sex, sex, sex. Women were playthings. Either that or they threatened men's jobs. Right now, she preferred life without a man.

With that thought, she turned over, luxuriating in the moment without any demands on her. She hadn't realized she'd fallen asleep again until brighter sunlight slashed across her face. She looked at the clock as she crawled out of bed. Almost noon. She trudged to the bathroom, slid her gown over her head and stepped under water as hot as she could stand it, hoping something in her world would soon start making sense.

In the middle of lathering herself with soap, she remembered that Hal's parents had asked to see her and Percy. Hal was going to come by after lunch and take Bea and Percy to the Meades' house.

She hurriedly rinsed off the soap and dried herself. After pulling on a flower-print dress and smearing on a little makeup, she hurried off to claim her baby from Nelda's. Percy clapped his hands and laughed out loud when he saw her walk in the door.

After a brief chat with Nelda's family, Bea took Percy home. She had barely finished feeding him lunch when Hal walked in the front door like he owned the place.

"Ready to go?" he asked.

"Soon as I get Percy's bottles made. Here, can you put this outfit on him? I had him dressed, but he spit up on everything. His diaper's wet, too.

Hal grunted. He lifted and held Percy at arm's length.

"Hey, little fellow, miss your daddy?"

"No, he hasn't. But a lot of good it would do him if he had." Bea opened the fridge and pulled out a quart of milk and began filling three nipple bottles for Percy.

Hal strolled around the room, Percy still in his arms. "By the way, I talked to Violet the other day. And she still says she'd be glad to take Percy and raise him as her own. That way, you wouldn't be saddled with him."

The bottle of milk crashed to the floor.

"Saddled with him?" She had shouted so loud that Percy started whimpering.

"That's it, Hal. You take Percy to your parents by yourself. I'm not going. And don't you ever walk in my house again without knocking."

Soon as she said the words, though, she felt ashamed. She loved Hal's parents like her own mama and daddy who were both now in their graves. She hadn't seen Mr. and Mrs. Meade since all of this with Hal and Violet had started, but she'd heard they were plenty upset with him.

"Never mind. Give me a minute to clean this mess and we'll go."

She cleaned the milk and broken glass, poured another bottle and they headed outside. Hal opened her car door and held Percy while Bea slid into the passenger seat, then he plopped the baby in her lap.

By the time they reached the Meade's, no more than six words had passed between them, and to Bea, that was too many. Hal parked in front of the small, three-room house. At the sight of it, pent-up emotion clutched Bea in the stomach. She and Hal had gotten married in that little house with all of his family surrounding them. With her Papa gone, and Mama in such bad health, Edith had been the only one from her family to attend.

Tall, white-haired Mr. Meade greeted them at the door with his Lord Davenport pipe in hand. The three-room house smelled of snuff and pipe smoke. Although Bea felt close to her in-laws, somehow she never had been able to call them anything other than Mr. or Mrs. Meade. Perhaps because they'd never offered an alternative.

Mr. Meade stuck the unlit pipe in his mouth and reached for the baby.

"Hey, little fellow. I thought you'd never get here. Grandma has banana pudding in the oven, browning the meringue. She makes the best you ever did taste."

He tickled Percy's belly. "Wait 'til it cools and we'll go in and steal some. Okay?"

He carried the baby inside. "Come look, Mama, look who's come to visit."

Mrs. Meade came in, wiping her hands on a bib apron. She tucked a sprig of sandy brown hair back inside the severe topknot on the back of her head, and smiled. The brown snuff she constantly dipped left her teeth with a permanent stain.

"My boy's here," she said, clapping her hands in greeting.

Percy, seemingly not bothered by snuff-breath, leapt into her waiting arms.

"Come on, little fellow, look here what Grandma has, your very own playground. See?"

She took him over to a quilt spread on the floor. Piled high were homemade toys lovingly cut from leftover pieces of wood, then sanded and smoothed down until they felt as soft as velvet. Grandpa had carved trains, horses, turtles, and a set of building blocks with letters and numbers in relief on the sides.

So much love in this household, Bea thought, and she knew that love encompassed her. She hugged them both, not knowing what to say next. Awkwardness silenced the room. Hal still stood at the door, a stranger in his own parents' home.

"You get along, Hal," Mr. Meade said. "This day is for the boy and our daughter."

"I'll be back in a few hours to get you." Hal said, looking rather like a fox caught in a hen house and released back out into the wild.

After Hal left, Bea and Mr. Meade enjoyed a bowl of banana pudding while Mrs. Meade fed some to Percy, then excused herself to the kitchen to wash the dirty dishes and put on supper.

Bea and Grandpa Meade played with Percy until he fell asleep.

"Hey, Bea," Mr. Meade said, "do you want to see my garden?"

For some reason, Bea sensed this conversation had been planned out in advance of her arrival.

Together, they walked through the kitchen where a pot of rice steamed on the stove. Mrs. Meade dropped pieces of floured chicken in a big cast-iron Dutch oven full of hot, sizzling lard. Even the aroma tasted delicious.

She and Mr. Meade headed out the back door, across the porch and down the steps to the yard. A small path on the right led to the back of the lot where a two-hole outhouse offered its distinctive aroma to the neighborhood. On the left, neat rows of tomatoes and bell peppers and hills of cucumber showed Mr. Meade knew his gardening.

"Almanac's never let me down. " Mr. Meade leaned over and snatched a stink bug off of a tomato plant."

Bea took his elbow and squeezed. "A man at work pooh-poohed planting by the moon. I told him my father-in-law swore by it and I knew no better gardener."

Mr. Meade laughed. "Yeah, some of these new kids think they know better'n us old-timers. I've done both, and I always have a better crop if I take the cycles of the moon into account. I swear by my Farmer's Almanac. That, and Farmer's Mercantile across from the courthouse. They have the freshest seeds around."

They both grew silent. The leaves on the sycamore trees rustled in the breeze. A few early volunteers drifted down to the ground.

"What's this I hear about you and Hal breaking up?"

"It's not me, Mr. Meade. It's your son. He's found another woman."

Mr. Meade shook his head. "This war has gotten people all messed up. All they think about is spending all the money filling their pockets and having a high-hill good time."

He leaned over and picked up a scrap of paper that had blown into the yard and tucked it in his pocket. "I swear, dear, I don't know what this world's coming to. Sometimes I feel that even though we were half-starved to death, families were better off during the Depression. They stuck close together."

"I don't know how I'm going to handle this." Bea had held the tears way too long and they would not be quenched any longer.

Mr. Meade pulled her to his chest and held her tight. "Don't give up on the boy, honey. He might come around to his senses yet."

"Doesn't matter if he does or not. She's carrying his baby."

He stiffened and released Bea to look her in the eye. "Hal didn't tell me that. He knew what I would say. That boy's been brought up better'n that. Reminds me of the time my sister Irene broke up with your brother-in-law Sol and married another man. Love does strange things to the heart, and not all of 'em are good things."

He stared at the garden bed. "You know who she is? He wouldn't tell me."

"She's a Winters. Family's got money, I hear. She works down at the shipyard in the personnel department. I saw her. She's already showing."

The pain on his face made her pain even harder to bear. She

loved this man who had grown so dear to her. So like Papa. As they headed to the rear of the garden, his steps were slower, more halting, as if he too had lost a zest for life.

"So what you going to do, honey? You know we'll help you out all we can. The County don't pay much for road workers, and now, with money going to the war, they're paying us even less. But we'll help you keep food on the table. Long as we got this garden and that milk cow out yonder, you and Percy won't starve to death."

He limped to the fence and stopped. "I never thought one of my boys would do this to a woman. My oldest, Al, drinks way too much, but leastwise he comes home at night."

"We'll be okay, Mr. Meade. I've started working at the shipyard and I've already been promoted to riveter." She held up her hands for him to see the dirt under her fingernails.

"That's just not right. A woman's place is at home taking care of her children and her hus—well, I guess times are a-changin'. I heard on the radio how lots of women are working now, how they have to, to keep this war going. So we can bring our fighting boys home safe."

"You know, Mr. Meade, I never thought I could learn how to rivet, but I can. My teacher says I picked it up really fast. Plus, you know Hal brought home a boarder. That helps with the bills."

He looked surprised. "You have a man staying in your house. And you without a husband? What's the neighbors think?"

"Probably the same thing you're thinking. I have to make it on my own now, Mr. Meade. I just hope you don't think less of me."

"No, no, of course not. You do what you have to do. And no matter what Hal does, you keep coming over here with that darling baby."

Chapter 22

After Hal left Bea at his parents, he made a couple of stops then headed to Cherry's Pool Hall, shrugging off the guilt he felt when he saw how happy Pop and Mama were to see Bea and Percy.

Cherry's looked as crowded as ever. Several looked up when they saw him, elbowed their neighbors, and a quiet uneasiness fell over the room. Squinting through the cigarette smoke, he saw Rufus over at the bar, his big hands wrapped around a bottle of beer.

"Hey, good buddy, what's up?" Like a dog lifting his leg at a fire hydrant, Hal raised his and eased onto the barstool next to his friend. "Everybody in here looks mighty serious today."

Rufus didn't have look to know it was Hal. "You ain't gonna like it none."

"I don't need any more bad news, friend. I just left my folks house and, right now, they couldn't think less of me. After I left, I ran into Johnny, Violet's oldest brother. He says despite what the other two brothers say, if I marry his sister, he'll shoot me dead right on a street corner. And that I better not tell a soul what he said."

"Was he serious?"

"Sounded like it. Now, I don't know what to do. Let her have a bastard kid and live in this town in disgrace. Or marry her and take my chances. Maybe he don't mean it. Who knows?" Hal raised his hands in the air.

"Well, if I tell you what I just heard, maybe you'll change your mind."

Hal looked up from the bottle of Lone Star the bartender had set in front of him, and over to Rufus. "What are the old biddies talking about now?"

Rufus kept his voice low. "What if I tell you I done heard . . . that one of them's been playing around with his sister since before she even become a woman?"

"What woman? Violet?" Hal asked, confused.

"Violet."

Hal was stunned. "You talking about one of the Winters boys? Which one?"

"Same one."

"Johnny? No way."

"Some folks say they wouldn't bet that baby is even yours. What I hear, it's more 'n likely his."

Hal jumped off his stool. "That's an outright lie," he yelled, and popped Rufus upside the head.

Rufus reeled from the blow but grabbed the bar and regained his balance. "I wouldn't lie to you, Hal. I'm telling you the god awful truth.'

"I don't believe it."

"Dave, come over here," Rufus motioned to a man down the bar. "Tell Hal what you told me."

Dave waved them off. "No can do, partner. Just leave me out of it."

"No, no, Hal needs to hear it from somebody other than me."

Dave shook his head. He pulled out a bill, tossed it on the bar and walked out.

Hal scanned the room, looking for someone who might confirm or deny the charges. He caught Tony's eye. Bea's foreman—he'd tell the truth.

Tony walked over, looking like he'd rather be anywhere than there. He put his hand on Hal's shoulder. "Can't say whether it's true, good buddy. I heard Violet's Uncle Harry, after a bunch of beers, bragging about how he'd done it to his sister. You know—to Violet's mama, what's her name? And he also bragged that he'd taught his nephew to do it to his sister."

Tony looked embarrassed. "He must've meant Johnny doing

SYLVIA DICKEY SMITH

Violet."

"How come you never told me this before?"

"Harry was very drunk. But a few days ago, other folks said they'd heard Harry brag about it when he was cold sober."

Hal shook his head.

"Whether he still does it to Violet's mama or not, I don't know. He said they did when they were both kids, and swears she wanted it as much as he did. Says he taught Johnny how to take care of his needs and keep it all in the family."

Rufus joined the conversation. "Heard that's why Violet sleeps with every man she sees. She figures why not."

Hal wished for a tornado to suck him up and drop him a thousand miles away. "But they're a good family, well thought of in this town."

"Well, believe what you want. But we hated to see you leave your wife and kid and step into that kind of mess."

Hal slung a dollar bill on the bar and stormed out.

Ten minutes later he strode up the walk of the Winters' house, passed the big columns across the front into the shady portico, and rapped hard on the door. He waited, listening, until he heard light footsteps head his way. Violet opened the door. She was dressed in a light pink dress, brown loafers, with her hair pulled back in a ponytail.

"We need to talk," he said.

"I can't leave the house. Daddy told me I couldn't go anywhere."

"What do you mean, told you not to go anywhere? I thought he'd washed his hands of both of us. You'll come with me. I'll answer to your daddy if I need to." He grabbed her wrist just as Johnny stepped up behind her and grabbed the other.

"Hey, I told you I didn't want to see your face around here. You've caused enough trouble. Go back to your wife and kid. Leave us alone."

Hal's chest felt like a branding iron left in a fire overnight. He never had been much of a fighter, but he'd never been this mad before, either. "You can get on your high horse all you want to, Johnny, but I need to talk to your sister. I can do it here right in front of you or we can go inside and talk."

"Whatever you got to say, you can say it right here."

Hal looked at Violet. She looked worried, and tried to shake herself free. Both men kept a tight hold, each gripping a slender wrist.

"Okay, don't say I didn't warn you." He stared coldly at Violet. "I hear Johnny has been playing around with you for years, that—"

"What?" Violet screamed, "Who told you that?"

Johnny rushed him and slammed his fist into Hal's jaw.

He landed on his ass and skinned his hands as he tried to break his fall. Before he got back on his feet, Johnny had yanked Violet inside. But Hal managed to grab the door before it slammed and followed the two into the foyer, repeating the accusation that Johnny fathered Violet's baby.

He hadn't seen Mrs. Winters standing in the hallway until after the words were out of his mouth. She looked pale in the dim light seeping into the cool foyer.

"What—what in the world are you talking about? My son's done no such thing. Tell him, Violet. Tell him your brother never touched you. He's a good boy. He doesn't do that sort of a thing."

The pain on the old lady's face made Hal wince despite his anger.

"Tell me who said that awful thing," Mrs. Winters said, her face growing redder by the minute. "I demand to know."

Hal was still angry enough to repeat what he had just heard. "Your brother Harry did. He's the one who bragged about it, also bragged that he'd done the same thing to his sister."

Mr. Winters evidently had heard the commotion. He showed up and grabbed Hal by the collar. "What the hell are you talking about? Harry only has one sister, and that's . . ."

Everyone in the room stared at Mrs. Winters, who looked like she wished she were dead. She sputtered, turned and dashed out of the room, Johnny on her heels and Mr. Winters close behind.

"Mother, wait . . ." they both called in unison.

Hal clutched his throat, thankful to breathe.

White-faced, Violet sped to the drawing room, Hal on her heels, and dropped onto the sofa. Her hands fidgeted in her lap, and a tear dripped off her chin. "What'd you go and do that for, Hal? Daddy and Momma never needed to know."

Anger tightened Hal's jaw. "*I* needed to know, dammit! Why did you tell me the baby was mine? Your lie has broken up my marriage. I'll never forgive you for that."

"Well, the baby still could be yours . . ."

"Yes, but . . . you told me . . . Never mind." He slammed out of the drawing room and ran right into Bernard and Horace, Violet's other two brothers—the two who swore Hal would marry their sister or else.

"I told you to never show your—" Horace started.

"You better get your ass in there and find out what's really going on before you make any more threats," Hal yelled. "Or maybe you already know about Johnny and Violet."

Too late, he sensed Johnny coming up behind him.

"You son of a bitch." He grabbed Hal's arms behind him while Horace and Bernard rolled up their sleeves and stepped forward.

"It's too late, guys," Hal sneered. "You can beat me to a pulp, but that don't change the fact that Johnny's been messing around with his sister."

"What?" Horace and Bernard stopped short.

"Violet," Hal said.

"Johnny? Tell me that's bullshit."

Johnny let go of Hal's arms.

"Go ask your uncle," Hal said as he straightened his shirt.

"Leave Uncle Harry out of it," Johnny bellowed. "He has nothing to do with this."

Hal, madder and braver than he'd ever felt before, held nothing back. "Seems to me, he has everything to do with it. Your mama admitted as much."

Bernard and Horace both spoke at once. "Our mother? Leave her out of this."

They all turned to see Mrs. Winters charge into the room, weeping as if someone had shattered her heart. Someone had—her son, Johnny.

She rushed straight to him and pounded on his chest, shock and disgust frozen on her face. "*He* taught you to do this to my daughter," she screamed. "You've ruined her, just like he ruined me. I'll never forgive you for this, Johnny. I rue the day you were born."

She slid down Johnny and collapsed into a heap on the floor. Bernard and Horace hovered over their mother, their shoulders trembling in grief.

Hal figured it was time he left. He turned, walked past the lot of them, brushing Johnny hard as he passed, and stormed out the door, leaving the whole mess to Mr. Winters to handle. Hal was done.

The baby wasn't his. The baby wasn't his. The baby . . .

He'd left his wife and son for a woman who lied, who knew he hadn't fathered her baby but insisted he had.

He had to face Bea, had to tell her Vi's baby wasn't his. And he didn't want a divorce after all, that he'd be moving back in. She'd be upset all right, but in the end she'd let him come home.

Oskar would have to go. He'd seen the way the man looked at Bea, treated her all nice and kind. First thing he knew, Oskar would beat his time.

A dark cloud crept in from the north and the sky turned black as night. Hal headed down the street, the half-covered headlights of cars already on. A block warden walked the beat, eyes upcast, scanning the bottom of the clouds. Cloud cover like this would make a perfect setting for an enemy attack from the air.

Something told Hal he'd just survived an air raid all his own.

SYLVIA DICKEY SMITH

Chapter 23

Hal showed up late at his parents' house to collect Bea and Percy, leaving her to wish she'd driven her own car. She hadn't built up the nerve yet to tell Hal she had her own, fearing he'd not give her any money to help with paying Nelda for babysitting.

Nor was she ready to drive with Percy in the seat by himself—plus, she still needed to get her license. Masil promised to take her for the test one day soon, but Masil hadn't felt well as of late. Bea needed to stop by and check on her.

Hal opened the passenger door and assisted them in, climbed behind the wheel and took off in a huff. She'd never seen him quite so agitated—even when he'd admitted he fathered another woman's child.

Afraid to say a word, she stared straight ahead.

Meanwhile, the baby fell asleep in her arms. She looked down at his angelic face and held him tighter.

Halfway home, Hal started to speak, but stuttered and stumbled over his first words and grew quiet again. Wanting to say, Spit it out! like she did to men at the shipyard, she wondered why, when it came to Hal, the words stuck in her throat.

Thick tension filled the car. Percy even stirred uncomfortably, as if he too felt the discomfort in his sleep.

A few minutes later, Hal tried again. "I just found out . . ." then stopped mid-sentence.

They drove past Tent City where kids ran in the street playing kickball. Hal slowed around them and then accelerated. "I just found out the father of . . ."

"Spit it out," Bea finally said, irritated. "You just found out what?

Who the father of Violet's baby is? We already know that. It's you."

"No, that's what she'd told me, but I just found out she lied. Her brother Johnny fools around with her. The baby's his."

She looked over, ready to smack him in the face and yell at him to let her out of the car, that she'd walk the rest of the way home. He just wanted to save his own neck, she thought. But the look on his face told her, this time he spoke the truth.

"I'm telling you this, but I don't want to ever talk about it again." Hal stared straight ahead, his hands tight around the steering wheel. "It's over and done with. We'll put it behind us and go on."

At first, Bea said nothing.

Not because she couldn't think of what to say, but because she couldn't think of what *not* to say.

After a few minutes of volcanic buildup, she exploded, but through gritted teeth, afraid she'd wake the baby. "Buddy, you have no right to call any shots. I'll talk about this all I damn well please, and I'll talk about it until I'm done. If you can't handle that, then go find someone else to stick it in."

After she finished, she felt as startled as Hal looked.

He parked the car in the lot near their house. Bea climbed out of the car with Percy in her arms. The movement woke him and he screamed to the top of his lungs, probably soaking wet.

"But, Bea," Hal said as he trailed along behind. "I thought it'd be better to just put it behind us. You know, forget about it and start over."

"Start over? Start over?" She spun on him. "There is no *starting over*. You've lost any trust I ever had in you. You're at zero—below zero. I don't know if I want to even try to rebuild trust in you. I'll do fine all on my own. I've got a job now. I've even bought my own car and learned how to drive. What do I need you for?"

She held Percy tight, ran inside and straight to her bedroom. She slammed the door, locked it, and stayed until she heard the front door close. Good, he'd left. But she found herself wondering where she'd found the courage to say all that. *Who are you and what have you done with Bea?*

A few minutes later the front door opened. Relieved to hear her sister Edith's voice calling her, she opened the door.

"I saw Hal leave. He looked upset. What'd you say to him?"

Bea stepped out, Percy on her hip. Snot ran around his mouth and dripped off his chin.

"Guess who the real father of Violet's baby is?"

Edith's mouth dropped open. "I take it from your question it's someone other than Hal," she said, laughing.

"Actually, I think right now her family'd be thrilled if Hal fathered her baby." She paused, took a deep breath and let it out. "It's her brother Johnny."

Edith looked like she'd hit the floor at any minute. "But he's—"

"Exactly. Seems they messed around in the woodshed and their parents didn't know." Bea didn't go on to tell what Hal said about Mrs. Winters. The poor woman had suffered enough. Some things were best left unsaid.

Bea led the way into the living room and sat in the rocking chair.

"Come on sweetie," she said to Percy, "everything's okay. Here, let me wipe your nose." She did, and Percy screamed louder. Bea took him to the kitchen and fixed him a bottle of water. He grabbed it with both hands and swigged.

With his screams quieted, Bea changed his diaper then returned to the rocker. "It's okay, baby," she said, patting his bottom, lulling him back to sleep.

"Let me guess, Hal expects to move back in with you and Percy. You going to let him?"

More thankful than ever for Edith's company, Bea admitted, "That's what he expects to happen. One minute, I tell myself yes, but then . . . To tell you the truth, I don't know what to do."

"Well, I know what you should do." Edith stood and danced around the room. "Tomorrow, soon as we get up, we're going out to the gypsy camp."

"Gypsy camp?"

"Gypsy camp."

Percy had fallen asleep so, to buy time, Bea carried him to his crib and slowly walked back to the living room. "Why would we go to a gypsy camp? I hear they're just a group of dirty thieves. We might not ever get out of there alive. Besides, I don't want to leave Percy again."

"We'll take him with us. He'll love it."

"But you still haven't told me why we need to go."

"I certainly did, days ago. I told you the women are great fortunetellers and palm readers. A friend of mine lives there, goes by the name Black Betty. She's told me about this Lady Silvania, who can take one look at your hand and tell you what you should do, what your future holds. She's the one to ask whether or not to take Hal back."

Bea pooh-poohed Edith with a hand gesture. "Nonsense. Don't tell me you believe in that stuff. Besides, I hear every one of them is a liar and thief. They talk different, they break the law, let their children run wild—"

"They're just people, Bea."

"People who are horse thieves and pig snatchers, not to even mention the so-called *fortunetelling*. I may not go to church, but I remember going with Mama and how the preacher preached against their kind."

"They're not all bad, Bea. Listen to their music and you can tell. So, you know how Hitler and his comrades are killing all the Jews?"

Puzzled, Bea looked at Edith. "Sure I do. Everyone knows. It's in the news all the time."

"Did you know he's also killed thousands of gypsies?"

"No, I didn't."

It was set. Bea knew that when Edith made up her mind, high water or hell couldn't change it. Besides, she confessed to herself she was a little interested to hear what Lady Silvania would say.

* * *

Soon as Percy woke up the next morning, Edith shuffled them into her car and took off. Thank goodness Percy's mood had improved overnight. He seemed ready for adventure. At least Bea hoped so. She certainly wasn't, but her stubborn sister made saying no impossible.

Edith drove outside the city limits toward Pinehurst Ranch and according to Bea, the certainty of being robbed, if not death. Percy patty-caked and babbled the whole way, oblivious to the dangers awaiting them.

"I can see you're still scared." Edith glanced over at Bea.

"I'll tell you what, I know this couple who lives not far from the gypsy camp. How about we stop there first? You can talk to them about their gypsy neighbors."

Fifteen minutes later Edith pulled into the large yard of a white, one-story house. Out back, Bea saw—and smelled—a pigsty.

No sooner had they stepped out than a small man with a wild mop of reddish-gray hair approached. "Hey, Edith! Glad you stopped by. Ya'll come on in."

He shook Edith's hand, then turned and shook Bea's.

"I'm Tinsel," he said, "and here comes my wife, Clara."

Bea smiled and introduced herself. Clara was a short pudgy woman with pink cheeks and short, curly brown hair. She reached for Percy before she even grew close enough. He dove in her arms with a chuckle.

"We're headed over to the gypsy camp to visit a friend of mine," said Edith. "My sister's a little nervous about it. We thought we'd stop to see what you could tell us about them, maybe relieve her fears."

Clara spoke first. "Tell her, Tinsel, about that time one of the gypsy men came over."

Tinsel pulled a white sweat-stained cloth from his hip pocket and wiped his forehead.

"There's about thirty tents over in that trailer park, all put in a circle, with a campfire in the middle. They do all their activities around that campfire. I have these fine little pigs—see out back?" He pointed. "Well, one day this gypsy man comes up and says my pigs are just the size they needed for a wedding celebration, and could he buy a couple? I said no, I needed them to feed my family."

Tinsel's laugh revealed a missing tooth on the right side of his mouth.

"The man said, 'Well, we've got a big gypsy wedding planned, and we need those pigs so we can roast them whole.' Said they were just right to put over the fire. I say, 'No, you can't have my pigs.' They'd beg me, said they'd give me a good price for 'em. But for what I could get eating 'em was worth more than the money. These days, we have a hard time buying that kind of food."

Clara spoke up. "Yeah, but finish the story, Tinsel." She looked at Bea, a twinkle in her eyes.

Tinsel smiled. "Clara and I talked it over, and we decided if we didn't sell them a couple of pigs, they might just take 'em anyway. So we sold 'em three. They were lucky to get those."

"So they held their celebration?" Edith asked.

Tinsel picked up the story. "I'll say. They barbequed those pigs on a spit over the campfire and had a big feast with dancing and music all night long. We never could get to sleep. The neighbors are a little leery of them because we've all heard stories about how they steal things. So we keep an eye out. We don't have much ourselves."

"So you better watch your pigs the next time they have a wedding." Bea smiled, took Percy from Clara and thanked them for their time.

As they drove away from Tinsel and Clara's farm, she couldn't help but ask her sister. "And the moral to that story is . . . ?"

"The moral is they have their traditions just like we have ours. The gypsy could have just stolen the pigs, but he didn't. He bought and paid for them." Edith sat behind the wheel with a smug expression on her face.

"Okay, miss smarty-pants," Bea asked, a little less afraid that they were walking into a lawless gathering of vagabonds, "how come you know so much about the gypsies?"

"My friend Black Betty's told me a lot about what it's like to be a Romany."

"A what?"

"Romany. They call themselves Rom, or Romany, instead of gypsy, and they still believe and follow all the old Romani ways. They keep to themselves, mostly, out of fear they'd lose their revered traditions. For instance, Black Betty's father doesn't believe in anything mechanical. Everything he does must be done with horses or other animals."

Edith stopped long enough to light a cigarette. She threw the used match out the window, then took up again right where she'd left off.

"He's a man who won't be spoken to in a rude way. If you do, he acts like you haven't said a word. When you talk nicely to him, he'll answer. He's a big stickler for rules, but if someone breaks a rule, he sits everyone down and listens to their side of the story. Their tribe is best known for breeding horses, doctoring, woodcarving, and wagon building.

"And anyone who isn't a gypsy is called a *Gadje*, someone they naturally mistrust, and believe it's okay to steal from. But they don't steal from each other."

Edith droned on. Bea listened carefully, but still in the back of her head had an image of a band of gypsies hitting her over the head, stealing Percy, and then trading him for suckling pigs.

Chapter 24

As Tinsel and Clara had said, thirty or more tents, each big enough to shelter a large extended family, ringed a big campfire. Over to one side, three men sat constructing wagon wheels. One worked on spokes, the other, on hubs, and another, on the felly, the outside part of the wheel under the iron rim.

Before Edith brought the car to a complete stop, the eldest of the men broke away from his group and came toward them. Bea did a mental assessment of what the man wore in case she needed to identify him later to the police: an old-world style shirt, topped with a leather waistcoat and a print-pattern handkerchief around his neck, stovepipe-leg trousers with rows of stitching around the bottoms and pipe seams down the sides. Both he and his outfit looked spotlessly clean.

As he grew closer, he waved his hand at them. "*Nash avri*, go way. You have no business here."

The sternness in his voice left no doubt in Bea's mind that they were unwelcome. She shook Edith by the arm. "Turn around. Let's get out of here."

Edith stuck her hand out the car window. "We've come to see Lady Silvania. Can you tell us which tent is hers?"

"No. Turn your vehicle and leave."

"Wait," Edith said. "I'm a friend of Black Betty. Is she here?"

Through the windshield, Bea noticed a heavyset woman sally forth like an heiress to vast Brazilian coffee plantations. Heavy gold ornamentation dangled from her ears and her wrists. She wore a long, red skirt that swirled as she walked, a low-cut white blouse, and a black scarf tied around her head.

"Frederick, leave 'em be," she yelled. "This is women's business. You go tend to the men's."

"Never mind him," the heiress said. She looked from Edith to Bea. When she saw Percy, she broke into a big smile.

"*What a bori odjus tinker!*"

She laughed and clapped her hands to match Percy, who clapped his in response.

"Good to see you Edith. How can I help you?"

Aha, Edith's friend. Bea let out a breath she hadn't realized she held. Evidently, women controlled women's business and men controlled their own, for Frederick turned and walked off, his back straight.

"Good morning, Black Betty. Thanks for saving us."

"Oh, don't pay any attention to Frederick. He sounds tough, but he ain't so."

Edith opened the car door and got out. "We came to see Lady Silvania. Can you show us her tent? I want her to read my sister's palm."

The woman pointed to the second tent over. To Bea, each tent looked like the next. The only difference seemed to be the number of children who played in front of each. But that theory didn't last long when a little girl ran off and the rest trailed after her. It seemed no one monitored their play.

"Come," the woman said. "I'll take you to Silvania. When I saw you come up, I figured you were here for *dukkering*—fortune telling—and Lady Silvania is the best they come. Ain't seen no one like her in all of Texas."

Edith motioned to Bea, who got out of the car and propped Percy on her hip.

Black Betty led them over to the tent she'd pointed out earlier and called out. "Silvania? Couple o' women out here for dukkering."

A muffled sound came from inside, but Bea couldn't make out the words.

"She says go on in."

Edith ducked inside.

"Here," the old woman said, and took Percy from Bea's arms before she could object. "Let me care for *tikni*. You go on inside. We be happy out here."

More than anything, Bea wanted to grab her baby and run all the way home. Instead, she stepped through the wine-colored fabric at the doorway and entered a hazy room choked with incense and the smell of stale coffee. Daisy-yellow, sky blue, and various shades of brown curtains hung suspended from the top of the tent. Cushions of varied colors lay on sofas and chairs. A lone lantern, perched on a small wooden keg in the middle of the room, cast a dingy yellow light over a strange deck of cards on the keg.

"You're jessin' me to read ya." The husky words crawled out of the shadows, leading a dark-skinned woman with even darker long hair and almost black eyes.

"I . . . I . . . Edith says I need it, yes ma'am. How did you know it was for me and not her?" Bea thumbed over at her sister.

When she stepped closer to the woman, she noticed deep wrinkles carved into her face. When the woman smiled, a gold tooth twinkled in the firelight.

"Ya got a powerful decision ahead, I kin tell jus' lookin' at ya." The large woman leaned forward, stuck her rear out and eased down on a small sofa covered with layers of multi-colored fabrics. Next, she picked up the deck of cards from the wooden barrel.

"I read palms, yes, but I also use Tarot Tzigane to help. Now, what you need know?"

At a loss for words, Bea stammered and stuttered until Edith took over.

"My sister here is in a dilemma. She needs help. She must make a decision about whether or not to take back a no-good philanderer of a husband."

Lady Silvania laughed so hard her belly shook.

"Not hard decision to make. You don't need fortuneteller to tell you this."

"He's not all bad," Bea found herself defending Hal. "After all
. . ."

"No need say more. *Kari* trouble. I see."

"The other woman's name's not Kari, it's Vi—"

The fortuneteller's laugh cut Bea's last word in half.

"Not woman. This." She pointed below to her private parts.

Edith looked at the woman wide-eyed at first, then said, "Oh, I
see, yes, he has tallywhacker trouble."

All three women doubled over with laughter.

After they recovered, Lady Silvania took Bea's hand, turned it
palm up and stared. With a long, red fingernail, she traced a slow line
from the outside of Bea's palm over to her index finger. The gypsy
sighed deeply.

"You are forlorn, a sad person. You need to be surrounded by
others. But even when you are, you still feel sad deep inside. When
darkness comes, you feel even sadder."

Bea sat up straighter.

"Your head often rules your heart, which can make you feel stuck
in a loveless situation."

That's impossible. There's no way she can know me that well, Bea
thought, and looked from her hand up into the woman's dark eyes.

"See this island on the fate line? It tells me you feel stuck,
stagnated."

She shuffled the set of cards, then turned over one labeled *Le
Fou.* The Fool.

"Oh, oh, someone play you *divi—stagni*—like fool nanny goat.
Know who do that?"

Bea didn't answer.

Once again, she reached for Bea's palm and studied it. "Hmm,
may be more than one, by chance."

"Two?" *Hal and Violet,* she thought—*two.*

"Or three, even. And look here," she said. "This is your fate line.
See how it starts at the bottom, and then stops midway up the palm?
That means you're not done yet. More for you to know."

"Like what?"

"*Husk kicker*, be quiet and listen. *Le Soleil*, sun, soon shine on dark inside. Fate up to you. Silvania only know tell you watch. Careful like. Someone not who you think—*you* not who you think."

"What? If I'm not who I think I am, then who—?"

"Shh, let her finish." Edith said, resting her hand on Bea's arm.

On and on the woman went, describing Bea to a T. Somehow, all this only made Bea more confused than when she'd come in.

The woman put the cards away, and they sat and chatted for a while. Edith asked a ton of questions about the gypsy population in the area, about their lifestyle, why they had such a bad reputation for not disciplining their children.

"You may see our children wild and undisciplined, but the Rom treat our children like adults. We let them do what they like."

Outside, Percy cried.

Bea made motions to get up. "I need to go, Edith. Percy probably thinks we forgot all about him." Bea and Edith thanked Lady Silvania profusely. As they left, Bea noticed Edith left an envelope on the keg. Outside, they collected Percy, excused themselves, and headed for the car.

"So," Edith said as soon as they got out on the main road. "Still think they're thieves?"

Bea smoothed down the baby's red hair with one hand. She studied her other palm, held open, facing up to the heavens for inspection.

"I still can't figure out how she knew me by just looking at these lines in my hand."

"Pretty dang on, huh?" Edith used her free hand to wave out the window to signal a right turn.

"I'll say. But now, what do I do with all that Lady Silvania said?"

"Well, for starters, I'd say try to get unstuck. Make a decision—any decision, and go with it. Trust to fate. What would happen if you turned Hal down?"

Again Bea focused on the back of Percy's head, as if the answer lay in the way his hair curled up on the ends.

"Do you know what she meant when she said I'm not who I think I am?"

Edith glanced over at her. "I've meant to talk to you about that."

"Then let's talk."

"Now's not the time. But soon."

Chapter 25

Bea asked Edith to stop at Perry Brothers so she could buy a couple of outfits for Percy. The few she had were now much too small for him. Edith turned down Fifth Street, passed behind Abe's men's clothing store, and parked.

Bea got out of the car and swung Percy on her hip while Edith collected their handbags, and off they went. Shoppers passed, arms loaded with parcels as if spending money might soon go out of style. Nowadays, people had money to burn and not enough to spend it on. Two boys, barefoot and filthy, walked out of one of the stores brandishing bright yellow pea-shooters. One picked up a pebble, put it in the shooter and blew. The pebble struck the rump of a stray dog wandering down the street. Startled, the dog turned and growled. The boys laughed, then, faster than the boys could turn and run, the dog had the culprit by the seat of his pants. The whole caboodle ran down the street yelling, screaming and growling.

"Serves him right." Edith said, and laughed. Percy laughed too.

They approached the Western Union office just as a middle-aged couple stormed out. The wife sobbed while the man removed his hat, threw it to the ground and stomped it, then dropped to the curb himself and cried like a baby. Bea knew what that meant. Someone in their family, probably a son, had been lost in the war, another native son whose name would soon appear on a list. What little comfort that must give a mother.

Bea squeezed Percy tighter. What did the future hold for him?

She turned from the couple and collided headlong into a woman exiting a beauty shop. Instinctively, Bea grabbed the woman and hung on to keep from falling, as did the other. Stumbling, holding on for dear life, Bea caught the faintest glance of the other's eyes—violet eyes. Bea regained her footing and stepped sideways, eager to escape. No way in hell would she offer a common greeting or apology to the woman who destroyed her marriage. She hugged Percy to her chest and with words as cold as her heart, ordered, "Come on Edith."

The three turned to leave.

"Excuse me, but you're Hal's wife, aren't you?" the woman called out to Bea's back.

Bea kept going despite the hastening steps behind her.

"Hurry, Edith, walk faster," she demanded and increased the speed of her own brisk steps.

"Please talk to me. Please. I owe you an explanation, really, and to tell you how sorry I am . . ."

Something stopped Bea dead in her tracks.

"I know who you are," she said, turning. "I really don't think we have anything to say to each other. On second thought, there're lots of things I'd like to say to you—"

"I don't blame you. I deserve every one of them."

Bea certainly hadn't expected that.

The young woman's shoulders slumped. "Please talk to me, or let me talk to you."

Bea turned Percy away from Violet, from the whore who threatened to take him away from her.

"I don't want your baby. I just want to talk to you, to tell you how sorry . . ."

Her voice broke. "I beg you. Can you walk down the street with me for a few minutes?"

Violet looked from Bea to Edith. At first, Edith also glared back, but then— "Here, give me the baby, Bea. You two go talk. We'll be looking around in Perry Brothers. Take your time. Percy and I will be fine."

Bea handed the baby to her sister and watched as the two headed off toward the department store.

Violet turned and took a step forward then turned to see if Bea followed.

She didn't. She couldn't. In mid-summer, with the humidity as high as the ninety-degree temperature, her feet were as frozen to the ground as if she stood outside in the same blizzard that created the block of ice in her chest.

Violet kept walking, looked over her shoulder, and motioned Bea to follow.

Then, without making a conscious decision, Bea's left foot took a step forward, followed by her right, and then another, until the two women entered the Steak and Shake.

Kids from Orange High School sat at the fountain, two of them wearing the Bengal Guard band uniforms. Violet strode straight to the back where she slid into a booth and indicated Bea to sit opposite her.

They ordered, and the soda jerk brought two Cherry Cokes. After he left them alone, Violet spoke first. "I never thought I'd be here talking to you, Mrs. Meade. I'm so ashamed. I did such a bad thing, but I didn't know what else to do."

Tears filled her eyes. She reached her hand down and rubbed her belly the same way Bea had done when she'd been pregnant with Percy. "I just didn't know where to turn."

Bea bristled. "You set your sights on what you wanted, regardless of what it did to anyone else."

Violet looked down at her soda and fiddled with the straw. "Not what I wanted, no. I like Hal, sure I do. But more than anything, I had to get away from . . . I . . . I never wanted to hurt you. I just wanted . . . I had to get away from . . ." What had been a teary-eyed, nervous demeanor exploded into gut-wrenching sobs.

Until now, Bea felt not one iota of sympathy for this woman who had stolen her husband, her security, and even threatened to take her baby. She'd been so consumed by her own grief she'd thought of Violet as nothing more than a loose woman, a whore, a home wrecker. Now she saw the woman across from her as much a victim as she herself. Bea realized she'd been trapped for a long time, for a lifetime, inside a grief so all-consuming it left little room for anything else, a grief half starved for some nebulous something that was missing. And she hadn't a clue how to fill that void. She'd barely made room for Percy.

Now, for the first time in her life, Bea put aside her own grief. She finished Violet's sentence from a place so deep within her she didn't know it existed. "From your brother. You had to get away from Johnny."

"It's true . . . my own brother is the . . ." She rubbed her belly again. "I guess Hal told you this baby isn't his."

Bea didn't answer. She didn't feel she needed to.

"Hal and I—we did—you know, but just one time. He wouldn't have, but I egged him on. I needed a father for my baby that wasn't my brother. You do understand that, don't you?"

"Even if that man had another baby *and* a wife?"

"I didn't know that at the time. Hal didn't tell me," Violet said. She took a deep breath then went on. "Johnny's . . . *bothered* me . . . since I was just a little kid."

Something about the look on the woman's face slashed right through Bea and touched a raw, bleeding part of her, something stolen from her a long time ago. Something nothing else could erase, or return to her, or make right.

The abuse Violet lived with for years, due to her brother's actions, now culminated in the ultimate shame of bearing not only a bastard child, but one who would carry the shame of incest all his or her life. Bea couldn't imagine anything worse than that. Even her problems seemed small in comparison.

But Bea hadn't suffered the same thing as had Violet—so why the connection? Why did Violet's loss of innocence and respect for herself, the immense weight of the shame she bore—why did it touch such a deep part of Bea?

Confused, she stared at the floor, flashing through the distant, indistinct shadows of her life. As bad as her brothers were, they had never done that to her, nor had anyone else. Yet something about

Violet's loss touched a deep memory inside Bea. A memory so elusive it flitted past her like a whisper on a windy day.

Violet interrupted Bea's thoughts. "I don't know how my baby and I are going to hold our heads up in this town. It's not me so much as it is my baby. I play over and over in my head what that day will be like. He—or she—walks around town while everyone knows the child has a daddy who's . . ."

Violet straightened her shoulders and shifted in her chair. "This has brought shame to my whole family. My mother has had a nervous breakdown and my daddy blames me for not speaking up. I don't know what I'll do with the baby—probably give it away, but I can't bear to think of doing that either. If I keep it, every time I look at it I'll remember who the baby's daddy is and what he did to me."

Bea reached over and clasped Violet's hands in hers. "One question I've been wanting to ask . . ."

"What?"

"No, it's too personal."

"Go ahead, ask."

"Since I heard who really got you—you know—with child, I've wondered why you didn't just take something, you know, to lose . . ."

Violet's face contorted in pain. "It's too late now, but I wish I had. My church teaches it's a mortal sin, and I believed them."

"I see."

"No, you don't see. I don't even see." She pointed to her belly. "They taught us to believe to abort a fetus is a sin, regardless of how I conceived it. But no one taught that what my brother did to me all those years was an even bigger sin."

"That doesn't make sense," Bea said.

"And Johnny won't be the one to pay for his sin. It'll be this baby that'll pay. What a birthright, eh? I don't know if I can stand it."

"So . . . What do you want from me?"

Violet's hands moved from Bea's, to the straw in her soda. "Understanding, I guess—from one woman to another. Hopefully, one day . . ." her voice sounded ready to break apart, ". . . forgiveness."

"I guess I can understand," Bea said slowly, "but I'm not quite sure I'm up to the forgiveness part just yet. You've torn my family apart. My pain is so great right now I'm not sure I can—but maybe . . . one day. I truly am sorry for what happened to you. No woman should have to go through what you live with every day. No child should carry that stigma all his life."

"Thank you. That's all I ask." Violet pulled change for the drinks from her pocket, tossed it on the table, said goodbye and walked out. Her shoulders sagged like they carried the weight of the world.

Chapter 26

Edith glanced over at Bea with a raised eyebrow. "What was that all about?"

"She wanted to ask me to forgive her."

Edith's fist banged the steering wheel. "She screws your husband, and offers to take your son away from you. Knowing all along that Hal wasn't her baby's father. So now she wants you to forgive her?"

"I know. It sounds crazy, doesn't it?"

"What did you say?"

"I told her it would be awhile."

"Well, I should think so."

Bea didn't tell Edith her feelings of confusion, how she identified with Violet in ways she didn't understand. How she felt so mired down in quicksand she thought she'd drown.

The day had grown hotter than usual, and both women sweltered in the hot car even though they rode with the windows down, the wind in their hair.

Bea's mind wandered to the brooch she'd pinned on her dress earlier that morning. She fingered it now, remembering the comfort it brought her the nights she cried herself to sleep. She didn't know where the pin had come from, or how long she'd had it. She'd asked Edith about it once, but her older sister only changed the subject.

At times, Bea almost touched a memory connected to the heart-shaped mother-of-pearl pin. Then, like a word on the tip of her tongue, the harder she tried to recall it, the more elusive the memory grew.

"Tell me more about this pin, Edith. You said it used to be yours, but when did you give it to me?"

Edith looked over at Bea, then back at the road. "Oh honey, it's just a pin. Why do you keep asking me about it?"

"I don't know. It's just . . . I don't understand why, when I cry at night, this brooch is the only thing that brings me any comfort. Did you know that I sleep with it under my pillow?"

"Under your pillow?"

"Every night."

Bea glanced over at Edith in time to see her chin quiver before she swiped her hand across her mouth.

"Oh honey, it's just a pin. But it was a favorite one of mine . . ."

She broke off as they drove up to Bea's house. Edith pulled over to the curb. Percy looked out and started to squirm and bawl, so that was the end of that conversation for the time being.

They got Percy to bed and then the two lay down themselves across the mattress in Bea's room. They hashed and rehashed the whole situation with Violet and her baby and Bea's decision whether or not to take Hal back.

"The truth is," Bea admitted, "I never loved Hal."

"I thought as much," Edith said as she turned on her side to face Bea. She propped her head on her hand.

"I could have learned to, I think, if Hal met me half way. I did my best to be a good wife, but regardless of what I did, he kept doing his own thing. We seemed to be on the edge of his interest. He came home when he didn't have anywhere else to go, and stayed only long enough to think of someone else he needed to talk to or go see."

"You met and married Hal while I was off with, let's see, which husband?"

Bea shoved on Edith's shoulder. "You're an awful example to your baby sister."

"I never claimed to set the standard, Toots," Edith teased.

"That's good."

"Anyway, before you so rudely interrupted me, I wanted to ask how you and Hal met. I never heard."

"We met at the carnival. Mama and Papa wouldn't let me go

alone, or even with a girlfriend, so I talked Ivan into taking me."

"Ivan? Our brother?"

"Hard to believe, but I guess I just caught him on a night when he had nothing else to do. Anyway, we rode the tilt-a-whirl and stumbled down the bright midway eating cotton candy, when Ivan saw a tall red-haired man come out of a sideshow. He yelled over at him and the guy came over. I learned his name was Hal Meade and he drove a truck for the Dr. Pepper Bottling Company.

"A couple of nights later, Hal came by the house and asked Papa if he could take me to the picture show to see Irving S. Cobb and Rochelle Hudson in *Everybody's Old Man*. He wore these brand new cowboy boots. We walked to the picture show and then walked home. By that time, the boots rubbed water blisters on his feet."

"Oh, no." Edith held her stomach, laughing.

"It's funny now, but it wasn't funny that night," Bea said, laughing too. "I can still see him later that night as he walked home in his sock feet, his new boots in his hand."

"So, if you didn't love him, why did you marry?"

Bea thought about that for a while. "I guess I married because he asked me. Isn't that what women are supposed to do? That's what Mama always told us. A woman's place was to marry and have children."

"That lesson never stuck with me, that's for sure," Edith said. "I married all right, but I expected the men to take care of me, instead of the reverse. I guess that's why I've had so many. Anyway, I guess since you never loved him, you're not too inclined to take him back."

"I don't want to," Bea said as she flipped over on her belly and propped herself on her elbows. "But I probably will for Percy's sake. I've got a job now, yes, but this war won't last forever. What then? Will they still let me work at the shipyard after the soldiers all come home and take the jobs?"

"Who knows?"

Bea sat up. "When the war first started, everyone in this town was thrilled to have a job and make money, but lately, I've noticed a swing in people's attitude. I went to work because I needed the money despite the crowds, the heat, and the snide comments from the men. But when I saw the commissioning of the DD 580, the USS *Young*, my chest swelled so big I felt like the destroyer had my name on the side. The people I work with seem more like family than my own brothers do. I might not fight in the war, but I sure do my part."

"Hold on a minute," Edith said, "I've got to go the toilet."

Bea sat deep in thought while she waited for Edith's return. When Edith flopped down on the mattress again, Bea picked up where she left off. "One problem is, when school starts, Nelda won't have as much time to take care of Percy as she has now."

"Someone said they have daycare at the shipyard. I've never heard a company do that for workers before. It's a great idea. You could put Percy there while you worked."

"I suppose I could. And now that I know how to drive and am buying my own car—"

"Or you could marry Oskar."

"What?" Bea was startled to hear Edith say that.

"He likes you, I can tell that. But if you don't want him, I sure do."

"How about Daniel? He's nice too," Bea said. "But he seems more your type."

Edith smiled, turned over on her back and stretched like a lazy cat. Soon, her eyelids drooped.

Bea, wide awake from the many shocks of the day, stopped talking and watched Edith fall deeper to sleep, hugging a pillow to her chest. Bea watched the corners of her sister's lips curve upward and wondered what she dreamed about.

How fortunate she was to have a sister like Edith. At times, Bea supposed, she'd taken the woman for granted, perhaps even looked down her nose at her, judged her for sleeping around with so many men. Bea didn't understand Edith's passion—unbridled and real. Edith held little concern for other people's opinion of her or her behavior.

She reached over and touched Edith's face with her fingertips. A woman ahead of her times, for sure. A heart as big as they come, with a love for her baby sister that surpassed any other love Bea had ever known. Sure, Mama and Papa loved her. But they were old, exhausted. They did what they could, but no one loved as deeply as Edith. There was nothing Edith wouldn't do for her. Their older sister Marie always turned her nose up at the rest of the family, didn't come around, thought herself better than any of them.

Sleep thickened Bea's eyelids and they drooped closed, too. Then, she heard the front door open and looked up to see Oskar in the doorway of the bedroom, looking in at the two.

He walked off, quietly, and then she heard him puttering in the kitchen.

She slipped out of the bedroom and joined him.

"Hungry?" she asked. "I've got some leftovers in the icebox."

"No, but I could use a cup of coffee if you have enough."

"I'll put on the teakettle. It won't take but a couple of minutes."

Oskar cleared his throat. "I do not mean to pry, but . . . your husband told me he'd be moving back in. Is that so?"

"No, that is not so." She didn't mean for her voice to come out in what was almost a shout. "Sorry. I didn't mean to . . ."

"I just wanted to know if I needed to look for another place to live, if he was coming back here."

"Well, for one thing, you lived here when he did—and it was his idea. And you've been nothing but kind and respectful to me and Percy."

Edith's words about Oskar flitted through her mind. Up until now, she'd been comfortable around the man, but now she felt heat rise to her cheeks and knew they must be red. She covered them with her hands. "And for another thing, why would Hal tell you he was moving back in? No, I have not agreed to that."

Oskar reached over and pulled her hands away from her cheeks. "I am sorry if I embarrassed you. Please do not be. You are a good woman, Bea Meade. Any man would be proud to have you as his wife."

"By the way," she interrupted, anxious to take the focus off her. "You remember meeting Daniel Baxter?

"Sure, why?"

"He asked about you the other day."

"About me? Why?" His shoulders stiffened and crease lines crossed his forehead.

"He said to tell you he might have a lead on your brother."

The teakettle started to whistle. Bea turned off the fire and poured the boiling water over the grounds. When it finished dripping, she filled their cups and joined him at the table.

Oskar sipped his coffee, but said nothing for several minutes, as if her question caused him serious concern.

"Bea, what's your opinion of this war? I don't mean to put you on the spot, but do you think any one person has a right to rule the world?"

"Like Hitler, you mean?"

"Hitler, yes, or anyone." He picked up a spoon and stirred his coffee.

"I don't know. No one has ever asked me anything like that before." She searched for the words to describe her thoughts about the war. She sipped her coffee, sat the cup in the saucer then picked it up again.

Oskar waited.

"It's hard for me to talk about the war our boys are fighting over there. Because . . . because I have my own war going on inside me. Sometimes I feel like there's this giant weight tying me down, and then at other times it feels like . . . the only way I know how to describe it is, I feel like there's this roar . . . of death fighting life. I don't understand it, yet it haunts me, especially at night when I try to sleep."

He raised his eyes and met hers. "Yes, I have heard you cry at night. I thought it had to do with you and Hal."

"No, it didn't start with Hal. It started so long ago I don't even remember the first time. Until I decided to go to work at the shipyard, I walked around in a breathing, heart-thumping body, but still, something inside felt dead."

"How does your work at the shipyard change that?"

"I guess I'm feeling better about myself. I always thought I couldn't do anything but cook and clean and take care of babies and husbands. Now, I know that's not so. I can drive my own car. I'm the best riveter on Tony's team. I hold my head up and don't let the men get to me. For the first time in my life I feel like I'm not invisible."

"What does one have to do with the other?" Oskar asked.

"I don't have a clue, but somewhere down deep, I know it does."

Bea looked at the clock, surprised at the hour and said, "We better go to sleep or neither one of us will do a good job tomorrow."

Oskar agreed and as they started out the kitchen, Bea turned back to Oskar. "To answer your question, no, I don't believe anyone has the right to rule the world, or to rule another person. Not even Hal."

Chapter 27

Morning came early for Bea. She dragged herself to her feet. Edith was still asleep on the bed. As she headed to the kitchen, she noticed Oskar had already left. Something about that didn't set right with Bea, especially after the way he had reacted the night before when she told him of Daniel Baxter's questions.

Nelda arrived before Percy awoke, so Bea busied herself getting dressed and ready for work. For the umpteenth time, she rejoiced with the freedom the vehicle—half rattletrap, half noisemaker—gave her. Baling wire held the right fender together, and it spewed exhaust with its every breath, but it ran. Still, she avoided using the car and walked instead when she could, to conserve gas. So far, her ration coupons had lasted until the next ones were available.

Streets that before the war had held little traffic at this time of day now teemed with people going to or from work. The war had given the whole town a purpose for living. It wasn't just *the* war, it was *their* war. They owned it lock, stock and barrel, and everyone did their part to win it. Besides having their own sons and daughters in harm's way, the latest news about the Germans rounding up Jew and gypsy alike and doing lord knew what with them riled folks up, inspiring them to work harder and longer to win the war. Not that the local folks cared much for the gypsy clan camped outside of town. Most people thought of them as little more than thieves.

Today she'd work on a dreadnaught destroyer. She hadn't done so before. Those jobs were reserved for the most experienced riveters, but the quality of her work had earned her the right to work alongside the best. She headed toward the gate. A new sense of pride made her feel lighter.

SYLVIA DICKEY SMITH

A preacher stood outside the gate and preached against the sin of gambling, right next to a group of men squatted in a circle throwing dice.

Men and women—couples Bea knew were not husband and wife—came out with their arms around each other. They laughed, talked, and headed to the Louisiana Bridge and across to Showboat Ruby's.

Inside, she collected her gear and proceeded to her work station. As she had been forewarned, Tony assigned her down into the hull of the destroyer under construction.

She looked down at the site where she would be working, her heart in her throat, scared out of her wits, fearing she'd never come up out of the hull alive. Swallowing that fear, she started down the long rung ladder into the depths, several stories deep. With each step, the heat and humidity grew higher. Droplights gave the only illumination, and a battery of fans provided minimum ventilation.

She couldn't help but think of Mama's preacher and his vivid description of hell. She figured she'd be there by the time she reached the bottom.

A vise squeezed her chest. A whiny voice inside her said *why are you doing this, Bea Meade? You don't have to put yourself through hell. You can eat crow and take Hal back.*

She hesitated, and in a moment of weakness, started up the ladder.

Oh yes you do have to do this, Bea Meade. Get yourself back down there and do your job, a stronger, more demanding voice ordered.

She stopped, then followed the second voice, and climbed down deeper into oblivion. By the time she reached the second bottom, two stories down, and found other hot and sweaty women doing the job they'd been hired to do, she settled herself and went to work.

One older man worked alongside them. Animosity toward the women radiated off of him with every rivet he threw.

"Watch him," the woman working beside Bea warned. "He'll throw a rivet at you when you're not looking."

The man glared at Bea, holding his rivet gun up, threatening.

"You throw one of those at me, I tell you right now, you'll get one right back," Bea warned. She'd put up with a lot, but she sure didn't plan to put up with that nonsense.

Evidently he didn't believe her, for later, when she looked the other way, he threw a rivet at her and missed. It banged down the hull of the ship and pinged against the floor, below. A man yelled up at them. "Hey, be more careful. That hot rivet almost hit me."

She turned her gun his way and threw one right back at him, her aim perfect. The rivet fell right down inside his bib overalls. She thought he'd scramble out of those clothes right then and there, in front of God and everybody.

Every other worker in the hull cheered.

Salty sweat dripped off her nose and into her mouth. She swiped it away with her sleeve. Maybe she could do this job after all. If she could reach her own back, she'd pat it.

At lunch, when she climbed up out of the hull, her eardrums felt numb from hours listening to the constant noise bouncing off the interior of the ship's hull.

Her path to the lunchroom took her by Hal's crane. She noticed it moving along the track and wondered if he sat inside working the gears and levers, and if so, what he must be thinking about the whole thing with Violet.

She hadn't gone far when a man yelled and threw his hand in the air. At first she thought she'd done something wrong, but as she drew closer, she picked up parts of what he shouted

"... this woman walks up ... boom swung around ... hit her ... over the side ... in the river ..."

A crowd gathered around him and along with them, a safety officer who barked orders. Several men jumped in the river, their arms wrapped around life preservers. Bea ran to the side and looked into the rough murky water below. A brown head bobbed, the water growing redder by the second.

Bea watched the men's long, quick strokes over to the woman.

One of them forced the life preserver over her head that, even from there, looked crushed something awful. The woman looked familiar, but with all the hair and blood, she couldn't tell for sure.

Several men on deck hauled the woman up. Water dripped from her limp body and splashed into the river. The soaking-wet dress clung to her swollen stomach in what otherwise looked like a slim body.

"Oh, no, the poor girl's pregnant," someone called from the crowd.

Bea heard a gasp and realized the sound came from her.

They eased the woman down on deck and stretched her out. Someone threw a blanket over her. "Let's keep her warm."

The safety officer stepped up and took one look, then pulled the blanket over her head. "She's gone, dead before she hit the water," he said, shaking his head.

"Who is she?"

One man Bea knew by sight only stood over the body underneath the blanket. "It's Violet Winters," he said. "I saw her head right into the path of that boom as it swung around. I yelled at her, but I guess she didn't hear me, because she just kept walking. Poor kid never had a chance." He broke down in tears.

"Violet Winters? She works in Personnel?" The safety officer shook his head in disbelief. "What the hell was she doing down here?"

No one answered his question.

"The operator sounded his horn. I heard it. I swear I heard it," a woman worker said. The crowd confirmed her claim.

Another stepped forward. "I swear she walked right into the path of that boom. I yelled at her and I know she saw me because she stopped for an instant, but kept walking. It looked like she wanted it to hit her."

Bea didn't have the heart to tell anyone her guess. Violet had chosen suicide as a way to escape the shame inflicted on her by her brother. Her hands shook so badly she crammed them down in her pockets in an attempt to steady them. When that didn't work, she grabbed her helmet and threw it across the deck.

"Bea, you're as pale as a sheet," her boss Tony said as she checked in with him soon after. "Are you sick?"

No words formed in her brain. She could only look at the ground and shake her head.

"Is it what happened a few minutes ago—with Violet?"

Bea broke down, sobs ripping through her like a summer storm.

Tony led her to the infirmary where the nurse had her lie with a cold rag on her forehead. As soon as she closed her eyes, the image of the men pulling Violet out of the Sabine River replayed in her head, the water dripping from her body over and over again.

None of this made any sense—none of it. What a tragedy—a young woman so victimized she took not only her own life but that of her unborn child as well.

The child hadn't been Hal's, but he had slept with Violet.

It bothered Bea that, like Violet, she too had allowed men to take advantage of her. Violet took her own life, but Bea still had time to repair hers. Right then and there she promised she'd never allow Hal, or any other man, to have such power over her again.

A few minutes later, she got up from the infirmary cot and returned to work.

At the end of the day, still numb over Violet's death, but exhausted from crawling into tight, hot places with her rivet gun, Bea wanted nothing more than to go home, put her feet up and relax. She hoped Nelda would have fed the baby and he'd be in a happy mood.

Her wish came true. After Nelda left, Bea slipped off her shoes and settled on the sofa with a romance magazine while Percy lay on the pallet playing with a rattle.

The last person she wanted to see or talk about was Hal. So when Ivan's oldest daughter Olivia came to the door calling, "Aunt Bea, I wanted to talk to you about Uncle Hal," Bea didn't want to invite her in. She had no desire to hear whatever her niece had to say.

Ivan, the oldest of Bea's no-good brothers, had never come

around to visit her and Hal. As a kid, Bea secretly called him Ivan the Terrible after her schoolteacher told them about the Russian Tsar of similar name and disposition. Like his namesake, her brother was given to rages and prone to outbreaks of mental illness. One such outburst had resulted in a family tragedy, the death of Olivia's husband in the front yard of Ivan and Molly's house.

Ivan had claimed self-defense and got away with it. How, Bea never understood. She had not seen Olivia since she had attended her husband's funeral. After that, any contact with Ivan was rare for Bea, as it was for most of the rest of the family.

Hal still somehow always got along well with Ivan and her other brother, Robert, but when he went to see them, Bea stayed home. She couldn't help but wonder why Olivia had shown up on her doorstep to see her.

"Did Hal put you up to coming here?"

"No one did. I came on my own accord. Can I come in?"

Bea opened the screen and stood aside as brown-headed, heavyset Olivia walked in, scanned the room and took a seat in the rocker by the window. "I know you and Uncle Hal have been having problems."

That understatement could win first prize in some kind of contest.

Olivia smacked on a piece of gum, popping it with every bite, and chewed as fast as she talked. "And what I'm saying is not meant to change what you do about your marriage at all or whether he moves back in with you or not. I just know he's made a lot of mistakes, but he's not a bad man."

"I know that." Bea cleared her throat.

"I've often wondered if you knew what a good man Uncle Hal actually is. With the father I have, of course, any man looks better, but that's beside the point. I often wondered if you knew that after every important event in my life—not some, I mean every one—Uncle Hal always popped over to my house for a few minutes. He'd hug me real tight, pat my back real hard and tell me how proud he was of me, and that he loved me. That always meant more to me than he knew. Uncle Hal is the only relative that does it. Not even my own father seems to care. But Uncle Hal does."

Tears formed in Olivia's eyes. She bent over and swiped them with her skirt tail.

"After about the tenth time, I began to expect it. If he didn't show within a day or two, I always wondered if he missed the event. He never did. He never missed anything. I was always thrilled to death when I heard his knock on my door. Nobody, I mean nobody, hugs as good as Uncle Hal."

Bea made no response.

"What I'm trying to say, Aunt Bea, is I think you should think twice before you give up on Uncle Hal. After all, he's Percy's father. I know he cares about you."

"How do you know that, Olivia? What makes you so sure? Just because he treated you nice doesn't mean he treated me the same way."

"Sure it does. He just doesn't know how to show you that side of him."

"Well, I haven't made up my mind about what I'm going to do. Whatever it is, I'll take into consideration what you've said." When hell freezes over, she wanted to say, but she saw no sense in being rude. Olivia meant well.

Bea felt certain she'd sat with her mouth open during much of Olivia's visit. After she left, Bea glanced over at Percy, now sound asleep, and wondered why she'd never seen that side of Hal. Why he'd never done anything to help her feel good about what she'd accomplished. He'd not even mentioned pride in her promotion to riveter. Everyone in the yard who knew her, and even some who didn't, had gone out of their way to congratulate her.

Instead, all those days and nights when she sat alone at home, Hal busied himself making others, like his niece Olivia, feel good about themselves.

She tucked that away in her heart when she heard another knock on the door.

Weary of company, wanting nothing more than to be alone with her thoughts, she went to the door.

Hal sat on the front porch, elbows propped on his knees, his head in his hands.

He looked up, his eyes red-rimmed.

"Did you ask Olivia to come tell me how great you are?"

"Olivia? No. Has she been here?"

"She just left. Come on in, you don't have to sit on the porch."

She saw him with different eyes than she had before.

"Guess you heard about Violet getting killed. They called it an accident, but . . ."

"I came up right after it happened."

"You did?" His eyes were wild, he looked like a wreck. "She didn't walk into that boom on purpose, did she? I couldn't live with that."

"She carried a heavy load of shame, but you didn't cause her death. The shame belongs to Johnny. You got caught in the serious troubles of another family. Her death isn't your fault." For the first time in her life, she felt sorry for Hal.

She also knew in that instant that their marriage hadn't had a chance from day one. His concerns were for everyone except her.

She'd agreed to marry Hal the day she slipped away without telling Mama she went swimming at Cow Creek. The other three couples begged her and Hal to go. Until then, she couldn't stand him. Every day when she came home from school, he sat in the living room talking to Mama and Papa like he belonged there. His persistence pleased Mama. She figured he must have something on the ball.

That day at Cow Creek, when her best friend said Hal looked good in his bathing trunks, Bea got nervous, worried about what she should do. Maybe the other girls might go after him.

The morning after she married, she knew she'd made a mistake.

After he'd talked for a while about Violet's death, Hal didn't stay much longer. He'd talked about how busy things were at the shipyard and how much pressure he'd been under lately with all that was happening to him, then said a simple "Good night" and left.

Not once did he mention her promotion to riveter, ask about Percy, or ask how she was holding up through all the turmoil.

SYLVIA DICKEY SMITH

Chapter 28

Marie stood behind the door and listened to Sol's phone conversation. She knew he'd dialed Irene's number. My God, how long could a fire for one woman smolder? It had been over twenty years since that woman got her hooks in him, and still he obsessed about her.

"Well, tell her an old friend called," he said. ". . . No, no name. Just tell her someone from Galveston wanted to say hi." He paused, listening, Marie assumed.

"I'll try again later. . . . Yes, she'll know who it is. . . . No, no number. Thank you." Marie heard him put the receiver softly back on the hook, then she stepped from behind the door, enjoying his look of surprise.

"So you called her again, huh?" Marie said. "She's doesn't want to talk to you. She didn't then and she still won't. You've pined after that woman your whole life. Give it up." Marie rattled the ice in the highball glass in her hand, downed the last drop, and stepped to the bar to prepare another.

"She'll talk to me."

"How do you know?"

"Because I heard her old man's been seen with another woman."

"For a man living seventy miles away, you keep pretty close tabs on her. So you think if her husband's messing around she'll come running to you?" Marie filled her glass half with water and half with vodka and added another tart slice of lime. "How many kids does she have now? Last I heard, four boys and four girls. And now the grandkids are coming."

"So?"

"She couldn't look the same as you remember. Beside, you don't even like kids. You think she'll abandon them for you? She's not like me. She won't give up her kids—like I did our baby."

"She's not a drunken sot like you are, either."

"You know why I drink, so don't start."

Sol took Marie's fresh drink out of her hand, and tossed it out the open window. "You drink too much," he said, and then left the room, out the back door, headed down to the beach.

The phone rang. Marie looked to see if Sol heard and came back. When he didn't, she walked over and picked up the phone. "Hello."

"Marie?" a woman's voice asked.

"Irene?"

"Yes, it's Irene. Has Sol been calling here? He's the only man I know who lives in Galveston."

"He's still in love with you, you know," Marie whispered into the phone.

"No, he's not. Sol's in love with the memory of the only woman who ever told him no."

"What?"

"It's true. Tell him to stop calling me, and see what he does."

It might work for Irene, but it wouldn't work for Marie.

How could she love and hate a man at the same time? If she ever figured that out, maybe she'd be free of the bastard. Until then, she'd fix herself another drink.

Chapter 29

Oskar sat in the break room and bit off a mouthful of sandwich but when he tried to swallow the food, it stuck in his throat. He took a swig of water and forced it down, then put the sandwich aside. His mind wasn't on eating—his mind was on Bea. Violet's death hit her hard, men said, and now he learned she'd gone home.

Around the yard, rumor spread how Violet knew what was about to happen when she walked into that boom. How horrible, for Bea to witness something like that, and know of your husband's involvement. Her heart must be breaking with the knowledge. Bea might feel like she did something to cause it.

He looked at the clock on the wall. Four more hours before his shift ended.

He'd fallen for Bea, but he also knew the time wasn't right for him to act on it. She needed to make up her mind about Hal without any outside influence. It hurt like hell when he saw how Hal treated her, and for the life of him, he didn't understand it. Hal was a nice guy, but when it came to Bea, he just didn't treat her like she deserved, like Oskar would treat her.

"Hey, good buddy, a penny for your thoughts," Daniel said. He'd walked in and pulled up a chair, and now flipped it around and straddled it. "I thought we had found your brother, but just as I approached him, the fellow took off in a dead run."

Oskar straightened in his chair, hopeful.

"We found the young man fooling around Hal's crane. I thought maybe he looked for you, since you're an oiler for that crane."

"How'd he look? Does he seem well?" He'd give anything to find the kid, for it would be one less thing to worry about, for both him and Mama.

"Oh, yeah, he looked fine—clean, decent clothes, clean-shaven. I figure he must be working at one of these shipyards, maybe even at this one, which explains how he gets in and out. But if he is, he's using another name. I've checked the records and you're the only Eichel. And nobody is named Wilhelm. With 20,000 employees, between this yard and the other two, it may take us awhile."

"Thanks. I appreciate your help."

"Don't mention it. Like I said, I figure I know what your brother's going through." Daniel stood at the window and stared down at the yard, as if hoping Wilhelm might pop into view. "You heard about the accident, I guess."

"Yeah."

Daniel stalled, as if to get his voice under control. "Bad scene. I really feel sorry for Bea, she witnessed the whole thing."

Oskar hadn't said anything to Daniel about his feelings for Bea, and wondered if he'd guessed. "She must be beside herself. It's driving me crazy that I still have four more hours to work. I'd like to go check on her."

"I'm sure they can find someone to fill in for you. I think if you went over to Personnel and explained they'd let you go early. I've got to get back out into the yard, but I'll keep an eye out for Wilhelm."

Oskar gathered the remains of his lunch and left for the personnel office.

No telling what Violet's death would do to Hal, either. Even though he wasn't the baby's father, he still had a connection with her.

By the time Oskar got back to the Meade's house, his quick pace left him breathless by the time he stepped in the front door.

There she sat, eyes unfocused, expressionless, rocking Percy, who was sound asleep and about to slip out from under her arms.

"You okay?" He spoke softly, fearful he'd startle her.

When she didn't respond, he lifted her arm and lifted Percy to his chest. "Come on little buddy, let's put you on the pallet so mama can rest." He eased the baby down on his stomach and patted his bottom until Percy settled back into a deep sleep.

Perched on the edge of the sofa, Oskar took her hands in his. "Anything I can get you?"

She shook her head, but still didn't bring her gaze back from wherever it had taken her.

Nor did she speak. He knew why. If she opened her mouth she might shatter into so many pieces she may never fit herself back together again. *Humpty Dumpty* didn't hold a lock on that kind of crash. Oskar respected that, but it didn't keep his own heart from breaking when he looked at her. He wished to take her in his arms and hold her until things in her world turned right. No woman had ever affected him this way before, and it hurt like hell.

He sat quietly and waited. When Percy curled up into a ball as if he were cold, Oskar went to his crib and collected a blanket and covered the little tyke. Soon, the baby's legs unfolded and he settled into a deeper sleep.

"Thank you," she said, her voice barely above a whisper.

"How about you? Anything I can get you?"

"Water would be nice."

"You got it." He hurried to the kitchen, thrilled she'd finally asked for something—anything. He filled a glass with cold water from the pitcher Bea kept in the icebox and brought it to her.

"I just had a visit from my niece," she said, her voice still a whisper.

"Whatever she said must have upset you."

Bea laughed a hoarse, hollow sound. "She told me how thoughtful Uncle Hal always treated her."

"Hal can be a good-hearted man. When he learned I didn't have a place to sleep, he insisted I come home with him."

"Then why doesn't he treat me . . . that way? I am not that difficult to live with."

"Quite the contrary."

When the first tears eased over the edge of her eyelids and rolled down her cheek, Oskar reached over and took her hand again.

"I don't know what to say. I wish I did." He wanted to say he'd never treat her like that, but he knew the time wasn't right. He didn't want to confuse her anymore than she was. He knew she and Hal must first settle their future with each other.

Meanwhile, he'd wait—but he'd still keep his eye on Bea.

Chapter 30

Hal propped his forearms on the bar, his head abuzz, wondering what the hell had happened to his life.

Regardless of how many beer bottles he emptied, he couldn't make the disgust he felt towards Violet and Bea go away. It wasn't that he loved Violet, he didn't. The truth was, he didn't love Bea, either. But he sure had expected her to take him back now that she knew Violet's baby wasn't his.

She hadn't, which meant now he didn't have a place to call home. The guys at the shipyard would laugh at him when the word got out.

Who the hell did Bea think she was, not letting him move back into his own house? He was an assistant team leader for the crane operators, for Christ's sake. He earned the money, so he should make the decisions. Not her. He put food on the table for her and Percy. He kept a roof over their heads. Bea didn't.

Maybe you weren't man enough for either one of them.

Nonsense. How about that steamy time in his cab when he and Violet both *went to town on each other?* Violet had used him, that's all it was to it.

You could've done more to help her, you know.

Help Violet? How could he? She lied to him to get away from her brother. Then again, sometimes he wondered if she lied about parts of that, too. Maybe she really liked it.

You didn't do enough for Bea, either. She needed you to understand, but you're too selfish to think of anyone but yourself.

That's bullshit. Bea only thought about herself. And for the life of him, he could never guess what she needed, much less wanted. A little appreciation went a long way, but did she ever thank him for anything he did for her? Hell no. She just bitched, over and over.

What bugged the hell out of him was that infernal crying while he tried to sleep. What man could stand that several nights a week? After all, a working man needed his rest, that's all it was to it.

At first, he tried to understand what she needed, what turned her on when he touched her, but it got to be too much work. He knew about the Vaseline. At least Violet's moans and scratches let him know he was still the man he thought he was.

He slammed the empty beer bottle down on the bar. "Okay, Sam," he said to the bartender, his speech a little slurred, "one more might do it."

"Might do what?" the bartender asked while drying a shot glass. "Don't you think you've had enough for now? Booze solves some problems, but just for a short while. Why don't you go home, sleep it off."

"Home? Where's that? Thanks to conniving women, I'm back to living with . . ."

Dammit, if Bea didn't like living with him, then she better find someone else to live with and listen to her cry. She was a looker— Rufus said so himself. She'd find another man to support her.

But the thought of his wife in the arms of another man made him want to hit something.

"Why don't you go home and get a good night's sleep?" Sam urged. "Tomorrow, you'll see things differently."

"Yeah, I'm going," Hal said, mumbling to himself.

He stood to go, but when the room blurred, he sat a minute longer.

Oskar seemed awful friendly with Bea. He hadn't given the man much thought, but come to think of it, he sure sounded German.

Chapter 31

Summoned to the security office without explanation, Bea hustled that way, her nerves taut. A million questions raced through her mind. Had she done something wrong? Were they going to fire her? Maybe they planned to demote her to materials handler and change her shift back to graveyard.

If so, Nelda might get fed up with all the changes and quit, or her mama might make her. If so, she'd have to find someone else to take care of Percy. If all else failed, she guessed she could go back to Hal. He still was hanging around, waiting for her answer.

The thought of his hands on her skin made it crawl.

Wait, what was she thinking? Security didn't handle schedule changers or demotion. She'd gotten all worked up over nothing. Maybe they still had questions about Violet's death. Out of kindness to the family, the authorities had declared the tragedy an accident, although some eyewitnesses swore Violet must have known exactly what she was doing.

"Come in," a male voice said when she knocked.

She opened the door to Daniel and Oskar.

"What's this about?" Bea looked from one of them to the other. "Is this about Violet's death? I told the other security guard what I saw. I don't know anything else."

"This has nothing to do with Violet," Daniel said, indicating a chair near him.

"No, thank you. I'll stand." She looked from Daniel to Oskar and back again.

"We understand you went out to the gypsy camp the other day."

Bea was puzzled at the question. "Edith and I did, yes. And the way the two of you look, that's against the law?"

"No, no, not at all," Daniel interrupted her. "Oskar and I are wondering if there's a German hiding out in the camp."

"A German? Why? Gypsies wouldn't hide a German," Bea said. "They're killing them, the same as they are Jews."

The two looked at her, their mouths open.

"What? You think just because I'm a woman I don't read the paper?"

"Excuse me, Bea," Daniel said, recovering. "You're right, but they just might be hiding someone out at their camp. That's what we've got to check out. And if someone is laying low there and doesn't want to be found, the gypsies would never let anyone know he was there. They seldom let outsiders in. But since you got in before, we thought you might be able to talk to them again."

"I'm not the one who got us in. Edith knew one of the women. She's the one—"

"We understand," Oskar said as he paced the room, "but the fewer who know, the better our chances. It would help me, Bea, if you could do this. I'd about given up finding Wilhelm. I figured he must have left town, if he'd ever been here in the first place. I need to at least find out if it's him living out there with the gypsies. If it is, I need to—"

"Your brother? You think Wilhelm is there?"

"—see if I can get him to follow the judges' order." He walked over to the window and looked out. "Yes, Bea, I think that's where Wilhelm might be hiding. I've looked everywhere else."

"This is ridiculous, I'm not a spy. I'm just a plain housewife who's . . ."

"Who's what?" The men looked at her, waiting for her to finish the sentence.

A sad little woman who lies in bed and cries herself to sleep every night and God only knows why, she thought, relieved she bit her tongue instead of saying it.

On second thought, she wondered if that image of herself was really still true.

Chapter 32

How she let them talk her into it, she'd never know. However, she had not promised she wouldn't stop and pick up Edith on the way. Despite Daniel's urgings that she go alone, as soon as Bea left the Security Office, she went straight to Edith's. Absolutely no way would Bea go without her.

But when she ran inside at Edith's house, she found her sister sitting on the toilet—in the throes of a miscarriage. Bea ran around to find some clean rags and took the pile to the bathroom.

"I'm so sorry, babe," she said. "I didn't know you were pregnant."

"I didn't know either, until now," Edith said softly. "It's probably for the best, anyway."

"Why? What do you mean?"

" 'Cause I'm not going back to that bastard who got me this way."

"Can't blame you for that."

"Why are you here this time of day, anyway?" Edith asked.

"I took off."

"Why?"

"Daniel and Oskar think Oskar's brother Wilhelm might be hiding with the gypsies. They talked me into going out and talking to Black Betty or Lady Silvania. I wanted you to go with me, but . . ."

"I can't imagine why they think that, but I sure can't go with you, not in this condition. To the gypsy, menstruating women are unclean."

"Why, for heaven's sake? I thought that belief went out with the Old Testament times."

"Gypsies believe a lot of things are unclean." Edith grabbed

Bea's hand and squeezed. "Don't worry about me. I'm okay . . . just weak. . . ."

"Should we take you to the doctor?"

"I'll be okay. I have some herbs to take to help with the bleeding. I guess this is just payback for my judgment of Marie."

"What does she have to do with this?"

Edith's face turned paler. "Oh, I'm always judging her about something or the other."

"You want me to stay with you for a while?" Bea stalled. She needed an excuse to not go to the gypsy camp by herself. What if they figured out why she came? Would they kill her and bury her body underneath one of those big tents?

"No, I'm fine. You go on. I'll lie around and rest until I get my strength up."

"No, Edith. At least come with me and I'll let drop you off at my house to rest up. That way I can check on you when I get back from the camp."

* * *

An hour later Bea drove into the outskirts of the gypsy camp and parked her old beat-up car, not far away from a group of playing children. A Roma, a gypsy man, was speaking to one of the boys. Bea marveled at how they conversed. The man didn't talk down to the boy, and the boy didn't act like a kid. An interesting way to raise children, she thought. She'd remember that with Percy.

The contagious music of a fiddler had gathered a crowd of adults enjoying his wild music. A few women danced to the strange tune, kicking their legs up and prancing around, arms entwined, laughing as though they had not a care in the world. Bea wondered what that felt like.

She didn't see the young boy approach, but before he could speak, an elderly man came up and put his hand on the boy's shoulder.

"Never mind," he said. "I'll handle this." The boy scampered off.

But when he spoke to Bea, the man's voice turned to a snarl.

"What can I do for you?"

"I ... I came out here a few days ago and talked to Black Betty. And then Lady Silvania read my fortune. I'd like to talk to either one of them again if I could." Relieved she'd practiced what to say all the way out, Bea's answer rolled pretty smoothly off her tongue, despite the quiver in her voice.

"We really don't take kindly to outsiders."

"I understand."

"What is it you want?"

"I had a follow-up question ... that's very important to me, and to a very good friend of mine. It wouldn't take long to ask it, and I'd be gone. And out of your hair."

He paused a moment, expressionless. Then, "Follow me."

He pointed her to a tent. "In there," he said. "Not sure she'll see you, but you can try."

Bea stared at the tent while, it seemed, a fur ball formed in the back of her throat.

"But aren't you going to take ..."

She looked for the man who no longer stood beside her. A quick glance around the campsite told her he'd abandoned her to her own devices.

Great. Just great.

She eased over to the tent and stopped at the entryway, not knowing whether to call out or not. Just walking in unannounced seemed like bad manners—not to mention risky. Inside, she heard several low voices speaking, but she couldn't make out much more than that.

Just get it over with, she told herself, took a deep breath, and opened the tent flap.

Smack in the middle of the tent sat Lady Silvania dressed in the same colorful outfit she'd worn earlier. But this time, the expression on her face wasn't pleasant. Tension in the room felt thick enough to cut.

Across from Lady Silvania sat a blonde young man. It was the same man she'd seen hiding around Hal's crane that night. The one she thought might be a German.

"Hello," he said, rising. "My name is Wilhelm Eichel."

Chapter 33

Bea gawked at the man standing before her. She recalled the night she'd seen him hiding near Hal's crane. Maybe if she looked long enough now she'd believe what she saw.

"Wilhelm Eichel? Are you Oskar's brother?"

"Yes, madam, Oskar is my older brother. I heard someone was asking for me, and when I looked out and saw you . . . I figured you must have been sent here by him. At least, you don't look like the shipyard security, or the local police."

Bea wasn't sure what to say.

"If that is true, then you can help me," Wilhelm continued. "Since I realized he had followed me here to Orange, I've found out where he works, but I have had no luck finding out where he lives. Do you know?"

"Wait just a minute, first things first." Bea raised her hand, palm out. "What on earth are you doing here? And how did you get in the shipyard without being seen by security?"

"Suffice it to say the fence has a hole in it. Am I right? Did my brother send you to find me?"

"As a matter of fact, yes, he's worried himself sick about you."

"Is it me, or the wrath of my father that sends him?"

Lady Silvania interrupted by suddenly getting up. She stepped over to the tent flap and pulled it aside. "Go get Sonia," she ordered someone outside. "She needs to be in here, too."

Within a couple of minutes, a young girl stepped inside.

"Get in here, Sonia. You're the one who started this whole thing when you fell for this gadje."

"Lady Silvania, were you aware that Wilhelm is a German?"

Bea asked, still trying to figure out who knew what and when.

"We know, yes. He told us, but—"

"Did you know that Germans are killing gypsies by the thousands over in Germany?"

"We not trust them, no. But we not trust anyone but gypsy."

"Why?"

"You not keep gypsy laws. Gypsy clean. You . . . unclean, defiled."

Bea looked down at her print dress, feeling a mite defensive. "I put this dress on clean this morning."

"Not *melalo*—dirty with dirt. You are *marimé*, defiled. We gypsy, or Rom, believe upper body pure, clean. Lower portions—genitals are marimé. Upper and lower body parts or anything touching must not mix. Gypsy washes hands more. Gadje wash babies and dishes in same pan."

The woman looked aghast. "Rom, we use different towel for face than nether regions. Even use different color soaps. Pregnant women must have separate dishes to eat from."

"What about a German? You don't have a problem with him in your camp?"

Bea looked from Lady Silvania to Wilhelm. "Do you know you can get in a lot of trouble letting him hide out here? The judge ordered him to join the Army, and he ran away."

"Rom not worry about what gadje do. We tend to our own."

"But he's not one of you, that's what I'm telling you."

"Wilhelm is now *familia*, part of our *kumpania*. He—"

"Part of what?"

"Kumpania. Like your union. All gypsy men in one tribe make up kumpania, which determines which man does which job. Most our women do *bujo*, that be fortunetelling. Rom women make more money than men by reading palms, telling fortunes, reading tarot cards. Gadje call fortune telling flimflam, swindle."

"Is it?" Bea had to ask, since she'd had hers read by Lady Silvania and still hadn't figured out what it meant. Maybe she'd spent too much time worrying about it.

"I didn't charge you, did I?"

"Not that I know of, no. My sister left an envelope, but—"

"Some flimflam, some honest." The old woman shifted in her chair.

"'Nother thing—chastity important to familia. Problem come, however, when gypsy girl fall in love with gadje. She not permitted to marry him. To Rom, gadje *marimé*—unclean. Despite that, girls fall in love with who they do. So sometimes girls do marry gadje."

Impatient, Bea wondered why her questions about a runaway young man were being converted to a discussion of beliefs and practices of the Rom. Then the M-word penetrated her brain. Marry? Oh, my God. Did the two Rom men buy the pigs for a wedding between a Rom and a Gadje—a gadje who just happened to be Wilhelm Eichel?

"Do you mean to tell me this German boy married one of your Rom girls? When?"

Lady Silvania nodded. She did not look especially happy about it. "Couple of weeks ago."

"So was it *his* wedding celebration you needed the roasting pigs for, those you bought off of Tinsel and Clara?"

"That be it."

Bea shook her head in disbelief. What a small world. Then she realized the risk the Rom had taken to hide Wilhelm.

"Did you know taking in a German boy running from the law could get you in a lot of trouble? The authorities in Seguin are looking for him right now. As is the Army. Not to mention the head of security at Consolidated."

Wilhelm spoke up. "I didn't mean to get these folks in trouble. I ran away with a small group of Rom because I couldn't fight the Germans, knowing that Dolph, my oldest brother, was on the other side. I thought it would be simpler, somehow, to get a job at the shipyard. And I did, using another name. One night while sitting around the campfire here, Sonia walked up and we started talking."

Wilhelm looked at Bea. "I do not wish to cause anyone trouble. I just want to stay here with Sonia. I hope you won't tell on me. If you do, the judge might stand me before a firing squad. But I am not a Nazi. I am just a young man born in Germany, who is now living here, whose oldest brother is on the other side . . . and who got in trouble . . . ." He drifted into silence, then shook his head. "Many Germans oppose that mad man."

"How old are you, Wilhelm?" Bea shook her head, struggling with what to do next.

"Seventeen."

"I don't think the judge will shoot you, but they might make sure you join the Army—or lock you in a cell instead."

"I thought Americans believed in freedom? This is why I want to become an American citizen."

Bea sighed. "Getting in trouble with the law didn't help that. And I hardly think marriage to a gypsy will qualify you for citizenship."

"You think they might send me back to Germany? I do not want that. Hitler and the Nazis have ruined my homeland." He looked at Bea, pleading in his eyes. "If I could talk to Oskar, he would tell me what to do. I know he would, that's why I tried to find him that night you saw me at the shipyard. Do you know where Oskar lives? I would not even mind being thrown in jail if they would just let me see him one more time."

Bea stared from Sonia to Silvania and back to Wilhelm. "Oskar's the one who sent me to see if you were here. I didn't really think you were. And I certainly didn't think you were the groom at the recent gypsy wedding celebration."

"So you do know Oskar?"

"He boards at my house."

"At your house? Are you telling me the truth?"

Lady Silvania stood. "This woman does not lie. I see it in her eyes." She turned and walked to her new son-in-law and patted him on the back. "Wilhelm does not either. So now it be all in your hands, Bea Meade. What you going to do?"

Chapter 34

When their shifts ended, Daniel drove Oskar to Bea's to await her return. Oskar was a little worried for her safety. He knew gypsies well, how they distrusted anyone who wasn't one of them. And he knew especially of their dislike for anything German, and rightly so.

His knowledge came from their boyhood days growing up in Germany. His younger brother had spent many a day playing with his best friend, Pitti, who lived at the gypsy camp outside their hometown. Wilhelm and Pitti were inseparable playmates, until the day the Nazis dragged Pitti and his entire disreputable, non-Germanic clan off to one of their death camps. One day they were there. The next, they were gone, their wagons and campfires deserted.

Oskar couldn't imagine the Rom ever giving aid to a German. But he knew they had given Wilhelm a ride from Seguin, headed in this direction. So maybe they knew where he was?

He warmed a pot of coffee and dug leftover fried chicken and biscuits out of the icebox. "Come on in here," he called out to Daniel who stood staring in the bedroom at Edith, who was asleep on Bea's bed. "We might as well pass the time eating."

"Might as well." Daniel said, as he walked in and took a chair.

"It's a good thing Nelda took Percy to her house." Oskar said, digging into the food, for worry always made him hungry. "Edith doesn't look well. Her breathing seems to be so shallow."

Their bellies full and their plates scraped clean, Oskar drew the sink full of hot soapy water and started washing their dishes while Daniel went back to check on Edith. She lay with her eyes closed, arms across her stomach, and a pained expression on her face.

He rushed in a minute later, horror on his face. "She's bleeding,

Oskar. There's blood all over the bed. Come look. He grabbed Oskar's arm and yanked. "Hurry."

One look at the blood-soaked sheets and Oskar knew Edith was in serious trouble. "We've got to get her to the hospital," he said.

Daniel looked from Oskar to Edith, worry lines gouged in his forehead. "You stay here and wait for Bea. I hope she finds your brother."

"Don't worry about me. Get that woman treated before she dies right here in front of both of us."

"I'm going." Daniel snatched Edith up in his arms, with only a moaned response from the unconscious Edith, her blood soaking his clothes. He kicked the screen door open, turned sideways and headed out.

Oskar stood at the screen door watching Daniel jog to the parking lot. The last thing he saw was exhaust as Daniel's car sped away.

He went into the bedroom, stripped the sheets from the bed and carried them to the kitchen. After filling the sink with cold fresh water, he rolled up his shirtsleeves, submerged the blood-soaked sheets and scrubbed.

Then he gathered a handful of rags and a bucket of water, hurried to the bedroom and started in on the mattress. He thought of Bea as he cleaned, and how he'd explain what happened when she got back from the gypsy camp. What was it about that bed? It was the one he'd heard Bea crying on many nights, and now the one that drained Edith's lifeblood.

Masil came in just as he finished. Thankful for the company, he told her about Edith and the bleeding and the sudden trip to the hospital.

"Sounds like she might be having a miscarriage," Masil said. "I've lost three babies that way. My husband and I had about given up, but now, I'm five months pregnant—farther along than I ever got before. The doctor thinks this one will go fine. That's what I came to tell Bea. I knew she'd be glad." She looked around the room.

"By the way, where is she? Did she go to the hospital with the guy that took Edith? With Daniel?"

"No, Bea wasn't here when it happened. She should be home soon if you'd like to wait."

"No, that's okay. Tell her I stopped by and I'll come back tomorrow. But do me a favor and don't tell her why I came, okay? I'd like to tell her myself."

Oskar promised.

Masil left and the house grew quiet once again. Weary from the day's stress, he stretched out on the sofa and closed his eyes.

He hadn't realized he'd dozed until the sound of footsteps coming up the sidewalk awakened him with a start.

Soft voices drew closer, and then Bea opened the door and came in.

Oskar thought he'd heard more than one person approach. Oskar stretched to the side to look around Bea, but there was no one else there.

She rested her hand on his chest. "I found a German in the camp. When I got there, I found him in the tent with Lady Silvania and a young gypsy girl named Sonia."

"So they *were* hiding someone."

"It's quite a love story, actually."

"Bea, I'm not really in the mood for a love story."

"Hear me out." She put her hand out to quiet him. "You know, of course, that the gypsies have no use for outsiders. But this outsider told them he was half-gypsy because of his real father."

Oskar's eyes narrowed. "I, too, am half-gypsy, as is Wilhelm. This is not something in Germany to be proud of."

He dropped to the sofa and buried his head in his hands. "Years ago, after a good beating from my stepfather, I asked my mother why he hated me. She said, 'It's not you, he hates, Oskar, it's me.' That's when she told me about this gypsy man who came through our town every year or so to repair wagons. My older brother Dolph had been three or four years old at the time, and had fallen asleep on his pallet the day she . . . went to bed with the gypsy. My stepfather found them and chased the gypsy down the street and out of town. I was born nine months later."

Oskar looked up at Bea. "My stepfather never knew that a few years later, the same man fathered Wilhelm."

"Wow, what a story." Bea collapsed on the sofa beside him, her arm around his shoulders. "I've heard the band outside of town called Black Dutch. Lady Silvania told me that they came to this country from Germany, generations ago. So their heritage can be traced back to German gypsies—*Sinti*, Lady Silvania told me was the name of their tribe of the Rom."

"Black Dutch? From *Deutsch*, meaning German." Excitement rose in his chest. "So perhaps they have some sympathy for others of German background?'

"Yes. And when the outsider asked to marry Lady Silvania's daughter, and he had some gypsy blood in him, he could do so according to gypsy law." Bea said.

"What outsider, Bea? You're driving me crazy with—"

"The gypsies recently held a big wedding celebration, roasted pigs and all."

"Did you find Wilhelm or not?"

Bea opened the screen door. "You can come inside now," she said, and held the door open for the newlywed to pass.

"Wilhelm!" Oskar yelled.

He jumped to his feet. "You don't look like a kid anymore. You've grown thinner, and what's that hair on your face?" The two rushed into each others' arms, each pummeling the other on the back.

"Oh, brother, am I glad to see you," Oskar laughed with joy. "Where have you been?"

"As Bea said, I've been living with the gypsies ever since I left home. Then I heard you had followed me here. I longed to see you— even considered turning myself in to the local recruiters. But, I fell in love with Sonia...."

"Wow, I can't believe this—my brother right here under my nose the whole time. If you knew I looked for you, why didn't you come find me?"

"I tried catching you at the shipyard, but we always kept missing each other. I ran into Bea one night," he smiled over at Bea. "Then this other man started sneaking around, keeping an eye on your work station. Daniel—Bea told me is his name. I didn't want to get you into trouble or get nabbed by Security. So I pulled back and decided to find out where you lived instead."

"I hate to disturb your family reunion," Bea said, "but where's Percy? Is he with Nelda, or what? And I should check on Edith . . ." She started for the bedroom.

"Nelda has Percy over at her house. But Edith . . ." Oskar was just remembering the scene earlier, which seemed like a dream.

"Your sister started bleeding real bad," Oskar explained.

"Oh no, I knew I shouldn't have left her here alone."

"Daniel was here too. He took her to the hospital."

"What? How long have they been gone?"

Oskar looked at his watch. "A couple of hours now."

"I don't know what to do." Bea paced the floor. "I feel like I should go check on Edith, but I don't feel like I can just leave you two here without . . . getting in trouble with Daniel. After all, he's security at the shipyard, and he's the one who arranged for me to go to the gypsy camp."

"I'm not going anywhere, if that's your concern," Wilhelm said. "I don't want to get into any more trouble than I might already be in."

Oskar turned to Bea. "You go check on your sister. Both of us will be right here when you get back. We can wait for Nelda. When she brings Percy home, we'll put him to bed."

Bea grabbed her purse she'd laid on the table when she came in and headed out the door without a backward look.

Chapter 35

Before Bea could back out of the parking lot, another car pulled in next to hers. Daniel sat in the driver's seat, but no one sat on the passenger side.

Daniel jumped out and met Bea running around the front in a panic. "Where's Edith?"

"The doctor said she's going to be okay. It was a close call though. She lost the baby, but it looks like she'll be fine and able to have more. They gave her lots of blood and something to help her sleep. She'll be out until morning."

Daniel's voice cracked. "We could've lost her, Bea."

"I didn't know you and Edith were so close," Bea said, surprised at the intensity in Daniel's voice.

He wiped his face with both hands and shook his head. "We're not."

Bea felt as if she saw an embarrassed a fifteen-year-old boy with his first crush.

She placed a hand on his shoulder and gave him a gentle squeeze. "As soon as she's better, you should tell her how you feel."

"They said it looked like she'd bled out without even knowing what happened."

Daniel took her by the elbow and guided her toward her house. "Now, I can't wait any longer. What happened out at the gypsy camp? Did you find Wilhelm hiding there?"

By the time they reached her front door, Bea had summed up her trip to the camp and the reunion between brothers.

"I don't know what you think, Daniel," Bea said, her confidence growing by the minute, "but in my opinion, these two guys are not the enemy. They haven't caused us any harm. Quite the contrary—"

"I agree," Daniel said, stopping Bea mid-sentence. "But Wilhelm does have to settle up with that judge in Seguin. He may have to go back and serve out his sentence until the war ends. Let's go inside and talk."

Bea stopped Daniel before he stepped inside. "Soon as we finish here, I'm going to the hospital."

"Tonight? It's late, Bea. She'll be okay until morning."

"You don't understand. Edith is the only one who has always been there for me. Now, she needs me. I couldn't sleep anyway, knowing she's in the hospital all by herself."

They went inside and found Oskar and Wilhelm putting clean sheets on Bea's bed over a towel covering the damp spot. "Oh, thank you, guys." Bea said. "Daniel says it looks like she'll be okay, but they're keeping her overnight, so if one of you can stay with Percy I'm going to sit with her overnight."

"I'll be here, anyway, Bea," said Oskar immediately. "Don't worry about a thing. Percy and I have become big buddies."

As they all returned to the living room Nelda came in with Percy, his eyes drooping closed. Edith's loss did something to Bea, for all she wanted to do was grab her baby and squeeze him tight. Instead she eased him into her arms and fussed over his clothes, smoothed his hair down, leaned over and kissed his cheek, fiddling with him until he squirmed and cried out.

"Come here, little guy, let Uncle Oskar rock you to sleep." Oskar took Percy to the rocking chair and within minutes Percy was snoring. "Unless Daniel needs me for something, I can take care of the baby until you and Edith get home in the morning," he said.

He walked to the bedroom with Percy and put him in his crib.

"What do you think will happen next, Daniel?" Bea asked, hoping against hope they had come to the end of the investigation.

"None of this reflects against Oskar because he really hasn't done anything but snoop around," Daniel said. "Wilhelm, I'll need you to come with me to the sheriff's office. I don't know the outcome, but I rather suspect they'll go easy on you, especially since you're turning yourself in. You are, aren't you?"

The sound of Wilhelm's audible relief filled the room. Everyone laughed, even Wilhelm.

"That sounds good to me," he said. "I need to accept responsibility for what I did, take the consequences, and get on with my life with Sonia. I can come back here, can't I?"

"Not sure 'til we get a copy of your immigration papers. Oskar says your Mother has them. Otherwise we just might need to shoot you."

Startled, Bea looked at the security officer. When she saw the twinkle in Daniel's eye, she popped him on the arm.

"Oskar, I don't think I'll need you tonight," Daniel said. "You stay here with the baby while Bea goes to the hospital to check on her sister. Meanwhile, Wilhelm, come with me. Let's get you processed." He started for the door, but stopped.

"Oh, and Bea, if Edith needs anything at all, please let me know."

"I will," she said, smiling. "She'll be glad to know you offered."

After everyone left, Oskar turned to Bea. "I am so proud of you, Bea, for finding my brother," he whispered. "But right now, I want nothing more than to take you in my arms."

Bea swallowed hard and took a step forward, but before she reached Oskar's outstretched arms, a knock sounded on the door.

Chapter 36

Bea opened the door and there stood Hal, hat in his hand and *beggar* on his face.

"I hadn't slept a wink, I figured I might as well come over here and talk to you. Can I come in?"

"My God, Hal, it's the middle of the night."

He looked into the living room and saw Oskar, standing close behind Bea. Hal stopped short, and his face turned red.

"Did I interrupt something?" He shot a look at Bea.

"Oskar and I were just talking," she said, then wanted to slap herself for not saying it wasn't any of his business.

"Oskar, if you wouldn't mind, I'd like to talk to my wife. Alone."

Oskar looked at Bea. "I need to shower and get to bed anyway. Bea, I'll see you in the morning. And don't worry about Percy. We'll be fine."

After Oskar left the room, Bea turned to Hal.

"Whatever you came to say, say it quick. Edith's in the hospital and I need to go see her." Irritation tinged her voice, but she didn't care.

"What's wrong with her?"

"That's really her business. I just need to check on her."

"You need me to stay here with Percy?"

"That's all been taken care of."

"I can stay—"

"I don't need you, Hal. Now, like I said, I'm in a hurry to get to the hospital."

He stiffened. "You said you'd get back with me about our chances of starting over. I'm here to get your answer."

She turned on her heel and went to the kitchen. "You know, Hal, I don't think so. I really don't think so."

"Why?" he whined, trailing along behind.

"Let's see." She started counting off on her fingers. "My days were planned around what you wanted, when you wanted it, and how much you wanted it. I never figured into any of it, nor did Percy. What I wanted—what we needed—didn't count."

"But Bea—"

"I know, all that wasn't your fault. I had no idea what I wanted, or that I could even want anything. Now, I do." She'd never spoken out like that before. By the look on Hal's face, it shocked him as much as it did her.

Hal looked like a mule not wanting to plow.

"That's why women were put here on this earth, Bea. As a help-meet for men. The good Lord planned it that way."

She tried not to laugh, for she knew he wasn't joking. He believed it to his toenails. Still, a chuckle bubbled up.

"Hal, you're still living in the 1800s. This is the '40s. Women have the right to vote. We hold jobs. We fight in the war. We provide for our families—and I don't just mean cook the damn food."

Heat rose to her cheeks. "Regardless of what you think, good things have come out of this separation and the war."

"What?" Hal looked dumbfound.

"For one thing, I like myself so much better now."

"But I don't," he cried. "Why can't you just be like you used to be?"

He stomped to the icebox and poured a glass of milk.

She heard Oskar piddling around in his bedroom, getting ready for his shower. In the small house, she figured he heard every word they were saying. But she didn't care. Now that she'd found her voice, she planned to use it.

"I've spent every day of my life putting myself last. I've lived in this world as a *good woman*. Until one day, thanks to you, that world came undone. I still don't know why I cry at night. But that doesn't make me a bad person. There's a reason for it, and if I do nothing else in this life, I'm going to find out why. Find out what I've lost. And it's not you I'm crying for."

"You'll be sorry, Bea. How are you going to get by without a husband? Your mama raised you to be that virtuous woman King Solomon talked about in the Bible. She'd roll over in her grave if she heard you say that."

"Maybe she has heard me. Maybe she'd agree with me. We'll never know. What I do know is I've made my decision."

He didn't say another word. Upending the glass of milk, he drank it, banged the glass on the table and marched through the living room and out the front door.

As soon as the front door slammed, Oskar appeared in the kitchen. He pulled out a chair, sat next to Bea, and clasped her hand.

"This may not be the best time," he said, "but . . . but—"

"But what?"

Although Bea knew her feelings for Oskar had grown and knew he felt the same way about her, the last thing she expected from him was a marriage proposal, but that's what she got.

Chapter 37

Edith elevated the bed and stared out the hospital window, lost in memories. Perhaps dealing with her own pregnancy brought into focus a time in her life she hadn't thought of in many years. She had been only thirteen when her long search had resulted in finding Marie's six-month-old baby in an orphanage in Baton Rouge, Louisiana.

She had gone to Hartburg, a tiny town in east Texas, to visit her older sister, Marie, who had moved there months before to help out their ninety-year-old invalid aunt. Or so the family believed.

When Edith arrived, she had learned the real reason. Marie had left Orange because she was pregnant, by her boyfriend Sol.

Edith had barely recovered from the shock of that news when Marie went into labor and, with the help of an elderly doctor who lived next door the baby came later that day. Edith's excitement over the baby's birth and her elation at being an aunt fell in a shattered heap when Marie announced she couldn't keep the infant baby.

* * *

"Please, please let me take the baby home to Mama," she begged Marie. "I can raise her like she's mine. I know Mama'll help me. I'm old enough, I can even get married, Clayton's ready to marry me. And we can adopt her—anything—just please don't give her away."

Edith cried for hours, but all to no avail. When Marie made up her mind, no force this side of a hurricane could change it.

"Honey, you're just a kid yourself. The best thing is for me to give her up for adoption. You can't take care of a baby. I can't either, without a husband, and Sol won't marry me. You know that."

"No, I don't know that," Edith yelled back at her.

"No matter, the decision is made and if you know what's good for you, you won't breathe a word of this to Mama."

"The baby is your own flesh and blood, Marie. She's here in this world, born. You can't just give her away like an unwanted puppy."

But Marie clamped her thin, stubborn lips together and wouldn't discuss it further. Edith stomped to bed.

The next morning, Edith awoke and realized she'd slept through the night without hearing the baby cry. At first she panicked, hoping the baby still breathed. She pulled a blanket from the bed, wrapped it around herself and headed to the front room where she'd left Marie and the baby sleeping the night before.

She tiptoed over to the makeshift crib assembled from a wardrobe drawer. Empty. Marie must have changed her mind and taken the baby to bed with her.

When she tiptoed over to look, no baby lay in the crook of Marie's arms.

Edith knew what had happened without having to ask, but the panic rising in her chest forced the words out of her mouth anyway.

"Where's the baby?" She shook Marie's shoulder. "Marie, where's the baby?"

Marie wouldn't answer so Edith ran around to the other side of the bed, grabbed her sister and shook her again.

"Marie, snap out of it, wake up. Where's the baby? What did you do with her?"

Marie hadn't been asleep. She'd been crying.

"She's gone, sweetheart. I couldn't keep her. You knew that."

"What do you mean she's gone?"

"Dr. Mosquito and his wife came early this morning and took her. A friend of theirs knew a good place for her. He said if I intended to give her away, the sooner I did the better it would be."

"Marie! I told you I wanted her. I begged you to give her to me. You can't give away your own flesh and blood. Tell me you didn't."

Edith fell across the bed, screaming. "How could you do that?

Give away your own little girl. She was beautiful, Marie. She looked just like me. Tell me you're joking. I don't want her gone. I want her back."

"That baby was never supposed to be born, Edith. I couldn't raise her by myself. If I tried, Sol would leave me."

"To hell with Sol. All he thinks about is himself—himself and money—and that—that Irene girl. I'm glad she didn't marry him. I hope he burns in hell. I hate him, I hate him." Edith stomped to the window. "Just tell me, where'd the doctor take her?"

"Sweetheart, you're too young. You don't have any idea what it's like to be unmarried and raise an illegitimate child. Those old biddies would eat me alive and her, too. The baby would grow up being called a bastard. Do you know what that means?"

"What?" Edith sniffed and looked at her feet.

"It means she doesn't have a father, that's what it means."

"She does have a daddy—stupid Sol."

"His name won't be on her birth record."

"I can put *my* name on it."

"Be reasonable, Edith. How in the world could you take care of a baby? Besides, if you took her home, I'd have to look at her every day. I couldn't stand that. I couldn't stand seeing her, reminding me of . . ."

"Of what? Reminding you of what?"

"My shame, sweetheart. You know what the church teaches about having babies out of wedlock."

"I don't care what they teach. You don't either, or you wouldn't have tried to get rid of her. It's bad enough you took some herbs and lost one of them in the outhouse that day. But now you're giving the other one away."

Edith wiped tears off her face, a plan forming in her head. "You don't want this baby, but I do. I'll find her and take her home with me. I'll be her mama. You just watch me."

Edith fled to her bedroom, dressed, grabbed her suitcase and stalked out the door without saying a word to her stupid jerk sister.

Marie begged her to not breathe a word to Mama.

Ha. Fat chance.

* * *

A nurse came into Edith's hospital room carrying another pint of blood. She exchanged it with the empty bag hanging on a rack beside the bed.

"Can't sleep, huh? Feeling any better?" She straightened the sheets and fluffed Edith's pillow.

"Bad dream," Edith said.

"Want me to give you something to help you get to sleep?"

"No, I'll be fine. Some things a person just needs to think about."

"Call if you need anything," the nurse said and left.

The quietness of the night returned. So did the memories.

* * *

By the time Edith got home from visiting Marie and Blind Aunt Gertie in Hartburg, she'd made a plan. She walked straight into the kitchen and over to Mama, who stood at the cabinet, a bib apron tied around her thick middle and her plump hands in a dishpan full of dirty dishes.

"Mama, Marie just had a baby," Edith said, choking on a voice full of tears. "And she's given it away, and I don't know where they took her."

Mama turned around and stared at Edith, disbelief in her eyes.

"Edith, go wash your mouth out with soap. Your sister's a good girl. She did no such thing."

"It's true, Mama. I wouldn't lie about something like that. I was there. I seen it be born with my own eyes. Poor little thing came out feet first."

"Then who's the daddy? Tell me that, young lady."

"Sol, of course. But he's not going to marry her cause he's still in love with Irene Meade. Now Irene's gone off and married some other guy, so there's no way she's going back to Sol."

Mama plopped in the kitchen chair, her eyes filling with tears.

"I never thought I'd live to see the day one of my daughters would have a baby out of wedlock—especially Marie."

"That's cause she tries too hard to be perfect, Mama."

"But the good Lord tells us to. When I get on my knees by my bed every night, I ask the Him to baptize my daughters with the Holy Spirit."

"Just the daughters, huh? Sounds like you've given up on Ivan and Robert."

Mama didn't reply. She stared off in the distance. Then, she roused. "Edith, if what you say is true, we need to go find that baby and bring it home. We can't let strangers raise one of our own. It's just not right."

"That's what I told her, but she wouldn't listen. Said you were too old to start raising another kid. I told her I'd help, but they took the baby while I slept."

"So it's a little girl?"

"Yes, it's a beautiful little girl."

Mama clasped her hands under her chin and closed her eyes. Her lips moved like they always did when she prayed. After a few minutes, she opened her eyes. "Somehow or the other, we've got to find that baby and bring her home where she belongs. Promise me, Edith."

She promised. And she knew how her boyfriend Clayton had been begging her to get married. If they did, when she found Marie's baby, maybe they would let her take her home if she could show them a copy of her marriage license.

It didn't take long for Edith to convince Clayton to marry her. He didn't have a job so he moved in with Mama and Papa, too. Then, Edith got busy. Focused on nothing else, obsessed, her days were spent investigating every orphan home in the area between Orange and Hartburg, to no avail.

Marie certainly hadn't made it easy for Edith to find the baby.

As much as she bugged old bald-headed Dr. Mosquito, he wouldn't reveal anything about the identity of the woman who had taken the tiny infant. Months passed without any progress. After exhausting every place she could think of, she went back to Hartburg. She went to the doctor's house, next door to Blind Aunt Gertie, and pounded on the door. There was no response.

Finally, his wife came around the house from the backyard, a hoe in her hands.

"I need to talk to the doctor again," Edith explained. "I'm still looking for my sister's baby. And I'm not going to stop until he tells me where they took her."

"I'm sorry, child," Mrs. Mosquito said. "The doctor passed a couple of months ago." She shoved wiry gray hair off her face with the back of her hand.

"Oh, no, he can't have. Not without telling me where they took the baby." Edith collapsed on the steps in tears.

"I've got to find her, ma'am. I've got to. Please, if you know anything about it, please tell me."

"You're the girl with the young woman who delivered that footling breach, aren't you?"

"Yes, that was my sister, Marie." Something in the woman' voice built hope in Edith's chest. At last she had found someone willing to talk to her.

The woman gave a heavy sigh, and then eased her stiff body down to the steps. Edith pounced beside her like a cat after her prey. When Mrs. Mosquito scooted closer and wrapped her arm around Edith, the smell of dirt and lavender filled Edith's nostrils.

"To tell you the truth, child, I've always felt bad about my husband helping give away that little girl," she said. "He told me how much you wanted to keep her. I figured someone else in your family would have helped you raise her."

"I begged her not to get rid of our baby, but she did anyway. Yeah, I knew Mama would help me raise her."

Edith stuck out her hand. "See my wedding band? That shows

I'm old enough to get married and old enough to raise a baby." Never mind that Clayton had joined the Army a month after they got married and had been gone ever since.

"My husband will likely turn over in his grave for me telling you this," the doctor's wife said. "But he's dead now. He can't hurt me—that is unless his ghost comes to haunt my nights. I can deal with a ghost better than I can stand to see you hurt like this, child.

"But before I tell you where to look, there's something else you must know. The night my husband came home from delivering that baby, he sat in the kitchen drinking coffee and puzzling over what he'd seen."

"You mean because the baby came feet first? I'll never forget that either."

"No, not that. He'd delivered footling breeches before. No, it was the afterbirth he puzzled over. He described the remains of another protective membrane, attached to the side of it. He said he'd swear your sister started out pregnant with two babies. And somewhere down the line, she'd lost one of them."

The image of Marie in the outhouse checking her step-ins to make sure she'd lost the baby flashed through Edith's memory.

"Now, young lady, if you still want to find that baby, you might check the orphanage in Baton Rouge, Louisiana. That's where they took her. With what's going on in this world, I doubt anyone has adopted that poor little thing."

Edith jumped up, kissed the woman on the cheek and ran down the road full of excitement.

Early the next morning, she boarded the train to Louisiana.

Chapter 38

A pudgy, middle-aged nurse held a whimpering baby wrapped in a threadbare blanket.

"All I do is hold this baby night and day, day and night," the nurse explained to Edith, who stood holding a suitcase full of baby clothes gathered from friends and neighbors. She'd told them Mama was adopting a baby and needed any of their children's outgrown blankets and clothing.

"It's like she's missing something," the nurse said.

"Maybe she's missing her mama," Edith offered.

"Maybe, but it don't seem like that's quite it. One night, I was desperate to get her to sleep. I'd tried for hours and nothing worked. This other baby in the crib next to her, he can't sleep neither, so I put him in the crib beside her. He goes sound to sleep, but she keeps crying."

The baby fussed now, and with great tenderness, the nurse held her tighter, as if her own body might supply whatever the baby missed from her life. "The crying continued. Not a wail, but a soft, painful whimpering that rammed a stake in my heart. I've never felt so helpless with a baby."

She shushed the baby now, cooing and trying to comfort. "Then one night, we had a newborn baby girl dropped off at the doorstep, crying to beat sixty. I scooped her up and put her right next to this little gal here, to help warm her, help her feel better. I'll be dang, this one's whimpering changed into a soft sound, almost like the purr of a contented kitten put next to its mama or sibling. Then she fell sound asleep and stayed that way till morning."

Young Edith's arms itched like mad, eager to hold her baby. She held out her arms. "May I hold her?"

With great care, the nurse transferred the baby into Edith's open arms.

Edith reached inside the blanket and ran her fingertips softly over the baby's smooth little arms and perfect, tiny fingers, then across her plump belly. She felt something hard and nudged the blanket aside. Attached to the baby's diaper, she saw Marie's heart-shaped pin.

The nurse smiled and said, "It came pinned to her blanket. I always felt like someone would come for her and figured the pin might help with identification."

"It was my sister's brooch." Edith fingered the pin, tracing the red-colored glass set in the middle. "After she tired of it, she gave it to me. The night the baby was born, I pinned it on her blanket. I'm thrilled my sister left it pinned to the baby when she gave her away."

"I'm glad you've come to get her. That's where she belongs—with her family. I've cared for many a baby before, lots of them twins separated at birth, which leads me to believe this baby may be a twin. You know anything about that?"

Edith stared at the nurse, lost in the day she and Marie sat in the outhouse cleaning up Marie's blood. She told the story to the nurse.

"That sure would explain all this loneliness the baby seems to feel, especially at night," the nurse said, gathering the baby's few meager belongings.

Edith thanked the nurse, promising she'd take good care of the infant, then held the baby close to her heart and walked down the wide steps of the orphanage. She took the next train back to Orange, arriving late that afternoon.

When she walked up the front steps, Mama saw her coming and met them at the door.

"You found her?"

Edith didn't have to answer, the grin on her face told the story.

"Praise be to God." Mama clapped her hands and danced a little jig. Arms outstretched, she reached for the sleeping baby.

Edith eased her into Mama's arms.

"What's her name?" Mama asked, caressing the baby.

"Beatrice. Bea, for short."

"Voyager," Mama said, softness in her voice. "Beatrice means voyager. That fits what this baby's been through. I figure she's not done voyaging yet, though. I'm an old woman, Edith. I don't know how we're going to raise this precious thing, but we're sure going to do the best we can and depend on the good Lord to do the rest."

She fingered the baby's plump hand. "We'll tell people I adopted her, but I'll need your help to take care of her, get her to school, that sort of thing. How's that?"

They made a deal, a deal Edith never backed away from. Her love and care of Bea so consumed her, she'd hovered and pampered over her until the day little Bea, grown up now, married Hal.

All through the years, Edith held the memories of those first months in her heart, suspecting they held the secret of Bea's unshakable nighttime sadness. Though she never knew it consciously, it seemed as if the darkness reminded Bea of being inside Marie's womb, a womb she'd shared with an equally tiny sister, until the day of Marie's miscarriage.

Edith swore to Mama and Marie both that she'd never reveal the truth of Bea's birth to her for fear she wouldn't feel wanted. Yet all those nights when Bea lay in bed and cried, Edith suspected why. The mind really could play crazy tricks on a person.

And deep inside, Edith knew the day approached when Bea must learn the truth of those times. Surely Bea deserved to know, to find relief from the loneliness she carried with her since the loss of her twin in the womb, and her own survival and birth. She shouldn't have to suffer with that mystery until she died, went to heaven, and God told her.

Chapter 39

When Edith woke the next morning and saw Bea standing near her hospital bed, she wondered if they'd both died and it was Judgment Day. If so, she just might be in trouble. As loose as she'd lived, the good Lord might not do her any favors.

"Feeling better, sis?" Bea leaned over and kissed the top of her head. "You scared the daylights out of us last night."

"Hi, Toots. I bet I did. Sorry."

"You look like you were in deep thought. What's going on?"

"I had a nightmare last night. It still seems as real as when it happened."

"Want to talk about it? Maybe it will help get it off your mind."

"I don't feel like talking that much right now. We'll talk later . . ." Edith patted her sister's hand, and then paused, staring into her eyes. No, she'd lied long enough about all this, and the secrecy had to stop. First, she must be honest with herself. Once she'd done that, maybe she could be honest with her niece.

Edith rallied. "What happened last night? All I remember is going to bed at your house and waking up here. The nurse said some tall, good-looking man brought me and stayed until they ran him out after visiting hours. Who was that?"

"It was Daniel Baxter. He and Oskar found you unconscious on my bed, bleeding to death. You were fortunate that Daniel got you here so fast. I could have lost you, sweetheart." She squeezed Edith's hand.

The booming voice of the doctor sounded from the doorway. Both women turned and watched the bald-headed man come into the room, hands shoved down inside the pockets of a white lab coat.

"We had a close call with you, young lady. It's a little early to know for sure, but I think you should still be able to have more children." He put his hand on Edith's wrist and checked her pulse. "Of course, we'll just have to wait and see. I am discharging you this morning, but I want to see you in my office next week. Okay?"

With instructions to rest, the doctor bade them farewell and walked out.

"You know what? I've been lying here kind of wishing I hadn't lost the baby. Maybe having one would be good for me. Just think, we could have raised our babies together."

Bea smiled. "I'll let you in on a little secret, Daniel is sweet on you."

Edith jerked her hand out of Bea's. "He is not. Why do you say that?"

"He's been worried sick about you."

An energetic-looking nurse bustled in and removed the empty transfusion bag still hooked to Edith's arm. Another nurse came in with discharge papers for Edith to sign.

On the drive home, Bea shared with Edith the events from the night before. They were both excited that Oskar had found his brother and were anxious to hear what the consequences for Wilhelm would be.

When they walked in the front door, Oskar wasn't there, but Nelda and Percy were in the kitchen. Nelda shoveled oatmeal down Percy's throat as fast as he demanded. When he saw Bea, he broke into a huge smile despite the mouthful of mush.

"Good morning, sweetheart," she said to Percy, kissing him on his sticky cheek. "Mama's home." The deep sense of responsibility she carried on her shoulders had found a new partner—the realization of how much she loved the little tyke sitting in the high chair in front of her.

Bea helped Edith ease into a chair. "Sit here, honey, and I'll get you a cup of coffee."

Edith looked up and smiled. "Can you make mine milk?"

"Milk, it is."

Percy kept up his constant babble between bites. "What a happy little guy you are this morning," Bea said. "I've missed you something awful."

She handed Edith a glass of milk and took a chair beside Percy. "Did Oskar leave when you got here?"

"Yeah," Nelda said. "He said he wouldn't be gone long. Are you going to be okay, Edith? I heard you all had quite a scare here last night."

"I'm a tough bird," Edith said, sipping her milk.

"You certain you don't need me today? I don't mind staying." Nelda fed another spoonful of food into Percy.

"Bless your heart, no, we'll do fine," Bea said. "Soon as Percy goes to sleep, Edith and I will take a nap. I notified work I wouldn't be in until tomorrow. Just come in the morning at the regular time."

After Nelda went home, Edith and Bea kept an eye out for the first signs of Percy getting sleepy.

A couple of hours later, and without a single sign of weakening, Percy played on his pallet while Bea and Edith lounged on the couch chatting about what life would have been like raising children together. After a while, Edith was the first one to doze off.

Bea heard Oskar come in. She motioned him to be quiet and slipped outside with him. "Let's sit out here on the back steps."

"I can't stay long." He smiled at her. "How's Edith? She going to be okay?"

"I think so."

"Daniel ordered me to check on her, and if I didn't, his offer to speak up for Wilhelm was off the table."

"Sounds like he likes her."

"I think so. But that's not why I came this morning. I came to tell you it looks like everything is going to work out okay for my brother. Daniel talked with the judge, who agreed Wilhelm would be of as much service to our country working here at the shipyard, and Daniel's speaking up for him with some of the foremen looking to hire more workers."

"They're not going to send Wilhelm to jail?"

"Well, it depends on whether he can keep himself out of trouble. One more incident and he'll serve time, I'm sure. I think the worst is over, though. He's smitten with this young woman named Sonia. I got to meet her this morning. She and Lady Silvania came in to talk to Daniel. Lady Silvania even gave Daniel a free palm reading. Said he'd soon be married himself, and said they'd roast a couple of pigs in celebration."

"No kidding." Bea laughed at the image of Daniel dancing to the music of a fiddle. "That's great news."

Oskar took her hand and held it gently in his own. "I do believe I love you, Bea Meade."

She looked at him, dumbfounded. What did she say? For one thing, she still had to file for a divorce from Hal. His parents were begging her to give him a second chance. After all, she and Hal did have Percy to think about, they said.

But the thought of staying with Hal made her sick to her stomach. Guess she couldn't ask for a better sign than that. They just didn't fit together. He wanted someone different than the person she'd become. She could no longer be the kind of wife he wanted. She'd tried, God, she'd tried, and it nearly killed her.

"I can't say yes to you right now," she said, running her finger down Oskar's chest. "It's just too soon. Can we talk about it later, when the war is over and things have settled down?"

"We can and will. We can take our time, see how this all goes. I just want you to know I care for you and will make you a good husband."

"You won't ask me to quit my job?" She flashed him a mischievous smile.

"I will not. And one more thing I have not told you. I love to do laundry."

Bea laughed. "Now you're really tempting me. But I can't make any commitment right now."

"I understand. I have to settle things with my citizenship, too. But I'll be around. Okay?"

"Okay." She smiled as she stood. "I better check on Edith."

"Don't fail to give her the message from Daniel."

"I won't. She needs that right now."

Oskar reached for her as they stood. He pressed his open lips on hers, making her body respond in ways no man ever had. It was the first time she'd experienced this feeling.

It wouldn't be her last.

Chapter 40

Edith watched through the window as Oskar walked off. She waited with baited breath, eager for Bea to come inside so she could ask what the two talked about.

Out on the back steps, Bea sat with her eyes closed, savoring the moment. But then Masil walked up. Seeing Bea with her eyes closed, she tiptoed up quietly, then tapped her on the shoulder, surprising her.

"Masil! You scared me half to death. Where've you been?"

Edith shifted over to the screen door, listening.

"Did they tell you I'm pregnant? I asked them not to, but—"

"You're pregnant? Oh, Masil . . ." Bea gave her friend a big hug, then leaned back, her hands still on Masil's shoulders. "I'm so happy for you. I guess Ernie's excited, too? It seems like forever since we've talked. Come on in and let's catch up."

Edith stepped over to the side table and made busy work straightening a lampshade. But when Bea and Masil walked in, Edith blurted out, "I'm dying to know what Oskar said. I tried to listen, but you talked so soft. . . . Did he mention marriage?"

Bea smiled. "Yes, Oskar hinted at that. He told me he loved me."

"Oh, good Lord, Bea. He's the nicest guy I ever met. You said yes, didn't you?"

"I told him no."

"You what?" Edith and Masil cried out in unison.

"I'm still married to Hal, you two know that. What am I supposed to do, become a bigamist?"

"As if Hal's waiting for you to let him move back in," Masil said.

"I saw him walking down the street the other night, a woman on each arm."

"What? Well, regardless, I can't get married until he and I are divorced. Besides, I refuse to marry anyone until I stop this infernal crying at night. *I* don't even want to sleep with me."

Bea chuckled when she said it, but Edith knew it wasn't funny.

"Well, did you at least leave the door open with Oskar?" Masil asked, butting in.

"I told him I wasn't ready for marriage yet. That I still had work to do before I committed to anyone again. That I'd messed up one marriage, and before I got into another, I wanted to give it a flying chance."

"Okay, good, you didn't give an outright no."

"But, that's just it. I don't know if I'll ever be ready . . . if I can't figure out whether I'm crazy or not. At night when I go to bed, unless I go to sleep right away, this heaviness creeps in and I start to cry. I know part of it is I'm tired doing what everyone else thinks I should, but it's more than that."

Percy let out a yell and Bea started toward the bedroom, but Masil stopped her.

"Here, let me."

Masil went and fetched Percy and brought him back to the kitchen. After the three women fussed over him and Bea gave him a bottle, Masil offered to take him home with her for a while. Bea agreed, knowing Masil was so excited about the idea of having a baby herself soon.

Outside, it was looking like a wonderful cool day in Orange. Birds were singing and a soft breeze passed lightly through the neighborhood. There was no sign that a war was going on anywhere in the world. Bea stood at the back door for a while, looking out, saying nothing.

Relieved, Edith was happy that Masil had taken off and the two of them were alone. The confession she owed Bea would be hard enough, without another person in the same room, listening.

"Come, sit beside me, Bea." Edith patted the sofa next to her.

When Bea did, Edith cleared her throat, then plunged ahead. It just couldn't wait any longer.

"Toots, I've dreaded this day forever. We should've told you the truth all along—*I* should've told you, regardless of what other people said. I don't know if knowing that truth will help or hurt . . . but I owe it to you to let you find out."

"You're scaring me," Bea said. "I don't have any idea what you're talking about."

On the edge of speaking, Edith stalled, "Give me a minute, let me check my bleeding. I'll be right back."

"Dammit, don't leave me hanging," Bea cried, but to no avail. Edith patted Bea's hand and took off to the bathroom.

"Hardly any blood at all," she said when she returned a couple of minutes later.

* * *

Bea held her breath, as Edith sat down again. Bea wasn't sure why, but was afraid that if she breathed, the world hanging by a thread might fall and shatter into a million pieces.

Edith sat beside her, took one of Bea's fists in her own hands and caressed it.

"Okay, here it is, Toots. I don't know why you cry at night, but I do know you do have something to cry about. That is, if you knew what I know. Maybe deep down you do."

"What do you mean?" Bea stiffened her back.

"I've always told you the truth about things, but—"

"I know you have."

"But I haven't told you everything. I don't know if withholding the truth carries the same sin as lying. I hope it doesn't." Edith's voice quivered.

"I can't believe you've kept a secret from me. Why?"

"It goes to a promise I made many years ago."

"You're not making sense, Edith." A knot formed in Bea's

stomach.

Edith cleared her throat. "It has to do with your mother."

"Mama?"

"No, not Mama. Your mother," Edith continued. "Mama never wanted you to know this. To her, she was your mother. Hell, most of the time, I felt like your mother, too."

"What do you mean? Mama was. She always called me her change-of-life baby."

Edith looked Bea in the eye. "Sorry, Toots."

Bea jerked her hands away.

"No, stay with me, sweetheart."

By the look on Edith's face, Bea knew truth sped her way, ready or not. Who would she be by the end of the telling?

She crammed her fingers in her ears. "I don't want to hear it," she cried. Resistance thickened around her, encased her in a bubble of protection.

"You must listen, Toots. I've finally gotten the courage to tell you what you should have known all along. If I don't say it now, I may never get the guts again. You'll never find peace until you know the whole story."

Bea wished she could stay ignorant, could go around the pain that awaited her. She didn't want to sit quietly and listen. She wanted to scream, run, hit something—anything, including her sister. She didn't want to know what left her so scarred, so lonely, so grief-stricken.

Bea walked over to Percy's pallet, picked it up, folded the quilt and put it in the corner.

Then, she crossed the room and sat by Edith again. She was ready now, for the first wrinkle of truth to ease through the cracks of her soul. She sat up straight, cleared her throat and said, "Tell me."

"Well, it happened when I was just a kid. And, of course, Marie was a couple of years older. Marie talked Papa into letting her go out to Hartburg and stay with his great aunt who still lived alone."

"That must have been Blind Aunt Gertie. I remember Papa talking about her," Bea said.

"That's right, Blind Aunt Gertie. Anyway, I had this boyfriend, Clayton. We were madly in love and planned to get married someday. We did, but after he got out of the Army, this horse he tried to break, broke his neck first. You never met him, you were too young."

Bea tightened her grip on Edith's hands.

"It's okay. It happened a long time ago. Anyway, when he and I were dating, we went downtown to Farmers Mercantile one day to pick up a saddle. While I waited in his beat-up old jalopy, one of Marie's former boyfriends came up and asked me about her. I said she was fine as far as I knew and why did he ask." Edith paused, then continued.

"He leaned over, put his head close to mine and whispered he knew she was having a baby. I swore to him Marie wouldn't do any such thing."

Edith chuckled and said, "I remember I stuck my tongue out at him. He laughed at me, but I knew Marie wouldn't do any such thing. She was the good girl. I'd heard Sol call her frigid one time. I thought that had something to do with making babies, but I wasn't sure."

"I'd be frigid too if I was with Sol," Bea laughed. Not a funny laugh, but one that revealed a deep dislike of her brother-in-law.

"But then I remembered. A few months earlier, I'd been in the outhouse one day when Marie banged on the door. Blood ran down her legs," Edith continued. "She wouldn't explain what happened—called me too young to know."

Edith took a long breath, like the worse was still to come. Bea shuddered.

Edith squirmed in her seat. "You know that brooch you've asked me about?"

"Yeah."

"It belonged to Marie first. But she gave it to me because I begged her for it."

"So you're the one who gave it to me?"

"No, not exactly. Marie gave it to you."

"Marie? When? I thought you said she'd given it to you. When did I get it?"

"You had it on you when I rescued you from an orphanage in Baton Rouge, Louisiana."

"An orphanage?" Bea's world lost its color and swirled into a huge gray mass. "No, stop, I can't handle any more of this."

She ran to the bathroom and slammed the door shut.

In a minute, she heard Edith on the other side.

"Okay, honey, that's enough for now," Edith said. "Marie needs to tell you the rest of the story. I'll stay with Percy for a couple of days. Take the bus down and see her. If it were me, I'd go unannounced."

Chapter 41

After Bea heard the front door close, she fled to her bedroom. She flipped the cigar box lid open and, as reverent as Mama in church, lifted out the heart-shaped mother-of-pearl pin and rested it in the palm of her hand. So often at night, she had held that pin in her hands until the clasp pricked her skin.

Tears ran down her cheeks, for the sacredness of the simple piece of jewelry touched a part of her she hadn't known before. Connecting her to a past she never knew.

Mama wasn't her mother. Then was Marie? Was Bea the baby she'd carried when her oldest sister—or maybe her mother—had gone to Blind Aunt Gertie's? If so, why didn't Marie want her?

Oh, Lord, she hoped Sol wasn't her father.

She remembered hearing Mama on her knees by her bed at night, begging God to forgive Marie for living in sin. For years, Bea thought living in sin and living with Sol was the same thing. Anyway, she had guessed God had forgiven Marie when, right after Bea's fifth birthday, Marie and Sol got the Pentecostal preacher to come over and marry them in the middle of Mama and Papa's living room.

Mama, so thankful her daughter was no longer a fallen woman, extolled the Lord for three days. She walked through the house singing *Praise God from Whom All Blessings Flow*. Bea never understood why God hadn't seen fit to *bless* them before then. It would have saved Mama a lot of prayers.

Marie went to Blind Gertie's and Edith had said she followed a few months later. But was Marie her mother? If so, when did Edith rescue Bea from the orphanage?

Edith had been the one always there for her. She walked Bea to school every day and met her outside the building in the afternoons to walk her home. She made sure Bea got a bath at least once a week and brushed her hair a hundred strokes every night. At night, when Bea cried, Edith held her in her arms until she fell asleep.

That still didn't explain the heavy loneliness. She'd had plenty of love—from Mama and Edith. Then why did she not know how to receive it, how to fill the void left behind by . . . something. What?

* * *

She sat on the bus to Galveston, watching the scenery fly by. She'd gotten the okay from Tony at the shipyard to take off a couple of days, although he wasn't happy about it.

Arriving in Galveston, she caught a taxi and went straight to the address given her by Edith. Butterflies churned her stomach. She'd never been to Marie's house, so when the taxi stopped in front of a fancy house on the beach, Bea told the driver he'd taken her to the wrong address. He assured her he hadn't, so she paid the fare, still a little dubious, and got out, small suitcase in hand.

She stood staring at the house, not taking a step toward the front door until the cabbie drove away. Waves lapped against the shore. The pungent smell of salt water and fish hung heavy in the humid air. Sea grapes lined the road, a seagull flew overhead.

Her pace hesitant, halting, Bea walked up what seemed like a half-mile-long sidewalk. She caught her breath and knocked on the front door, praying Sol wouldn't answer.

He did.

"What do you want?"

He was taller than she remembered. In his day, he must not have looked too bad. He still maintained a thick head of white hair combed back in a pompadour, but carried an air that suggested an over-inflated opinion of himself. Perhaps it was the way he lifted his nose while looking down at her.

"I've come to talk to Marie. My real mother."

He started to close the door in her face, but Marie came up

behind him. "No, Sol, let her in. It's time."

He turned and stalked to the back of the house, letting off a string of curse words as long as the sidewalk out front.

"I swear, I don't know what his problem is," Marie said, smiling at Bea as if they both knew she didn't care.

Perfectly groomed, every hair on her hennaed-head in place, a martini in her hand and a stagger in her step, Marie took Bea's arm. They went into a formal living room furnished with an elegant snow-white sofa and matching red velvet chairs. A round, marble-top coffee table fit between the three pieces. Original oil paintings hung on the walls.

Bea realized her mouth had dropped open as she stared. She closed it and perched on the edge of the sofa, wondering how anyone could be comfortable living in what looked to be a museum.

"I knew this day would come someday," Marie said, slurring her words. Bea wondered how many drinks Marie had consumed so early in the day.

"You're here for answers, I guess." Marie straightened a rich-looking maroon skirt over her knees. "Before we even start, though, I want you to know I've always felt terrible about what I did to you."

Not expecting such an open response, Bea had steeled herself for this moment. She'd figured she'd have to fight her way in and then confront Marie. This reception took the wind out of her sails. Bea wasn't sure what to say.

"Edith made me think you're . . . my mother. That you gave me up because . . . Sol—or I guess I should say, my father—wouldn't marry you if you had a baby.

Marie bowed her head. When she looked up, tears streamed down her cheeks.

Bea squeezed her heart shut. She didn't know this woman. She wasn't about to let Marie's tears keep her from getting what she came after—the truth. For the first time in her life, she felt like it was okay to put herself first.

"Yes, Bea, Sol is your father," Marie said at last. "I should have told you many years ago, but he wouldn't let me." She stopped, shook her head and continued. "No, I'm not going to put the blame on him. I could have gone against what he wanted—but I didn't. I needed a man to take care of me, or so I thought."

From the corner of her eye, Bea noticed Sol had returned and stood outside the doorway, listening. When he heard that from Marie, he headed to the kitchen. The back door slammed behind him. Bea hoped it hit him in the butt.

"You see," Marie said, tears choking her voice. "Being pregnant and unmarried was much more a shame then than it is today. It still is—for the woman, that is. Not as much for the man involved.

"I loved you, I really did. And that's why I've stayed away from Orange all these years. It hurt too much to see you and to know my younger sister had more guts than I did. That she had gone to get you and bring you home. But what no one knows but me is . . ."

What? Bea wondered. *Is there something that explains this unquenchable loneliness I carry in my heart?*

Bea held out her hand she'd kept rolled in a fist. Slowly, she opened her fingers to reveal the mother-of-pearl brooch. "Where did this come from?"

"It belonged to me, but when Edith was little, she begged me for it. I finally grew so weary of the whole thing, I gave it to her. She wore it constantly. She called it her 'sister' pin. Then, the night you were born, Edith took it off of her blouse and pinned it on your blanket. I left it there the next day when . . . when I handed you over to the doctor. It was my way of letting you know . . . you had a sister."

"That makes no sense. I already thought I had two sisters, but the fact is, I've never had a single one."

"You did."

"No, I don't. One is my aunt, and the other is my mother."

"I'm not talking about Edith or me. I'm talking about your dead sister."

"My what?" Bea sank back on the sofa.

"When I learned I was pregnant, I told Sol. I was delighted that now he'd marry me. But he refused."

Marie's eyes grew moist. "Women know what to take when they need to end a pregnancy, Bea. We've known what to do since the beginning of time. It's the only way we have to control our own body. Women do what they must."

An image of Violet, and what happened to her, came to Bea's mind. What choice did she have about Johnny and what he did to her? Other than to try to trick Hal? Unable to live with the shame, she'd chosen death over a life soon to grow even more miserable.

Then she remembered Edith sitting on the toilet bleeding. Had she'd taken something to rid herself of an unwanted pregnancy?

Marie's words jerked her to the present. "This big gush of blood came running down my legs. I ran to the outhouse and, sure enough, when I pulled off my under drawers, I saw the bloody clot in them."

"I thought you were pregnant with me. You didn't lose me. I'm not dead."

"You're right. The baby I lost wasn't you, it was your sister."

"How could you tell it was a girl?"

"I couldn't, really, I just always felt like it was. But at that time, I didn't know I had been carrying twins. Not until a couple of months after the miscarriage when my stomach kept growing. I learned that sometimes a woman's body can lose one and carry the other one to full term. That's what happened to me."

"So I was a twin? You tried to end the pregnancy, but only lost my sister and not me?"

Bea sat in the chair, her mouth hanging open. "Did you name the other baby—my twin sister?

"I called her . . ." Marie's voice broke. "Sally."

"*Sally?* When I was little . . . I had . . . an invisible friend that I called Sally."

Bea sat in silence and let the whole story sink in.

As she did, she felt something move in and fill the void inside her.

She managed a tiny smile. "So . . . that's why I've cried at night.

Deep inside, I've been grieving the loss of my sister. Like a part of me had been cut out and left bleeding, and no one ever talked about it. I've grieved the other half of me. I knew something was missing, but I never knew what. All these years, I've felt I had to steel my emotions to maintain any sense of control over my life."

"I know words can't make up for all the pain you've been through, Bea, but I am so sorry I gave you away. I wished a thousand times I'd kept you, and said to hell with Sol, but I'm not strong enough."

"I'm learning we're stronger than we think we are." Just saying the words gave Bea a new sense of strength. "But what does all this have to do with you never having anything to do with the family? Acting like you were better than all of us."

"Shame. And I felt I had to hide my mistakes, else someone think ill of me—or lose Sol."

Bea stood. Marie did too.

At first they just looked at each other, both unsure what to do next.

Bea realized she was mad, and that her fists were clenched. "I want to hate you, Marie, for what you put me through."

"And you have every right to do so."

Marie looked at the floor, her shoulders slumped, without defense, as if she'd waited years for this.

"I didn't know what to expect when I came here, but I didn't expect this." Bea wasn't ready to let go of what she was feeling, and she didn't want to keep it inside.

"I did guess I'd find out something terrible, and that I'd hate you by the time I left. And I don't know if I ever want to see you again."

Bea's fists unclenched and her fingers tingled from the pressure of the grip. Her palms itched. She needed to hit a wall.

Chapter 42

Bea stormed out of Marie's house. Suitcase in hand, she took off down the road to find a place to sleep before night set in. No way was she prepared to go home yet. She needed time to think, sort out what she'd heard and how she felt—about everything.

She walked two or three miles before she reached a main street and another mile before a sign *Room to Let* caught her attention. A small bulldog stood in the front yard, his leg hiked, peeing on the sign. An old man with a big, broad brimmed straw hat hoed a flower garden around a wide wraparound porch.

"Sir," she asked, and stepped across lush green grass. "May I inquire about your room? Is it still available?"

He looked up, squinting against the glare of a setting sun. "Yes ma'am, it is, by the night or by the week."

"Hopefully, for just one night, I need to get home tomorrow."

"If you don't mind my asking, where is that?"

"I live in Orange."

"Then you, or your husband, work at the shipyard. My son went up there last year and got a job right away. Come on in. I'll show you the room and you can decide."

Bea had never traveled out of town by herself before, much less rented a room. She marveled that she did it now. If Mama were still alive, what in the world would she say about this new, bold Bea?

Oh, my God. Her mama *was* alive. She'd just met her.

"Here's the room, miss. The rate sheet is there on the table. Check it out and let me know. If I don't hear from you in a few minutes, I'll figure you decided to rent it for the night. I don't like to bother folks so I'll be on my way." The man turned and hobbled out.

"Rent's due in the morning, on check out," he said with a wave over his shoulder.

Bea turned and took in the small, adequate bedroom. A white chenille bedspread covered the bed. Chintz curtains hung from a window overlooking the backyard.

In the corner of the room, a small rocking chair invited her over. Weary, she dropped her bag on the floor and slid into the chair.

Mama. She felt disloyal calling anyone that except the woman who raised her.

Perhaps she'd get used to the idea of Marie being her mother. Then again, maybe she wouldn't. Right now, Bea carried not one bit of respect for the woman. But when she got right down to it, except for the alcohol, what difference was there between them? The woman who gave birth to Bea had no backbone. She'd given up everything for a man who never loved her. She even gave up her daughter for that man—gave up two daughters.

As a result, Marie spent her life numbing herself with booze so she could live with the price she'd paid.

How close had Bea come to doing something similar? Not give up Percy, she'd never do that, but the sacrifices she'd made for Hal were innumerable. The biggest sacrifice was that she hadn't learned who she was or what she stood for. No longer would she allow herself to be vulnerable, dependant on a man. She wouldn't sit and wait for a man to bring home money to pay the rent. No more feeling ashamed for the loneliness she had carried for so many years, or other people telling her what to think or do.

A mockingbird outside the open window sang a song, the notes pure and clear in the late afternoon air. She felt just as free at that bird, as light-hearted. She was a survivor who, from this day forward, thrived on her own—whether she ever married again or not.

The sun set, but the sky still held onto a red-orange afterglow when a quick knock sounded. Bea found a tray of sandwiches and a glass of milk on the table outside her door. Egg salad never tasted so good. She wondered who made the wonderful mayonnaise as she swallowed the last bite of sandwich and drained the final drop of milk.

After a short stroll, she crawled between crisp white sheets, turned out the lamp on the bedside table, and slept— a sweet, undisturbed night of sound, peaceful sleep.

The next morning, she awoke with the same mockingbird on her window sill, singing its little head off.

"Good morning to you, too," she said, smiling and stretching. "It is indeed a glorious day. And today I know who I am."

She went to the bathroom down the hall and took a few minutes to freshen up. The old man had left a bowl of fresh fruit and warm biscuits for her on the kitchen table, along with a note saying he'd gone to town and would she please leave her payment on the dresser in her room.

* * *

The three-mile walk back to Marie's house went much faster than it had yesterday. When she rang the doorbell, she hadn't even broken a sweat, but her heart felt like she'd been in a foot race.

Marie opened the door. Her red-rimmed eyes revealed her night hadn't been as peaceful as Bea's.

"Where is Sol?" Bea asked, looking around her into the house.

"He's out back."

"Good, we need to talk. You may not want to hear what I have to say, but I'm going to say it anyway. So I hope you'll hear me out."

"Come in. Let's sit by the kitchen window so I can keep an eye out for Sol. That way, he can't sneak in on us and listen."

"That's terrible, Marie. How do you stand it?"

"You get used to it, honey. Now, tell me, how are you handling all this?"

"I've just had the best night's sleep I've had in a lifetime."

"Really? I didn't sleep a wink for thinking about you."

"Tell me something, Marie."

"Anything."

"Why have you stayed with Sol all these years? He treats you awful."

A look crossed Marie's face that Bea didn't understand. "Oh, Bea, you know how I was raised. Mama taught you the same thing. Good girls find a boy, marry them, and that's it. A wife's there to take care of the husband. He's the king of his castle. You've made your bed, you lie in it."

Marie paused, took a deep breath and blew it out before she spoke again. "You sacrifice who you are just as though you'd been nailed to that blamed cross Mama always talked about."

"Oh, my God, Marie, that's exactly what I did. I don't know how many times I told Hal I'd live *anywhere*, as long as he was happy. Hoping if he was, he'd be there for me. The other day it hit me. What about my happiness?"

"Sounds familiar." Marie stared off in the distance, but when she spoke, Bea knew Marie tapped into the deepest, darkest crevice of her soul.

"You want to know why I drink so much? Because I hate the beach, I hate sand, wind, fishy smells. I never wanted to move here in the first place, but Sol did. So," Marie held her palms toward the ceiling, "here we are."

"I've got an idea, Marie. Come home with me."

Marie shook her head. "Sol would never let me go."

"I'm not talking about Sol *letting* you do anything."

Marie was silent.

"Marie, do you know how good it feels to be a woman who survives and thrives on her own? I'm doing it, and it feels great. I've got a job I'm good at. I've got a precious baby, Percy—your grandson—and even a man interested in me who just might work out. But if he doesn't, my life will still be full. Come stay with us until you get on your feet."

Unknown to them, Sol had slipped into the room when they weren't looking. He snorted, stomped forward and glared at Bea.

"Humph. I see she's still here."

"Sol," Marie said, "what do you think about me going home with Bea?"

"You're not going anywhere." He turned and stomped upstairs.

Marie looked at Bea. "See what I mean?"

Bea stiffened. She wanted to say much more, but figured she'd be wasting her time. Maybe it was too late for some people. But it wasn't too late for her.

She stood, taking Marie's hands in hers. Her mother's hands.

"It's going to take a while for all this to sink in for me. I've wanted to know all my life why I cried at night. Not knowing that, at some level, that I missed my twin sister. At least this pin you gave me shows at one point in my life you did claim me as your daughter."

"Oh, I've always claimed you," Marie said softly, patting her chest, "right here."

Bea kissed Marie on her cheek, picked up her bag and walked out the front door without a look back.

So all this time her grief had been over the loss of an unclaimed twin sister, a sister no one ever acknowledged existed. Everyone deserved that—to count.

She thought she'd fallen even further from grace when she hated Violet. Yet Violet had been a victim, too. Perhaps it was impossible not to hate or to love God, or anyone else, when you had no idea who you were. One thing she knew for certain. She must get to know herself. Now that she knew who she was, and why she'd always felt incomplete, it just might be possible. Her climb out of this spiritual void, this wilderness, might take years. Then again, it might take no time at all.

She thought about Oskar and Hal. She knew if she let Hal move back in nothing would be different. She'd soon fall back into that old pattern, because he couldn't stand it any other way. Oskar . . . He might make a good husband, but then again, no law said she had to be anyone's wife. Oskar must wait, and if he wasn't willing to do so, too bad.

All those years, she had cried hoping someone would scoop her up and hold her—like she counted for something. But the person who mattered more than anyone was Bea Meade. So perhaps her fall hadn't been from grace after all. Maybe it had been a fall into self-discovery.

That thought vibrated so loud and clear throughout her body she thought someone surely called her name. Someone had and it wasn't just someone, it was her.

"My name is Bea," she said, "and I deserve love."

Chapter 43

Bea took the bus home, happier, and yet at the same time sadder than she'd even been in her life. By the time the bus arrived in Orange, Bea felt certain she'd explode if she didn't talk to Edith soon. Suitcase in hand, she hurried home, but instead of Edith greeting her at the front door, Masil did.

"So, did she admit she was your mama?" Masil asked.

Bea stepped inside and saw Edith. "You told her?"

"Sorry, Toots," Edith said. "I figured I'd kept the secret too long already. No sense in hiding it any longer."

"Don't blame her," Masil said, caressing Bea's shoulder. "I nagged her till she told me where you'd gone. Bless your heart. That must've been tough."

Bea smiled. "I'm fine, and I'm glad you told me, Edith. So many things make sense now—like my infernal crying at night. And no, Marie wasn't mad. She actually looked relieved."

The three sat on the floor in a circle around Percy, who lay on the quilt with a rattle in his mouth, while Bea recounted the trip in detail and summed up with, "Marie drinks too much, she hates the beach, and she hates and loves Sol at the same time."

"The story of her life," Edith said, and headed to the kitchen to make coffee while Bea and Masil played with Percy.

"You think she'll ever leave him?" Masil's eyebrows arched in question. "I can't imagine Marie staying with him—or ever wanting him in the first place."

Edith walked back to where they sat and handed each of them a cup and saucer and returned with her own. "Careful, the coffee's extra hot," she said, resuming her seat beside them. "No, she'll never leave him. Somehow that man got his hooks in her and she can't get free. She's maybe as much a victim in all this as you are Bea. When she gave you away, she swore she only did it for your sake, but I knew she hoped Sol might marry her if she didn't keep you."

"And that's what happened, five years later?" Bea asked. "I remember their wedding in Mama's living room."

Edith counted on her fingers and said, "It took that long for him to give up on Irene Meade ever coming back to him. It took Irene having her first child with someone else."

"Don't you think it's weird that I had a child by a Meade, and I'm the child of a man who loved a Meade? I'll bet that drove Sol crazy."

"Made him more determined to never come back to Orange, I guess," Edith said. "I always saw the Nelson and Meade families more like star-crossed lovers than friends." A harsh, bitter laughed escaped from her throat.

Bea looked over at her sister—no, her aunt—and saw the woman through new eyes.

"Thank you, for . . . for . . ." Bea stopped to gain a semblance of control over a floodgate of emotions threatening to steal her words, words she must say.

Edith grabbed her hand and squeezed.

"I know I thanked you for telling me, Edith, but thank you for raising me, too. I know you're the one who did. Mama was already too old."

"You're not mad at me?" Edith's eyes grew misty.

"Why? You did the best you could, and I don't care what you or anyone else says, you'll always be my sister."

They stood, wrapped their arms around each other and cried until Edith finally laughed and stepped back. "We're quite a pair, aren't we?"

"Sisters forever," Bea said.

The screen door flew open and all three women turned to see Daniel, red-faced and out of breath.

"Bea, thank God you're back, Oskar needs your help."

"What's going on? Where is Oskar?"

"Out at the gypsy camp, but things aren't looking too good for him. Folks have shown up calling for his arrest. Word's spread that he's a spy."

"That's nonsense. Oskar's not a spy." Bea's cheeks felt hot.

Daniel had a serious look. "No, Bea, he's not. But folks these days panic anytime anyone uses the word German. There's a group of vigilantes out at the gypsy camp calling for blood. They're pretty worked up."

Daniel glanced over at Edith, but spoke to Bea. "I don't think Edith should go."

"You go on to the gypsy camp," Bea said. "Those of us who can come will. Give us just a couple of minutes."

Daniel left as Bea grabbed her car keys.

"If he thinks I'm staying behind," Edith said, "he doesn't know me like he thinks he does."

Bea knew better than to argue with her.

Masil sprang to her feet. "I'll check on Nelda." She turned and ran out the front door.

She returned a few minutes later. "No one's at home."

"Then we'll take Percy with us." Bea propped her child on her hip, grabbed a handful of diapers, and the three women piled in her old '37 Ford.

The gypsy camp sat just five or six miles outside of town, but the trip seemed to take forever. Bea's hands sweated and she gripped the steering wheel so tightly her fingers ached.

Percy reacted to the tension in the car by being fussy. He kept slapping away Edith's hands when she tried to sooth him, while Masil hummed some silly ditty that made Bea want to pull her hair out.

What would Bea do when she got there? What would she say? Would anyone listen?

Chapter 44

At last, they saw the camp. Just outside it, twenty or thirty townspeople huddled in a circle, clearly agitated, talking among themselves.

"What do you thinking they're planning to do?" Edith asked. She sat beside Bea, holding Percy. "People around here ain't afraid to take the law in their own hands. Remember when that Baptist preacher shot the sheriff dead on a street corner, and then got away with it?"

"I don't know, Edith. I'm scared to death. But we can't sit back and let them hurt Oskar or anybody at the gypsy camp. They haven't hurt anyone."

"Wasn't too long ago you were scared of the gypsies yourself."

"That's before I met them."

The mob was edging closer to the camp.

Bea pulled over to the side and parked the car, then opened the car door and stood on the running board for a better look.

She saw more than she expected. At the front of the still-growing crowd stood a familiar figure—Hal.

Masil and Edith, holding Percy, got out.

"I'll be damned," Edith swore.

People in the crowd started yelling. "I hear these gypsies are German, too," a man in the middle of the crowd hollered. "You can't trust a German or a gypsy. Put 'em together and no telling what they'll do—rob you blind, that's for sure. These people ain't like us, and they don't belong here!"

Then they saw a solitary figure—Daniel—standing in front of the group.

"Wait a minute, folks," he yelled over the others. "Ya'll know me. I work in security at the shipyard. Trust me, I wouldn't lie to you when I say these people are harmless. Don't run off half-cocked and do something you'll live to regret."

Another man from the rear yelled out, his fist pumping the air. "Let's tar and feather 'em is what I say. Run 'em out of town."

Bea exchanged a panicked glance with Edith and Masil. No one tarred and feathered anyone anymore.

"That's right," another called out. "They don't belong here with decent folks."

"No telling what kind of secrets they've already sent back to Hitler and his henchmen."

"Yeah. And that Oskar guy works right out there at the shipyard. He might've already sabotaged our ships."

"I heard tell someone found a two-way radio on the beach. My guess is it's his."

Pushing and shoving, Bea fought her way through the crowd to Daniel. "How'd this get started?" she yelled in his ear.

He pointed to the angry man standing across from him.

"Hal?"

"So I hear."

"He knows better than that, he's just being spiteful. I can't believe people would take his word about that."

"Evidently, this mob does."

"This is ridiculous. Where are Oskar and Wilhelm?"

"Lady Silvania and the others have them over there in their tent trying to protect them. I'm afraid they're at risk, too. I don't know what else to do."

Overwhelmed, helpless, Bea felt her legs get weak, and she wanted to collapse to the ground. But instead, She shoved her way over to Hal, and stood in front of him, her feet planted, a look of fury on her face.

"Did you do this? Did you get this started?"

"Hey, all I did was tell the truth about Oskar, someone else found

SYLVIA DICKEY SMITH

out about Wilhelm. You can't blame this on me."

"What truth?"

"He's a real German, born in Germany I found out. And he stole my wife. No telling what else he might've stolen."

"That's the stupidest reasoning ever come out of your mouth. Do something, Hal. Make these people go away."

When he didn't, she turned and stomped off. Behind her, she heard him rabble-rouse the crowd. "We don't have to put up with people who're different," Hal yelled. "We're Americans and we can do something about it."

Bea climbed up on a gypsy wagon and stood in the back, watching the crowd grow more hostile.

"Bea, Bea, down here." She followed the voice and saw Edith holding Percy, who screamed at the top of his lungs.

"Give him here," she said, took Percy and held him tight. "Shh, shh, it's okay, honey, Mama's here."

Nothing she did calmed Percy or quelled the crowd.

When someone started yelling, it took a minute before she realized the words came from her mouth.

"Go ahead, kill them!" she shouted.

No one heard her.

"Kill them I say," she screamed.

A few people in the crowd saw her and stopped, grew quiet and punched their elbows into their neighbors, who also grew quiet and looked up at her.

"If you're going to kill them, go ahead and get it over with. Kill them all."

"Yeah," one yelled.

Once begun, the words rolled out of her mouth. "You're right, they are different than we are. And that's reason enough to kill them! We need to kill everyone who is different than we are—kill them all." She pumped her fist in the air, saying the same thing over and over again.

Percy kept screaming.

One by one, the crowd's attention moved from Hal to the small blonde woman standing on the back of the gypsy wagon.

"And you know what? After you kill them, you can kill me too, because you see, I'm different, too. Guess what? I'm a bastard. I was born without a father—and then, my mama didn't even want me and gave me away to strangers. So you sure better not trust me."

She glanced down at her red-faced son. "And I guess while you're at it, you might as well kill Percy here, too, because I sure don't want him to grow up without a mama, like I did."

The crowd grew quiet, fifty or more pairs of eyes focused on her.

As silence fell over the crowd, Bea scrambled for something else to say. She continued, unsure where her words or her thoughts headed.

"You can kill me and my baby, and Oskar and Wilhelm, and then all these gypsies who live here, but then you'll have to start killing each other, because you're different, too."

She pointed to the man down in front of her. "Look at you, Jack, you've got blue eyes. and Matt standing there next to you, his eyes are brown—so you'll *have* to kill him. And Ruth, look there next to you. That woman is fat, and you're thin. Of course, she'll have to die. And you, Sarah, you're blonde, but Glenda there next to you is brunette."

She sucked through her teeth. "Yep she'll have to die, too."

She paused, then "Don't you see, folks, we are all different, but that which makes us different is just as important as that which makes us the same as everyone else."

She paused to catch her breath, but still, no one spoke.

"I've felt bad about myself my whole life because I felt different than other people. I am different, but I'm also just like you. Yes, Oskar and Wilhelm were born in Germany. Does that make them evil? They're here in this country because they, too, love freedom, and the ability to live their lives without fear of being gassed to death. What's wrong with that? What about the Irish, Dutch, Italian? Our parents came here for the same thing, but we're not killing them."

Spent, Bea stood for a minute, then dropped her arm to her side. "That's all I've got to say. Do what you will, but whatever you do, you'll have to do it to me, too."

No one said a word, while Percy still screamed at the top of his lungs.

Bea watched as the crowd divided down the middle as someone walked through.

It was Oskar.

He headed straight for her, never taking his eyes off hers. When he reached the wagon, he climbed in and took Percy out of her arms. As soon as he did, Percy looked up, saw Oskar and stopped crying.

Laughter echoed from the crowd.

Leave it to a baby to accomplish what she couldn't.

Just when she thought tension had eased, the crowd parted again, but this time, they stepped even further back, as if an undesirable passed.

Hal. He looked up at her, disgusted. "You're not the same woman I married," he said. "I don't even know who you are anymore."

He spat on the ground and made to turn, then looked back at Oskar. "You can have her for all I care," then shoved his way through the crowd, who gave him ample space in which to pass, and watched him saunter to his waiting car. Hal climbed in and drove away, alone.

One by one, the crowd turned and walked off.

Oskar put his arm around Bea's shoulder and squeezed. "Thank you," he whispered into her ear. "I didn't know you had it in you."

"Neither did I," she said, laughing.

Edith ended up leaving with Daniel, and Masil rode with Bea and Oskar. When they drove into the Riverside parking lot, Masil said goodnight and walked home.

Bea, Oskar and Percy went inside. Oskar fed and cleaned Percy and put him to bed while Bea made a pan of cornbread to crumble into glasses of milk, and got out a couple of spoons.

She and Oskar were starved by the time she got supper ready.

They ate while they recounted recent events. Then they sat and talked for hours, about each other, about their past, and what the future might hold for them.

Later, when she yawned, he excused himself, promising he'd be back the next day.

"But where will you sleep?"

"Wilhelm and Lady Silvania have invited me to sleep there. It doesn't look right for me to stay here tonight if Edith isn't here."

She didn't complain when he put then his arm around her waist and brought her to him. She loved his earthy smell, and she breathed deeply, content and aroused, for the first time in forever—at least since he'd kissed her that one time. When he lifted her chin and lowered his lips to hers, she knew he was correct. No way could she resist him if he lay asleep in the other room. One of these days, she wouldn't resist, but the time had to be right.

After he left, Bea lay alone in bed, events of the last couple of days playing through her thoughts.

She glanced at the bureau and the cigar box where the brooch lay. Should she get it and stick it under her pillow?

No, something told her she'd sleep fine without it. From now on, she'd live her own life. She may one day be with another man, even marry again—but not right now. First, she'd get reacquainted with that child wrapped in a threadbare blanket and left at the orphanage so many years ago.

She propped the window open, and a hint of the coming fall drifted in on a cool breeze. She loved the change of seasons. Somehow it gave her hope that life went on and things changed for the better. She shivered with delight, certain she could fly.

THE END

Acknowledgements

No work ever stands alone. Multiple people contribute to the wealth of information it takes to produce any work of historical fiction like *A War of Her Own*.

However, there are specific individuals I must thank who helped make this work possible. Critique partners Earl Staggs, Randy Rawls, Joan Upton Hall, Joy Nord, D.C. Campbell, Jaime Roton, and Manfred Riemann were always there for me, offering suggestions for improvement, correcting my mistakes, and pushing me forward. Also, Helen Ginger and Earl Staggs both helped to edit the manuscript and offered valued suggestions for improving it. You gals and guys are number one in my book.

My husband, Bill, never failed to encourage and inspire me, and help foot the research bill. Thanks, Love, for doing all the housework so I could write.

I would also like to acknowledge one incredible editor and all-around neat person, Philip Martin, of Crickhollow Books. His knowledge, experience, and guidance has been invaluable. Working with him is indeed a delight.

Of a number of books about the homefront in World War II, Louis Fairchild's excellent work, *They Called It the War Effort: Oral Histories from World War II, Orange, Texas* (Eakin Press, 1993) offered especially valuable and detailed information about those years and made them come alive for me.

About the Author

Sylvia Dickey Smith is a story catcher, award-winning author, and fifth-generation Texan. It has been said that she sees everything and misses nothing. Born backward—feet first and left-handed—she's done most things backwards ever since.

Six years on the Caribbean island of Trinidad led to the discovery of a deep love for understanding different customs, cultures and folklore. Returning to the U.S., she took her first freshman class at age forty and later graduated with a B.A. in Sociology.

She went on to earn a Master's Degree in Educational Psychology and became licensed as a professional counselor and marriage and family therapist. She owned and conducted a private practice, served as an adjunct professor, wrote curriculum for virtual textbooks, and served as an expert witness for administrative law judges, along with other related management positions within the human services field.

Today, she spends her time as a full-time writer. In addition to her latest work, *A War of Her Own*, a historical fiction set during WW II. She also is author of the popular Sidra Smart mystery series, along with many published short stories and nonfiction essays.

She lives in Georgetown, Texas, not far from Austin, with her husband, Bill, a full-bird Army Colonel, retired.